I0590656

THE PAINTED

PHOENIX

Sarah Kay Moll

A NineStar Press Publication

www.ninestarpress.com

The Painted Phoenix

Copyright © 2020 by Sarah Kay Moll
Cover Art by Natasha Snow Copyright © 2020

This is a work of fiction. Names, characters, places, and incidents are either the product of the author's imagination or are used fictitiously. Any resemblance to actual persons living or dead, business establishments, events, or locales is entirely coincidental.

All rights reserved. No part of this publication may be reproduced in any material form, whether by printing, photocopying, scanning or otherwise without the written permission of the publisher. To request permission and all other inquiries, contact NineStar Press at the physical or web addresses above or at Contact@ninestarpress.com.

Printed in the USA

Print ISBN: 978-1-64890-039-6

First Edition, July, 2020

Also available in eBook, ISBN: 978-1-64890-038-9

WARNING
This book contains sexual content, which may only be suitable for mature readers, use of homophobic language; discussion of off-page drug use, addiction, and prostitution; suicide ideation; graphic violence; domestic violence; child endangerment and child abuse; murder of a side character; off-page murders of side characters..

With paintbrush in hand, Nate Redfield takes a city full of ugliness and makes it beautiful. His quiet, empty life is a refuge from a harrowing past, and although he has nothing to love, he also has nothing to lose. Standing up to the syndicate is a good way to end up with a hole in his head, but Nate is not afraid to die.

For once in his life, he's going to do the right thing, even if it kills him. And it probably will.

But the most dangerous criminal in the city—a man whose sadism and ruthlessness have become local legend—decides to spare Nate's life. On the streets, Ras is a cold-blooded syndicate enforcer, and makes no apologies for it. But he pursues Nate with a tenderness like nothing Nate has ever known. While no amount of violence could compel Nate to betray his moral compass, love leaves him defenseless.

The vibrant portraits Nate paints tell every story but his own: a lost little girl who thinks of him as a father, a lawyer who tempers justice with compassion, a crime boss and an art thief, and the killer who stole his heart. Ras offers him the love he's yearned for all his life, if only he is willing to close his eyes to the violent truth. But his story is not one of compromise. It is the story of an indomitable spirit, rising like fire from the ashes of his past.

This one's for you, Mom

THE CAT SCRATCH CLUB. 2005

Ink on paper

Nate Redfield knows he's going to die. He's known it for a while now—woken up with it, gone to sleep with it, held it near to his heart. It's not suicide, not exactly, but it might as well be. He might as well be putting a gun in his own mouth when he pushes open the doors to the Cat Scratch, the seedy strip club where Alan DiCiccio conducts his business.

He walks past the stage, strippers swaying, sliding their G-strings down their long, supple legs so a handful of men can spend their Friday afternoon appreciating the view. The bouncer at the back of the room gives him a nod and steps aside so he can push open an unlabeled black door and walk into what serves as DiCiccio's office. Behind him, the bouncer's heavy footsteps follow, and then the door clicks shut.

"You're late," DiCiccio says. "I hope you's got some extra cash to make up for it."

DiCiccio looks Mafia, through and through, with a New York accent and an unnecessarily formal black suit. But he's not Mafia. There is no Mafia in this city, only the syndicate with a monopoly on crime and the muscle to keep it that way. DiCiccio works for them, so Nate does too. Or he did, anyway. Until today.

"I quit," he says, and with those two words, his heart begins thumping, fast and heavy like someone's banging the hell out of a snare drum in his chest.

"You quit?" DiCiccio leans forward over the scattered cash and bags of white powder on his desk to stare at Nate. "You fucking quit?" He looks up at the bouncer. "Bobby, am I hearing this shit right?"

"He said he quit," Bobby responds. He's a tall, beefy guy with stubble and a couple of big gold rings Nate imagines he wears just for the scars they leave on his victims. "You heard him right."

"Okay..." DiCiccio draws the word out. "I'll humor you, Nate. Why the fuck do you think you're going to quit sellin' for me?"

Nate is silent for a moment, gathering his courage. "'Cause it's wrong," he says, standing still to give away no hint of the fear scrabbling inside him like some desperate animal.

"Oh, it's wrong, is it?" DiCiccio puts his hands behind his head, leaning back in his chair. "You think it's wrong, Bobby?"

"No, boss. I think it's his fucking job."

"That's right. It's your fuckin' job. Which I gave to you as an especial favor to my friend Troy. And now you come and you throw it in my face."

"You told me the pills wouldn't hurt anybody," Nate says. "You said they're not real drugs, and it's not gonna hurt anybody that bad. But that's not true. And I'm not gonna do it anymore."

He thinks of the girl who used to buy from him every Tuesday, dark eyes, a bitter laugh. She was found dead from an overdose just a few days ago, and since then, Nate has been building his courage for this confrontation. He's not going to walk away alive. But better him than another person like her.

"Nate, look. I like you; I really do. You're a nice guy. But you come here and you tell me you're not gonna do your job, and you really leave me no choice. You get what I'm sayin'?"

"Yeah." Nate's high voice comes out rough and raspy.

"No." DiCiccio shakes his head. "I don't think you do. What I'm sayin' is that you get out there and you do your fuckin' job, or Bobby here's gonna have to fuck you up." He puts his elbows on the desk and leans forward. "You understand that?"

Nate looks at the glinting rings on Bobby's right hand, so thick and heavy he might as well be wearing a pair of brass knuckles. Nate's not afraid to die, but he wishes it wasn't going to hurt so much.

"I get it," he says.

DiCiccio shakes his head sadly and glances at Bobby, jerking his head at Nate.

Bobby nods, solemnly, like they're making a bank transaction—not playing around with someone's life—and that just pisses Nate off.

A hot wave of anger crashes over him, and as Bobby approaches, he lunges forward, driving his fist into Bobby's gut and then bringing a knee up hard between the hitman's legs. Bobby makes a sharp, wounded noise, going to his knees, and Nate drives a hard kick to his ribs. He's been in enough fights to know how to move and how to make sure the other guy isn't getting back up anytime soon.

"That's enough."

It's not DiCiccio speaking, but a low melodic voice Nate's never heard before. He steps back from the groaning thug on the floor and looks up. A man stands in the doorway, his messy dark hair falling over his forehead, and he smiles at Nate. It's the damnedest thing, this smile. It doesn't fit the situation at all. It's the kind of friendly, amused smile he might give Nate if they were walking their dogs in the park and the leashes got tangled together. It's strange and surreal and almost familiar. And the adrenaline is stretching seconds into minutes into hours and highlighting every detail of this man who—Nate somehow just knows, from his arrogant stance and the tilt of his chin—now controls every aspect of the situation.

"Who would like to explain to me what's going on?" the man asks.

"Jesus fuckin' Christ, Ras," DiCiccio says. "Make a little noise next time you walk in a room, you sneaky bastard."

And Nate freezes, his earlier fancies iced over with fear because this is Ras, second in command to the syndicate boss and meanest motherfucker in the whole city. He's heard a lot of talk about Ras—anyone who's spent time in the criminal underworld has. The gossip rags love him. Their stories are sensational and exaggerated, but the rumors Nate hears on the streets— tales of sadism and deadly skill—make him think there is some truth to them.

"DiCiccio." Ras doesn't sound happy to see the drug dealer. "What's all this?"

"Motherfucker attacked me," Bobby moans as he picks himself up off the floor. "The little faggot fights dirty."

Nate winces. He's used to that word, but it still wounds more deeply than any other.

"He attacked you, did he?" Ras sounds unamused.

"He thinks he can quit," DiCiccio says. "He comes in here givin' me some bullshit story 'bout how what we do is wrong, and he's just not gonna do it anymore."

The corner of Ras's mouth twists upward, and he glances at Nate. "What we do *is* wrong. I can hardly fault him for being honest."

"I'm not doin' it anymore." Nate's mouth feels dry and sandpapery as he waits for Ras's response.

"Great for you, you're a big fuckin' hero." DiCiccio rolls his eyes. "You got any last words, big fuckin' hero?"

"Fuck you," Nate growls, anger coursing through him so hot he doesn't feel the fear anymore—it's burned away like a paper shell around something hard and relentless as iron.

DiCiccio raises his gun in one sallow hand. The bang of the gunshot is so loud Nate can almost feel it, a tangible burst of pressure. But nothing hurts. Nate looks down and is startled to find himself intact.

DiCiccio drops the gun and stumbles forward, collapsing on the carpet. A pool of red seeps out from under his head, a bright spatter painting the far wall.

Ras has holstered his gun, but clearly, he can draw so fast he may as well still be holding it. He turns to Bobby and raises an eyebrow.

"I swear to god I had nothing to do with it," Bobby says, backing away as Ras approaches. "DiCiccio was the one who stole from you. I told him not to. I told him!"

Nate's not stupid, he knows this isn't going anywhere good. So while Ras pulls a little knife from his pocket, he darts out the door, sprinting for the parking lot. He draws in a shaky breath when the sunshine falls over him, so bright and carefree, but he can't spare even a trembling second because he's got to fucking run for it. He zigzags through alleyways, ducks into stores, and indiscriminately boards busses and trains, traveling across town in the wrong direction for a couple of hours before he feels safe enough to get on a train headed home.

He's not an idiot—he knows that in this town, no one can watch a syndicate enforcer do a hit and walk away. He's probably only delaying the inevitable, and as he watches the shining city outside the windows of the train, he wonders if he's ever going to see it again. It seems fraught with fragile beauty, the blinding splashes of light reflected in storefront windows and the metal of the cars streaking by on the interstate.

In his entire life, he has only ever had one true love, so it makes sense that as he nears the edge of his lifetime, he has only one regret. He left her behind because he had no other choice, but he could no more stop loving her than he could stop his blood from flowing through his veins. And even when his heart has beat its final rhythm, that love will endure. He knows that much is true, even as he believes in nothing else.

INFANT. 1997

Pencil on scrap paper

Most of the chairs in the maternity ward waiting room in the large, impersonal hospital are empty at three in the morning. A woman's muffled yelling comes from down the hall, but the nurse at the reception desk doesn't look up from her crossword puzzle, so Nate assumes it must not be an emergency. He's been here for twelve hours now, watching the daytime talk shows give way to infomercials as the night drags on.

Troy was there at first; he was the one to drive them to the hospital when his sister Traci's water broke. Troy's a shitty brother to Traci most of the time, but he's curious enough about the first child to enter their family that he's been unusually attentive through the tail end of his sister's pregnancy, if not as closely involved as Nate.

Traci's gynecologist took a regressive, disapproving attitude toward single mothers, so Traci had grabbed the closest available man—in this case, Troy's lover—to attend appointments with her. At first Nate had gone out of curiosity and because he was used to doing whatever Troy told him, but he quickly became fascinated with the fuzzy, indistinct images on the ultrasound screen, the blobs of white that were a hand or a foot or a face. He started to feel a connection to the unborn child, and even to Traci. He spent the last few months lifting heavy objects whenever it seemed she might have need of it, trying to get her to take prenatal vitamins, and worrying her brief stint of sobriety would end before the baby was born.

Troy watched him with a fond bemusement while remaining unattached to the prospect of his soon-to-be-born niece. "If I didn't know better, I'd think you were the one who knocked her up," he'd say, then slap Nate on the ass as though to drive home the point that Nate wasn't likely to knock up any woman at all, let alone his boyfriend's sister.

Now, Nate turns off his phone to avoid seeing Troy's number light up the screen. Troy wants him to come home, but he's determined to stay as long as it takes.

It's not a shock when the nurse steps into the waiting room asking for him.

"She's pushing," the nurse tells him. "Do you want to be there?"

Nate shakes his head. "Don't think she wants me to. Sorry."

The nurse frowns, confused. She must be assuming he's the dad—hell, Traci probably told her as much.

"Of course," she says. "I'll keep you updated."

She hurries back down the hallway. Nate follows after a few moments. He stands beside the door numbered 321, his back against the wall, its white plaster scratchy through his thin T-shirt. He listens to the murmur of voices, and then Traci screams, just twice. A long silence spools out unbroken, and Nate holds his breath. And then the squall of a baby angry at the sudden shock of cold air on her skin.

Nate smiles and allows relief to overtake him.

After a moment, the door opens again. The nurse seems startled to see him there but quickly recovers.

"Come in," she says. "Your wife...doesn't feel ready to hold the baby. She said you would."

Nate is a little surprised Traci would go so far as to imply that Nate was her husband, but he's willing to go along with almost anything to make this easier for her. He follows the nurse into the room where Traci lies limp under a white blanket, and the baby fusses in the arms of a woman in bright pink scrubs.

"Take off your shirt," the woman in the scrubs says. "Skin-to-skin contact is essential for newborns."

Nate hesitates. He's sixteen and still scrawny, his limbs long and awkward, but he's more worried about the track mark located in the crook of his right arm. But the baby begins to cry again, and more than anything, he wants to soothe that pitiful sound away.

They put him in a reclining chair and place the baby girl on his chest. Immediately, she stops crying and nestles against his skin, and suddenly nothing else matters. His worry about the exposed track mark, his anger at Traci for refusing to hold her daughter, his anxiety about what Troy will do when Nate returns home all bleed away to nothing as the child lets herself relax in his arms.

The girl is nothing less than perfect, two tiny arms and two tiny legs, dark eyes and umber skin. Her head is coated in black hair, and he strokes it once, hesitantly.

Her blind trust creates in him a fierce protectiveness, an urge to step between her and every sharp edge of the world. The soft rise and fall of her breathing, the frantic beat of her heart against his own, inspire a kind of emotion he's never felt before. Lying there with the infant on his chest, he whispers all sorts of impossible promises, to guard and guide and love. And love and love and love.

DEATH #4, SERIES. 2005

Charcoal on paper

Nate's stop arrives too soon, and he gets off the train, walking back to his home like a condemned man back to the gallows. It would be smarter, maybe, to cut his losses and run for it, abandoning everything he has. But that would feel too much like defeat, and Nate has never in his life stopped fighting when he still possessed the strength to continue.

Outside the front door to his studio apartment, Nate bends over, his hands on his knees, breathing deep gulps of air and trying not to throw up as the day's events wash over him. He unlocks the door with a shaking hand and steps inside.

Ras is sitting on Nate's ratty gray sofa.

Just sitting there, idly flipping through one of Nate's sketchbooks. He looks up, smiling pleasantly, and Nate's insides get cold. It's much scarier than a menacing scowl and a brandished weapon would be.

Nate raises his chin and meets Ras's gaze, though inside he's trembling with terror. "Get the hell outta my house," he says, and that sinister smile just gets wider.

"I have to admire your tenacity." Ras gets up off the couch with a predator's fluid grace. "And you're a very good artist. I may keep some of these."

Nate's temper flares blindingly hot. "Don't fuckin' touch my stuff."

Ras takes something out of his pocket. With a little click, a shining blade about five inches long springs out from the handle. He advances on Nate, lazily twirling the knife in his hand, but even though they say on the streets that Ras is a fucking karate master, Nate's not going down without a fight. He lunges forward with all his might. Ras casually sidesteps, as easy as dancing, and Nate's momentum sends him stumbling into the back of the couch.

He turns and, in a heartbeat, Ras is on him, feral glint of teeth and a fluid sweep of his arm that ends with the knife pressed gently to Nate's throat. A little bead of blood wells up where knife and skin meet, hot and sticky on Nate's neck.

"You are fun," Ras says. "I could do this all day, but my father always told me not to play with my food. So, lucky you. I'll make it quick."

Anyone else would be afraid. But Nate is fire—licking, crackling, burning bright even in the cold shadow cast by this pale specter of death. He might be about to die, but sometimes it feels like he's been about to die his entire life. A cold night on the streets, an overdose, or the shining blade of a knife—does it really matter?

"You think you scare me? With your fucked-up smile and your little knife?" Nate laughs with the genuine ease of someone who knows his heavy burden will soon be set down. "I been waitin' for you my whole life."

Ras hesitates, puzzled.

"Don't touch my art, asshole," Nate says, and he doesn't look away. Ras might not think they are equals, but he is wrong. "You don't deserve it."

A long silence follows, and Nate knows this is it, his final moment, but he refuses to close his eyes. Instead, he stares directly at the evil creature looming before him with unflinching defiance. And as he watches, Ras...changes. Like the throwing on of a mask, like the pulling back of a shroud—he can't tell which face is real, only that this one is distinctly *different*, in a thousand tiny ways, from the monster who was about to cut his throat.

And Ras pulls the knife away. He steps back, taking a black cloth from his pocket and wiping away the little bit of Nate's blood on the blade. When his eyes meet Nate's—a quick, upward glance—he seems uncertain. He doesn't smile. He looks nothing like the killer who was about to cut Nate's throat.

He looks just like a shy boy who stood on a street corner in the Warrens, all those years ago, selling drugs and watching the city with sad, soulful eyes.

"Jude?" Nate whispers, as all the fear and adrenaline come back in a dizzying rush along with the shock of recognition. He struggles to stay on his feet, feeling like he might throw up.

"Don't call me that," Ras says with the strange, youthful vulnerability he—Jude—always used to wear. "How do you know that name?"

Nate jams his hands into his pockets so Ras won't see them shake. "We, uh, we met. When you used to sell dope in the Warrens. We only talked a couple times but...I knew you. Everybody knew you."

"I see." Ras twirls the little knife between his fingers. "I hope you realize I'm not that person anymore. Jude de Haven might have let you live, but I won't."

Nate's a little unnerved by how Ras talks about himself, like the person Nate knew then is a separate individual, distinct from the person he's now talking to, though they share the same body.

"You saved my life, Jude," Nate says, and Ras flinches very slightly at the sound of his name—his real name. "And I never got to thank you for it. So, thanks. Even if you kill me now, I probably woulda died earlier if you hadn't saved me."

"My name is Ras," he protests, but he's stopped toying with the knife, and has actually closed it, hiding the blade away.

"You probably don't remember me at all," Nate continues, "but I remember you, Jude. You were kind, and you helped me."

Ras flinches again, taking a step back. "Don't call me Jude. Jude is dead."

"That's a goddamn shame." Nate leans against the back of the couch with feigned ease. "I liked him a lot better than I like you, you fuckin' monster."

"You don't know when to quit, do you?" Ras raises a sly eyebrow, and just like that, the strange vulnerability is hidden again. He shifts, again *changing* from Jude to Ras, from the shy, kind boy to the gleeful, dangerous stranger. The transition is dizzying in its speed, and when it's over, Nate feels like prey caught in a predator's claws.

"Guess not," Nate says gruffly.

"I like that." Ras looks him in the eye and grins slow and lazy as a cat. "I have a proposition for you. I think you'll like it."

Ras in Restaurant, Smiling.

2005

Graphite on paper

Nate goes through the next few days in a kind of a haze, turning Ras's proposition over and over in his mind. It's a simple enough idea—an art gallery as a money laundering scheme, and Nate would be one of the people supplying the art. The money would be good, Ras assured him, and he wouldn't be hurting anyone. He'd just be doing the one thing that makes his soul sing. Something he does all the time anyway, even though no one's ever paid him or showed all that much interest before.

There's not much to do besides brood on the possibility since Nate quit his job and hasn't had much luck finding another. The track marks that haven't faded after a year of sobriety—probably due to the fucking black tar heroin he used to get so cheap—are easily hidden by long sleeves, as are most of his tattoos and scars. Only the feather on his neck and the thick concentric circles of scar tissue on the back of his right hand are visible in an interview. But he's sure who he is and what he used to be is written across his face. No one's going to hire him, except maybe a criminal like Ras.

Ever since their encounter, he's been trying to draw Ras's face, but each of his attempts has ended up in the trash. Usually, he has a good memory for faces because he finds them so interesting, and back when they frequented the same scene, he used to be able to draw Jude without much trouble. But something about Ras, his bearing, or the angle of his chin, or the shape of his eyes, is all wrong, like he's a completely different person than the one Nate used to sketch with quiet longing in every pencil stroke.

Even more than his rapidly dwindling supply of cash, the need to get that portrait right at least once is what finally brings him to call the number Ras scribbled down for him before leaving.

*

The restaurant where he meets Ras is elegant and expensive, with tall crystal vases in the center of each table and more silverware laid out on actual cloth napkins than someone could really need for one dinner. Most of the words on the menu look like they're in French or something.

Ras appears completely at ease, his hair messy and his smile as oddly compelling as Nate remembers.

And that's what it was, Nate realizes, watching Ras speak to the waiter. The smile. Sinister but genuinely cheerful. A playful song that hits a few minor notes. He's never seen anything quite like it, and he wants to make Ras smile at least once more, so he can memorize it, and draw it. It shouldn't be hard. Ras smiles at everyone, even the busser who comes to fill their waters, giving out his attention like candy on Halloween to anyone who comes asking. Nate tends to hoard his own, rarely making eye contact, scowling at anyone who steps into his personal space.

"White or red?" Ras asks, glancing at him. Nate gives him a blank stare.

"White or red what?"

"Wine."

Oh. Now Nate feels like a complete fucking idiot, his face flushing with shame. "Right. Um, I don't drink. So, whatever. And, Ras, I gotta be honest; I don't fuckin' speak French." He gestures at the menu. "I don't know what the fuck any of this shit is."

Ras laughs, but it feels friendly, not mocking. As he starts to talk about what's on the menu, a tall, chubby woman in a sleek black suit jacket and slacks approaches their table with a smile that looks more like a grimace.

"Ras," she says, her voice slightly shrill. "It's such a pleasure to see you."

Ras grins, and this time it's all teeth, like a shark. "The pleasure is mine, Anita."

She gives an anxious laugh. "I'm sure it is."

She grabs the bottle of wine a waiter is about to hand to Ras and clucks her tongue. "Oh, no. We can do better than this. I've got a chardonnay that would be just perfect. And you have to try the red snapper. It's unbelievably fresh."

"Do you like fish, Nate?" Ras asks with a raised eyebrow.

"Sure," Nate says, shrugging. He really hopes Ras is going to pay for this meal because there aren't even prices listed on the menu, like if you have to ask, you probably can't afford it.

"Good." Ras hands their menus to Anita and tells her they'll both have the fish. She gives him a wide, insincere smile and hurries off.

"She's fuckin' terrified of you, man," Nate says.

Ras grins like Nate just gave him a compliment.

"Thank you. I do try. Anita owes the boss a lot of money, and it's past due."

"Shit," Nate whispers. "You gonna kill her?"

"Not right away," Ras says casually. But he must notice the shudder that goes through Nate at the cold admission because he changes the subject. He talks cheerfully about the city, and the things he loves about it— watching the sunset over the skyline from the ferry that goes around the bay, the artisan market by the water's edge, the vibrant nightlife downtown—and Nate is content to listen and sip his water and gradually forget that cold grin in favor of this warm smile.

It's not until they finish eating and Ras is drinking his after-dinner whiskey that he brings up the reason for their meeting. It had been easy enough to imagine they were just two friends having dinner together. Whether that was something two friends generally did with each other, Nate couldn't say. He'd had very few friends in his lifetime, and almost none as an adult.

"Have you given any thought to my offer?" Ras asks. And his demeanor is still so friendly, so open, Nate doesn't feel the pressure or fear he thought he would in this moment.

"Yeah, I thought about it a lot. I just...I dunno. Don't think I can."

"Why not?"

Nate hunches his shoulders like a turtle slipping into a shell. "I don't really show people my art. You're the first person to see any of it in a long time, except for the guy who does my tattoos."

"Is that why you hide your tattoos too?" At Nate's puzzled glance, Ras adds, "You're always tugging on your sleeves, like you're trying to make sure they won't ride up and show your forearms."

Nate has never noticed himself doing that, but as he looks down at his hands, he realizes he's caught in the act right now. He flushes with humiliation.

"It's not the ink," he says softly. "I like my tattoos. It's... I got track marks. I been clean for a year but they ain't faded much. Think it's the fuckin' black tar that did it."

"You've been sober for a year?" Ras raises his eyebrows. "That's impressive. You must be proud of yourself."

Nate shrugs. "Don't cancel out all the fucked-up shit I did for the dope."

"You're too hard on yourself," Ras says with complete confidence. "That's why you don't want people to see your art. You think it's not good enough."

Nate scowls. "It's 'cause my art is a part of me, and I don't fuckin' trust other people to see it." The words come out with more vehemence than he'd intended. "Look, I'm sorry, but I'm not gonna do it."

"You're saying no?" Ras sounds slightly startled. It's probably not something he hears very often. "Are you sure? I would very much like to have you work on this project."

Even though he phrased it as a desire, the way he says it is just like a command.

"No," Nate says. "I won't do it." *You can't make me.*

"I understand." Ras sets down his empty whiskey glass, surprising Nate with a graceful retreat. "I'm not going to push you into it if you'd rather not."

"Okay." Nate's a little shaky with relief and something else he doesn't understand. Disappointment?

"I've got a little business to settle with Anita." Ras is momentarily cold as ice, sharp as glass, and then the sunshine is back when he smiles at Nate. "You have my number, just in case you change your mind."

It's a clear dismissal. Nate thanks Ras for the absurdly expensive dinner and gets up to leave. It's not until he's outside, pulling on his coat in the chill air, that he realizes he never asked if he could take a picture of Ras, to draw from later.

He hurries inside in time to see Ras step into a back room, pulling Anita with him.

Nate knows this kind of thing happens a hundred times a day across the city. He tries to harden his heart, to look the other way, to *just not care*. It's not like he knows Anita, or that she would rescue him if they were in similar situations. But he just can't let it go.

He crosses the room, trying hard to make it look as though he belongs despite feeling extraordinarily out of place in a ritzy restaurant like this. When he leans against the door, in a pose he hopes is convincingly nonchalant, he can hear the faint sound of Anita begging, though he can't quite make out the words. He wonders if she's going to die tonight, if he'll be standing right here, helpless, when she does.

It's not like I know her. Why should I care? Why should it have to be me?

But even as he tries to rationalize it, her sobbing intensifies, and he knows what he has to do. He pushes open the door and steps inside, shutting it behind him.

Anita is on her knees in the center of the room, her face streaked with tears, while Ras sits in front of her, a little knife in one hand and Anita's wrist held firmly in the other. He looks up at Nate and raises an eyebrow.

"I'm a little busy. Do you need something?"

"Let her go. Nate stands tall, his hands clenched into fists by his sides.

The corner of Ras's mouth twitches upward in a cold smirk that Nate immediately loathes. "Or what?"

"I'll call the police," Nate growls, though he knows the futility of the threat even before Ras laughs. The police force in the city has been coerced by the syndicate and bought by the Bancroft family—an open secret.

"Nate," Ras says. "I have a lot of things to do this evening. Would you like me to cut *your* throat or do you want to get the hell out of here and let me do my job?"

Ras wears the same cool indifference as several days ago when he ambushed Nate in his apartment after Nate's desperate run through the city. He expects fear, thrives on it. But Nate is getting tired of his bullshit.

"I ain't movin'. Nobody deserves to die just 'cause they owe money."

"I wasn't going to kill her." There's a distinct note of petulance in Ras's voice, like Nate is threatening to take away a favorite toy.

"He's going to cut off my fingers," Anita says, breathless with terror.

"I'll do what you want," Nate offers. "I'll work for you, just like you asked. If you let her go."

Ras studies him for a long moment, and then he grins, wide and wicked. "A hero. A knight in shining armor, charging in to save the day. I like that."

Nate swallows, hard, because Ras looks like the Big Bad Wolf right now, and Nate gets the feeling Ras would like to devour him whole. Through the churn of emotions in his chest he can't tell if that's a good thing or a bad thing.

"Fair enough," Ras says. "You come to work for me, and we'll call it even."

Anita sobs with relief as Ras releases her, and darts to the other side of the room. She throws her arms around Nate and buries her face in his shoulder, her whole body shaking. Across the room, Ras catches Nate's eye with a wry smile that makes Nate feel like Ras can see right through him, down to his bones.

"I'll call you," Ras says and winks at Nate before slipping out a back door.

*

Nate walks the half mile from the bus stop into the kind of neighborhood he's never lived in, a suburban utopia with mini mansions that stretch over rolling hills—boxy faux Victorian-style houses built in the last ten years—and giant gleaming SUVs in every driveway. His sister's house is no different, her family's own little slice of prosperity. He knocks timidly on the pale-blue door to her home and waits.

"Oh. It's you." Nate's brother-in-law sighs, standing in the doorway. "We're having dinner, Nate. Do you need something?"

As the pastor for an evangelical church, Aaron disapproves of everything about Nate, but reluctantly paid for rehab when Nate asked. Not out of his own pocket, but rather funds he convinced the congregation to raise.

"Sorry," Nate mumbles, shamefaced like he's ten years old again when the pastor at his childhood church would glare down at him and tell him he'd sinned. "I shoulda called. I just wanna talk to Becky for a little while. I'll wait out here if you want."

Aaron's gaze sweeps up and down the row of tidy houses with their little lawns boxed in by white picket fencing like in a story.

"I'm not going to have you sitting on our front lawn," he says. "Come in. We are compelled to charity."

Nate doesn't reply, following Aaron into a house that always smells vaguely of soap and lavender. Aaron tells him to wait in the parlor, but it's too late. Nate's nieces have already spotted him from the adjacent dining room, and they leap out of their chairs, food forgotten, to come greet him. They chatter at once, about school and church camp and what they learned in Bible study, and Nate sits on the couch and tries to listen to them both.

"Girls." Aaron's quiet, steady voice is enough to silence them immediately. They sit straighter, shoulders squared, and look obediently up at him. "That's enough. Go finish your dinner, and then go upstairs and get ready for bed."

It's not their bedtime, of course, but Pastor Etson wants them out of the way before their scruffy, gay, ex-addict uncle can contaminate them with his "lifestyle." Nate tries to always keep in mind what Aaron has done for him, but the bitterness never quite leaves him.

The girls drag their feet as they leave the room, casting reluctant glances back at Nate.

Becky comes in from the kitchen in a flowery apron, her hair pulled back in a plain ponytail. She looks so much like their mother that a little part of Nate wants to curl up into a ball and disappear at the sight of her. He wonders why he came here, out of all the places in the city he could go, and for a few moments, he desperately wants to get high so he won't have to feel all of this anymore.

"I should go," he says, getting up. "Sorry I bothered

you."

"No, Nate, please." Becky hurries over to him and puts a hand on his arm. "Stay. Let's talk."

He remembers when she went with him to his first NA meeting, how she'd been so anxious about going to *that part of town*, but she sat in the little metal folding chair beside his and held his hand the whole time. And when it was his turn to go up and say his name, she cried, clutching her purse and letting the tears run down her face.

She guides him out into the backyard, and they sit together on a porch swing, looking into the dark night. It's unusually warm for late fall, the air pleasant and crisp around them.

"Do you want to talk about it?" she asks, touching his hand.

"Don't talk about it," she says, and now she's eleven years old, and Nate is nine, and he's wiping away tears while she changes the bandage on a burn on his hand with the kind of ease that only comes from experience. "If you don't talk about it, it's like it didn't happen."

It's always like this with Becky—the past and the present merging hazily together.

"I, uh..." He sifts through the mess in his head, trying to figure out what he can tell her. "I met a guy."

She frowns at him, her brows drawing together in a familiar look of disapproval.

"Not like that," he adds. "I mean, I met a guy who runs an art gallery. He wants to show my art there."

"Oh!" Her face lights up, and she claps her hands together. "That's wonderful, Nate. I'm so happy for you."

She had the same smile when he was sober for six

months, then a year, the same smile when he got his GED. But he also remembers the way she smiled at their mother, and he finds he can't forgive her, even now. With her unmarked skin and her sweet, wholesome family, she represents everything he could have been, if only he hadn't been such a fucked up, worthless, rotten kid. If only he had been an angel, like her.

ART MUSEUM SKETCHES, VARIOUS.

2005

Graphite on paper

The art gallery sits on a street full of other galleries, trendy, expensive jewelry boutiques, and stores selling handcrafted furniture for thousands of dollars apiece. Despite the affluence of the clientele, it maintains a studiously bohemian vibe, with overpriced cafes and kitschy decor. Nate glances longingly through the window into a warm coffee shop but pushes his hands into his pockets and forces himself onward. He's already late. He's never been to this part of downtown before, and he missed a train on the way.

He reaches his destination, an unremarkable white building with wide windows currently blocked by sheets of canvas. Finding the door unlocked, he gingerly pushes it open and steps inside. The room is all white walls, divided into open cubbies to provide more space for displaying paintings.

A tall, skinny man stands in the center of the room, staring at a canvas hanging on the far wall. Nate doesn't like it much, a mixed-media monstrosity of sparkles, feathers, and gaudy paint. It might have worked if the coloring—a burnt orange and vibrant purple—wasn't so jarring.

"No," the man says, shaking his head so that his hair, which resembles a blond tumbleweed, flops around his face. "No, no, no. This just won't work."

"It's the color," Nate says, surprising himself. "The colors are all wrong."

"Well, shit." The man turns to him with a sheepish smile. "You're totally right." He glances at the wrapped canvas tucked under Nate's arm. "Sorry, I'm not looking for new talent right now."

Nate hesitates, his cheeks growing warm. "You sure? Ras said to come here, and I know I'm late but—"

"That guy does not know how to take no for an answer." The man sighs as he takes the painting from Nate. He carefully unwraps it, muttering to himself as he does. "Well, you're already here. I'll look at it, but I already told him I'm not going to put something on display in my fucking gallery just so he can—"

He goes silent as the last of the canvas is revealed, and Sierra's face stares out at them from the dark background. Nate isn't sure if this is the best of his paintings, but it's the one that feels the most alive and real. In it, four-year-old Sierra looks like a bird in the breathless moment before she takes flight, in a canary-yellow shirt and blue shorts. Her arms and legs are stick thin with knobby elbows and knees—it was always so hard to get her to eat. Her skin is a light brown, her hair inky black, and her dark eyes have a kind of quiet desperation strikingly out of place on such a young countenance.

"Well, holy shit. I owe you an apology. Ras, too, apparently." The man curls his nose at the thought. "I thought he was just trying to get into your pants. But this is actually something."

The first half of that barely registers, because hearing someone say his art is "actually something," in that gentle, awestruck way, is almost more than Nate can bear. He's kept it hidden like a shameful secret for so long he would have been grateful for indifference. Praise is too much to accept.

"I'm Leo." The man holds out a hand, his grin a wide arc across his face. "Leo Morelli. It's a pleasure, Nate, it really is. You got any more stuff?"

"Yeah," Nate murmurs, still stunned. "Yeah, I got a ton. But it's all at my apartment in Bayside, and I don't got a car."

"Not to worry," Leo says. "I'll drive you."

*

Leo is silent, studying the paintings on the walls of Nate's one-bedroom apartment, moving from one to the next with deliberate attention, like he's in a gallery instead of a shitty walk-up in the Warrens that reeks of pot. Nate doesn't smoke, but the smell constantly drifts in from his next-door neighbor's.

Nate shifts his weight, hands clenched into fists. He feels naked, vulnerable, before such a studious examination.

"They're not really that good," he mumbles when Leo finally turns to him.

"On the contrary," Leo says, looking like he happened upon a pot of gold. "They're remarkable, Nate. Your technique is a little rough, but the colors more than make up for it."

Nate looks away, letting the words crash over him. *They're remarkable.* Does this guy mean it?

"Where did you study?" Leo asks.

"Study?"

"Yeah. Where'd you learn to paint?"

Nate hunches his shoulders, jamming his hands into his pockets. "I had a high school teacher taught me a little. I didn't go to any art school. I didn't—I mean, I don't fuckin' know shit. I just fuck around with paint."

"I beg to differ," Leo says. "Your portraits are absolutely haunting. That one of the little girl is by far the best too."

For the first time, Nate allows himself to smile. "Really?"

"Yeah. And, hey, I think I see some Postimpressionist influences here."

Nate's confidence evaporates. "Maybe, I dunno. I look at art books and go to the museum, but I'm not a smart guy. I just like to look, that's all."

"Look, Nate." Leo leans against the tiny slice of kitchen counter by the sink, studying him. "You're humble. I like that. Most artists as good as you aren't. But your technique is a little rough around the edges, and you really need an education in art history."

Nate shrugs. "So? I don't have money for classes, if that's what you're askin'."

"Yeah, I got that vibe," Leo says. "Starving artist and all that. Very romantic unless you're living it. I'm not an artist, and I can't teach you any technique. But I do know my way around the museum. How do you feel about Thursday afternoons? We'll get you up to speed in no time."

Nate steps back warily. "Why?"

"'Cause you've got so much potential, and I don't want to see it go to waste. And because every artist should know the traditions they come from. Your work is really reminiscent of van Gogh—you should at least know who he is."

Nate snorts. "I know who van Gogh is. I'm not stupid."

"My point still stands. So, what do you say?"

Nate shrugs to hide how desperately he wants it. He's hungry for it, eager to understand the connections and evolutions of each artistic movement, but it's an overwhelming task to undertake on his own. Having a guide would make all the difference. "Sure," he says half-nonchalantly.

"All right." Leo grins. "Let's get this stuff to the gallery. Then, we'll hit up the museum."

*

Leo seems to know where every painting in the museum is, leading Nate through a tour that doesn't seem at all random, giving a lecture that doesn't sound improvised.

"The Postimpressionists were all about emotion and symbolism," Leo says. "Most of the big names—Gauguin, Seurat, Cezanne, and, of course, van Gogh—generally worked independently. They didn't think of themselves as leading an artistic movement together. But they did."

Nate nods, trying to absorb all of it.

Leo stops in front of a painting Nate has visited on his frequent trips to this museum.

"You see," he says, gesturing to the bent figure of a man working in a field of waving wheat, thick dark lines curving to create his figure. "This is one of the reasons you put me in mind of van Gogh. The bold outlines and the expressive brushstrokes. You're familiar with this one, aren't you?"

"Yeah," Nate says absently, letting his eyes wander over the canvas. "'Course I am." But before Leo's lecture, he never had the language to explain the style he loves so much.

"Van Gogh made this one early on in his career," Leo continues, leading Nate farther down the hall. "Most of his early work is more like that, rugged brushstrokes and coarse, earthy tones. In 1886, he moved to Paris and met Gauguin and a few others who were also rebelling against the Impressionist style. After that is when you see the really famous ones emerge. You know, the irises, starry night, whatever."

"Are you really just making this up as we go?" Nate asks.

"Nate." Leo gives him a stern look, stopping in front of a woodblock print Nate particularly likes, portraying a dancer in sweeping lines, her long skirt flying whimsically. "This is history. *Your* history, as an artist. You should pay attention."

"I am. It's just...you really know all this off the top of your head?"

"I've got a PhD in art history, with a special focus on Expressionism and Postimpressionism. So, yeah. I know this off the top of my head."

Nate glances over at Leo, taking in his unkempt hair, his torn jeans, his AC/DC shirt.

"Don't look so surprised," Leo says.

"Sorry," Nate murmurs. "So, are you a professor or something?"

"Nah. I'm a consultant. Right now, I'm working for the syndicate, but I've been all over."

Leo gives him an easy grin and lowers his voice, so Nate has to lean in to hear him. "Last year I had a gig "reappropriating" indigenous art from museums in Mexico. Before that, I rigged a major art heist in Canada. That one made the papers—you might have heard of it."

Nate shakes his head. "I don't really read the papers."

"Well, it was a big deal," Leo says, sounding slightly annoyed. "Anyway, I wouldn't usually take on a project as small time as this gallery, but the syndicate boss is very persuasive."

"Did she threaten to break your legs?" Nate asks.

Although the identity of the syndicate boss is shrouded in mystery, her cruelty and ruthlessness are well documented. She's the shadowy figure behind the syndicate's power, while Ras is its face and its fist.

Leo laughs. "No. But then, I brought her a gift she couldn't turn down."

"What was it?"

"Here. I'll give you some idea."

Leo leads Nate down a corridor to another section of the museum. The walls are covered with dark, fantastical paintings, depicting suffering with intricate scenes, the colors vivid and haunting.

"This is a Goya," Leo says, gesturing to one of the paintings.

Nate nods. He's heard the name somewhere before.

"I gave her one of his paintings."

"Wow," Nate says. Even he has some idea of what a museum-worthy piece of art might be worth. "Really?"

"She's the kind of woman who makes you lose your head. You know what I mean." Leo hesitates. "Or maybe you don't. I get the vibe that you play for the other team."

"Yeah," Nate says gruffly, though it's been a long time since he's played for any team at all.

"Well, this whole gallery thing is my attempt to impress her. You're a big part of that—my diamond in the rough. So make me something amazing, okay?"

"I'll try," Nate mutters, trying not to squirm under the weight of Leo's expectations. "I don't see how this is supposed to make any money though."

"It's not. I'll explain."

Leo leads him out into the sculpture garden, and they sit on a little bench against a wall, where they can see if anyone approaches from any direction. Leo lowers his voice again, so that, to the outsider, they would seem to be having a casual conversation, difficult to overhear.

"The boss makes a lot of dirty money. The problem is, it's mostly cash, and that doesn't spend very well when you want to buy a new Ferrari. They need a way to clean that cash, and that's where we come in."

"How?"

"Who can say what a painting is worth?" Leo leans back, completely at ease as they discuss his illicit occupation. "Someone could pay ten grand for something you make. They pay it in cash, maybe, but in this city, that transaction makes it legit. The boss can take the cash and the bill of sale to the bank the next day and deposit it, and no one can pin anything on her for it."

Nate sighs, studying the sculpture before them, sheer white and curving delicately like lace, as tall as he is and wider than he can stretch his arms. "Figures. No real gallery would want my stuff."

"Ah-ah." Leo waggles his finger. "That's where you're wrong. I'm in charge of this gallery. I may not control where the money goes, but I wouldn't let you in the door unless you were the real deal."

Nate nods, only half convinced. "I don't like it that my art is bein' used for somethin' like this."

"Sure, it's crooked." Leo shrugs. "But it's giving us both a chance to start something new. You wouldn't be the first artist in history to jump through hoops for a rich patron, after all."

Nate wonders uneasily what other hoops Ras might think up for him to jump through for this chance to show his art to the world.

Dark Street in Ghost Town.

2005

Graphite and watercolor on paper

Perhaps there are worse places in the dark city than sitting before the syndicate boss, having earned her full displeasure, but there aren't many. Scarlett Bancroft looks down at the unlucky man with less pity than most people would feel for an insect. He's crossed her; he's carried away more than a kilo of cocaine that belonged to the syndicate and shipped it somewhere up the river through a clever series of sleights of hand. She needs to know who it went to and why, who is trying to wake her sleeping dragon. One of the cartels, maybe? Or the Bratva, who have established themselves as aggravating rivals who refuse to stay across the ocean in Russia.

"Who paid for it?" she asks the culprit, the only member of the operation they've caught so far. "Who hired you to steal from us?"

Phil—the unlucky drug smuggler—swallows hard but holds her gaze. His hands are bound to the arms of a sturdy wooden chair, his feet lashed to the legs. He's pale, fingers trembling restlessly, but he's holding firm. "If you kill me, you ain't never gonna find it."

"I'm not going to kill you," Scarlett says. "Not yet. I'm going to let Ras play with you first."

Phil's hands clench the arms of the chair, and he clears his throat. "Ras is my friend."

"His loyalty is to the syndicate," Scarlett says, though that isn't quite the truth. Ras walked away from the syndicate once and might do so again, except that his heart and soul belong to her.

Phil shakes his head, his lips pressed into a grim line.

The door opens, and Ras stalks in with all his dark glee, moving fluidly as a shadow. Fitting, as he is her shadow, her second in command. Her knife in the dark, her pet monster, her dearest love.

"Phil?" Ras raises his eyebrows in surprise. Of course he didn't read the email she sent explaining the situation—he rarely bothers to check Scarlett's notes, preferring to operate on instinct rather than strategy. "What did you do to piss the boss off so much?"

It's pitiful, Scarlett thinks, watching the way Phil perks up in Ras's presence, his eyes suddenly big and hopeful, mistaking Ras's charm and generosity for empathy.

"We're short more than a kilo of cocaine," Scarlett says. "He was sneaking it out of the city."

Ras's eyes flick to her for a moment, and she reads his expression well enough. *Are you sure?*

She gives him the slightest of nods, and she tells by his brief moment of hesitation that he doesn't like it, but he trusts her judgment.

Ras raises an eyebrow, glancing at Phil. "Why would you do that?"

"I didn't," Phil protests.

"Tell me who you work for," Scarlett says, "and I'll let you go with a warning."

Phil hangs his head for a long moment. Then he looks up, his eyes on Ras. "I swear to god I had no idea it was there."

Ras sighs, flops into a nearby desk chair, and puts his

feet up. "This is boring. "He glances at Scarlett. "If you let me cut off a few of his fingers, he'll talk faster."

Phil goes a shade paler, and Scarlett shakes her head. *Not yet.*

She's never sure how much of this is an act for him. His gleeful bloodlust is unsettling, something she'd hoped would be tempered as his mind recovered. But some days, she wonders just how well healed the break is, even all these years later. There are moments when he seems closer to the desperate teenager she remembers than the man she wants as the father of her child, but they are rare enough for her to forgive and forget.

"I'm a good guy," Phil says, on the very edge of babbling. "You know me. You know I'm not a traitor."

"I know what the boss tells me." Ras pulls a switchblade out of his pocket and idly plays with it, flicking the blade out and folding it back in.

"Because you fuck her," Phil says, his voice raw, furious. "Is she good? Is she worth it?"

Scarlett glances at Ras, the corner of her mouth quirking slightly up with contained amusement. This isn't the first time someone has implied she fucked her way to the top, but usually they're smarter than to say it when Ras is nearby.

"Go ahead," she says. "Show him that his words have consequences."

Ras gets up, looking to her again. For a moment she thinks of what he must have been like at fourteen years old, the same kind of knife gleaming in his hand, looking to his father for orders. Only, the leader he follows has changed.

"Make him sing for me," she says.

He gives her a gleeful smile, twirling the knife in his fingers as he approaches Phil, and gets to work. It doesn't take much blood to make Phil talk, naming a high-ranking member of the Bratva as the leader of his operation.

"Is that everything we need?" Ras looks languidly up from his knife. She nods, and he gives her a vicious grin. "So can I kill him now?"

"Make it quick. We were supposed to be at dinner half an hour ago."

He draws his knife across the prisoner's jugular before the man's frightened protest is fully voiced. Scarlett sighs to herself. She would prefer something less bloody, but she has to let Ras off the leash sometimes, or she wouldn't be able to hold him back at all.

"Let's go," she says as he glances back at her with blood spattered across the front of his shirt and the self-satisfied smirk of a cat who's dragged a mouse to her doorstep like a tiny offering. "You know your mother hates it when dinner is late."

He tilts his head and frowns, no longer a smug cat but now a chastised puppy, and despite herself, she feels guilty. Of course he is violent, and of course he is bloodthirsty. He was exactly what she needed when they first started out, when they first stood in the syndicate office in a skyscraper high above the city and plotted for all of it to be theirs. Through it all, he has been ever faithful by her side.

"You did good," she says, relenting. "Thank you."

He grins at her, wide and exuberant, and does a little bow before following her out into the night. She drives them out of the dark, abandoned warehouse district and merges onto the freeway that loops around the curve separating Ghost Town from Bayside, before it crosses the river into the district where his mother lives.

"I met someone." Ras pulls his bloody shirt over his head.

"A man or a woman?" She's not happy he's taking yet another lover, but by now, she's used to it.

He chuckles, shrugging on a white button-up shirt. "You always ask that first. A man, this time. An artist."

"Have fun," she says dismissively.

She's comfortable enough with their polyamorous arrangement, but only because she's secure in the knowledge that only she and Ash will ever really own his heart. And Ash has become like a brother to her, so it's easier to share. The three of them have found a simple harmony, but Ras keeps disrupting it by bringing other lovers into the fold at a whim of his exuberant heart, his passion impossible to contain. And he manages it, somehow, drawing on his relentless reserves of energy.

"I knew him before," Ras says hesitantly. "*Jude* knew him before. But...I can't remember." He glances at her, a touch of vulnerability in his shining eyes. "Why do you think that happens?"

She puts her hand on his thigh, her other resting on the steering wheel. This isn't the first time he's come across someone who he simply can't remember, someone he knew when his mind was still broken into two opposing pieces.

"It's normal," she says, though it's not. She wants to make him feel better because she knows this wound is beyond healing. "For someone who's been through what you've been through, it's to be expected."

He hums a noncommittal answer, turning to glance out the window.

"What's his name? Did I know him?"

"I doubt it. His name is Nate. The one who DiCiccio was going to kill."

"You and your big heart." She shakes her head. "It's going to get you killed someday."

"You love it about me," he says, his hand slipping up her thigh.

"I love that you're ruthless." She turns into the long driveway that leads up to his mother's house. "I love that you're dangerous."

After they park, he comes around to her side of the car and lifts her into his arms without warning.

She laughs, pressing her palm to his chest. "What are you doing?"

"Nothing," he says solemnly. "I just want to hold you. Because I love you."

She puts her arms around his neck and lets herself be carried up the wooden stairs and into the huge Victorian mansion where he grew up and where his mother still lives. He's given to both excessive displays of devotion, and small, quiet gestures that make her heart sing. She has a hard time with the way he falls head over heels for someone new. But when he sets her down in a kitchen filled with red roses, a jewelry box on the counter with an ornate ruby necklace inside, he looks at her with that shy, eager half smile she remembers from the time he went by "Jude," and her heart aches with the desire to be nearer to him.

"I stole it for you." He nods to the necklace.

"I love it," she says softly. *I love you.*

RAS #1, SERIES. 2005

Graphite on yellow sticky note

Nate's days fall into something of a comfortable routine. Thanks to Leo's connections, he got a job teaching figure drawing at a museum two mornings a week. He doesn't feel nearly qualified enough to be a teacher, but Leo talked him into it somehow, and he's actually starting to enjoy it. He likes interacting with the students.

After classes, he usually spends the rest of the day at the gallery, upstairs in the loft where the "artist in residence"—a title that still makes him giddy—gets to work. Leo insisted he have the space when he found out Nate was working out of his tiny studio apartment. He's not paid a lot, but it's enough to get by, and he has all day just to work in the gallery or go out in the city and sketch things.

Today, he doesn't have any classes, so he wanders through the museum for several hours, retracing the steps from Leo's latest lecture. Leo somehow always knows exactly what masterpiece Nate needs to see to inspire him on whatever he's working on. He gets back to the gallery just as it's closing, but that's okay because he has the key and permission to come and go as he wants. He says goodnight to the staff and heads up to the loft.

When he reaches the top of the stairs, he freezes. Ras is already there, his back turned to Nate, examining the sketches on the table.

"My white knight," he says without turning around, and his voice is tinged with a fondness that sends a strange sort of queasiness through Nate. "How are you?"

"I'm okay," Nate says, trapped in the doorway as though strung on a web.

Ras turns and gives him a smile that is half the glee of a spider approaching his meal, and half something else entirely. "Do you like working here?"

"Yeah." Nate's voice is a little raspy despite his sincerity. Something about Ras's presence, the dark look in his eyes, makes Nate's heart race, and his palms start to sweat. "I guess so."

"Draw something for me." Ras's tone is that of a man who is very used to getting his way.

Nate swallows the lump in his throat, but he looks Ras in the eye. Ras may not think they are equals, but he is wrong. "I don't work for free."

"Fair enough." Ras looks amused. "Draw something for me, and I'll buy you dinner."

"You treat everyone like this? You didn't used to be such an asshole."

Ras raises his eyebrows, startled. But then he laughs, and his laugh is rich and melodic and carefree. "I truly have become a monster. Asking you to dinner...what could be worse?"

"You didn't ask me," Nate says, crossing his arms. "You told me."

"I see." Ras still looks more amused than contrite, dipping forward in a mock formal bow and giving Nate a trickster grin. "Nate Redfield. Will you do me the honor of joining me for dinner?"

Nate looks at him warily. "I dunno. Last time you took me to dinner you almost killed somebody."

"I was multitasking." Ras looks slightly annoyed. "I am a very busy person. And I wasn't going to kill her."

Nate gives Ras a skeptical glance.

"You're right," Ras says with a look of contrition that is half undermined by the playful glint in his eye. "My full attention should be on you. This time, I promise not to spill a single drop of blood."

"I wanna draw you," Nate says cautiously, but something compels him to add, "After that...maybe."

*

"Hold still," Nate says.

His hand is paused above the sheet of paper covering the large drafting table. His fingers are smudged black from the charcoal, the barest outlines of Ras's distinctive features taken shape on the page. He's not handsome, with his sharp nose and strong features, but he has a definite allure. Nate finds his eyes drawn again and again to Ras's pale skin, his shock of black hair. And his eyes, which are this unbelievable shade of green, a green that makes Nate think of a picture in his eighth-grade textbook of a forest somewhere in China. He used to stare at it while the teacher droned on and on, putting his finger on the impossible green of the leaves and thinking *someday, someday, I will go there.*

He never went to China though. He's never even been out of the city. He had a foster family once that took vacations, but he was a difficult kid, so they left him behind to watch the dog. They'd leave in a flurry of swimsuits and beach chairs and come back trailing sand, a sheen of salt on their skin.

"I *am* holding still," Ras says indignantly, just as he leans forward to try and see the drawing.

Nate laughs, a rough, sweet rumble that startles him because it's been so long since he last made a sound like it. "You're moving right now."

"Fine." Ras sits up primly in the chair. "I'll be still."

And he is. For about a minute. Then he leans back, puts his feet up on an empty chair, and pulls a little switchblade out of his pocket. He plays with it, flicking the blade in and folding it out. At the first click of the shining knife, Nate's heart leaps into his throat, but Ras is looking up at the ceiling absentmindedly, and Nate realizes it's not a threat. He's just fidgeting.

"You're fucking scary, man," Nate says, but the thing is, he's not, not really, or Nate wouldn't have said anything at all.

Ras looks from Nate to the knife in his hand, eyebrows raised, then apologizes and puts it away. "My mother is always telling me not to do that. I forget sometimes."

"You got a mother?" Nate asks incredulously, then feels like a complete idiot when Ras laughs. "I mean, you're fuckin' Ras, y'know. You have any idea how people see you? You know what they say about you, right?"

"Yes, actually." Ras gets up and moves to stand by Nate, putting his hand on the back of Nate's chair just behind Nate's left shoulder so he can lean down and study the drawing. "They say I'm the most dangerous person in the city, and it's true. But it's not the whole truth."

Nate's heart races as Ras's fingers brush— accidentally? —against his shoulder. He swallows his fear, his heart beating like the wings of a hummingbird, sending vibrations through his chest.

"What's the whole truth?"

"What do you think? Does this"—Ras gestures to the drawing—"look like a picture of a monster to you?"

The man in the drawing is smiling and the glint in his eye could be charm or malice or something else entirely, something Nate doesn't want to name for fear of crushing it. The charcoal brings him to life in black-and-white, and the stark contrast suits him. He is so different from the boy Nate once knew, but at the same time, Nate feels a breathless certainty Jude is still there, somewhere, behind the smiling mask.

"I dunno." Nate chooses his words carefully.

The way things had been going, DiCiccio certainly would have shot him if Ras hadn't crashed that shitty little party. Instead, Ras decided not to kill him, bought him dinner, gave him a place to show his art. And now, he's even posing so Nate can draw his face, because his features are too compelling not to draw at least once. Nate wants to set aside the blue canvas on the easel by the window and pick up a fresh one to paint something else. Something green.

And that feeling scares him more than Ras's little knife.

*

It's close to midnight and Ras and Nate are tucked into an intimate table in the back of a posh bar—all leather seats and dim lighting, a woman in a sequined dress singing a slow jazz song in one corner. Ras is drinking whiskey, and Nate has some kind of fancy soda with elderberry and lavender and who knows what else. He's not sure how he's still here, except that he's been having more fun hanging out with Ras than he has had in a long time.

"Come back to my place with me," Ras says. "Just for a few minutes. I want you to see the view. I'm going to commission a painting of it."

Nate shrugs and agrees. It seems harmless enough.

*

Ras's apartment is nothing like Nate thought it'd be. He expected the king of the underworld would have a decadent palace, plush red furniture for half-dressed women to lounge on, cocaine in serving dishes. The spare, clean lines of the modern black-and-glass furniture give the open space a luxurious austerity. It suits Ras somehow.

They're on the top floor of the skyscraper, the city spread out before them—twinkling yellow lights in the dark—and Nate immediately understands why Ras wanted him to paint it. Nate has never seen the city like this except on postcards and the one time Troy took him to the top of the city's tallest building.

They had stood on the observation deck, a cool spring wind tousling Nate's hair, and Troy actually put an arm around him for a little while, the green tendrils of tattoo ink on his chin curving when his lips turned upward into a smile just for Nate. It had been easy to pretend it was a date, and that afterward maybe they would go to dinner, and make love like people did in movies and books.

Nate had wanted to stay up there forever, the city so distant. But, instead, he closed his eyes and let himself pretend that was his life, for a little while.

"It's beautiful, isn't it," Ras says. "I want you to make two paintings of it, one in the day and one at night. Those would be just for me, not for the gallery."

"Sure," Nate says, still half in memory. "I can do that."

"Come here." Ras sits on the floor by the window so confidently it seems more normal to imitate him than to sit in one of the chairs or on the couch. "When you're on the floor like this, it feels like the sky surrounds you. Like there's nothing between you and the city."

The window stretches in every direction around Nate, the glass so clean and clear it's barely there at all. Suspended in the air with Ras, it's like a magic carpet ride, like they might dip and twirl along the yellow lights of the city, and then fly up to run their fingers through the thin air around the stars.

"So what do you think?" Ras asks. "Are you ready for the art show to open?"

Nate hunches his shoulders like a turtle trying to slip into his shell. "I gotta be honest with you, Ras. You were the first person to see most of my stuff in a long time. I don't fuckin' trust other people, and I don't like them to see what I make."

"That seems lonely." Ras looks thoughtfully out at the city. "Making all those things for no one to see."

It is pretty fucking sad, Nate thinks. But he just shrugs.

"I'll add a little incentive, if that helps," Ras says. "Is there anything you want?"

An icy shiver runs down Nate's back as he realizes there is something he could ask for, something it would be trivial for Ras to acquire. Ras might not be a drug dealer like Nate was, he might not stand on the sidewalk covertly trading little baggies of narcotics for folded, grubby cash, but most of the drugs in the city pass through his hands.

The craving, the hunger so deep it's an ache in Nate's bones, awakens. A yawning mouth never sated, a starving, savage beast.

"You probably got the best dope in the city." The words come out smooth, practiced, even though his insides are shaking with shame and self-loathing and the manic hope that he might get high soon.

Ras glances at him, tilting his head. "No. You can have anything else you want. But no drugs."

Nate lets out a single, shaky laugh of relief, trying to collect every scattered piece of himself and puzzle them together again. His muscles feel weak and wobbly, like he just fought a battle.

"Why not?" he asks when he can breathe again.

"Because I like you," Ras says, as though it could ever be that simple. "And I don't want to ruin your life."

"Thank you." Nate means it.

Then Ras actually touches him, just a brush of his fingertips on Nate's shoulder. It makes Nate keenly aware that he can't remember the last time a man deliberately touched him in any way at all. When he meets Ras's eyes, there's something there. Not a spark, not a flame, but something resonant and less volatile. Like a low chord, it thrums through him.

"I probably used to sell you dope all the time." There's something like regret in Ras's voice. "Is that how you knew me?"

"You still don't remember?" Nate can't help but feel a little crushed. His memories of Jude—of their very few encounters—are still fresh and vivid in his mind. But at the same time, he's relieved. Jude saw him at his worst, at the lowest, most broken time in his life.

Ras is quiet for a moment, looking out at the city. "A mind is like a sheet of glass. Once it's broken, you can try to put it back together. But there will always be pieces missing."

Nate nods. He's not sure how to respond. It's cryptic, but also deeply tragic, something jagged held close to Ras's heart.

"When I was in your apartment," Ras says, "I have to admit I looked at a few of your sketchbooks. They are very beautiful."

Despite the compliment, Nate winces. Those sketchbooks are like diaries, but with pictures instead of words, and they chronicle the darkest parts of his life, delving into the ugliest reaches of his soul.

"There's a little girl who shows up often," Ras says. "Is she your daughter?"

"Not really. I mean kinda, 'cause my name's on her birth certificate. But not like... I mean, I never fucked her mom or anything. I was just there. I was the only person she had."

Ras raises an eyebrow. "Your name is on her birth certificate?"

"Yeah," Nate says past the lump in his throat. He misses her, desperately, and he knows she's probably in trouble and there's nothing he can do to protect her. Going to find her would mean going to find Troy, and Troy would get him high, and then he would lose everything.

"When she was born, I was standing outside the hospital room. The mom—Traci—she and I got to be friends while she was pregnant. I kinda took care of her, even though it wasn't my kid. Nobody else was there at the hospital to look after her, so I stayed and waited for the baby to be born."

Ras nods for him to continue, watching him in a way that makes Nate feel like he really cares about the story.

"So when the baby came, it was just me, standin' out in the hallway in case Traci needed me. I heard the baby cry, really loud, and then the nurse came and got me. Thought I was the dad. Turns out Traci didn't want to hold her new baby. She wouldn't even look at her. So the nurse gave me the baby."

Nate chuckles, glancing at Ras. "Fuckin' crazy, right? I was some dipshit kid, I didn't know nothin' about how to hold a baby. But she stopped crying when I held her. She looked up at me with these dark eyes, and I told her I was always gonna love her and always gonna protect her, and—"

Nate's voice breaks, and he bows his head to hide the overwhelming emotions crashing over him.

"You really are a hero." Ras's green eyes are wide and gentle. Everything about him, the relaxed tilt of his shoulders, the kind turn of his lips, speaks of openness, of guilelessness.

"I'm not." Nate hunches his shoulders and draws his knees to his chest, staring out at the dark city. "I ain't seen her in years. I send clothes and food and stuff, but it's not the same as bein' there. And I was just a selfish junkie back then anyway. I was no good for her."

"I find that hard to believe." Ras's hand settles on his shoulder, a brief press of warmth that leaves Nate wishing for more. "What's her name? Tell me a little bit about her."

As Nate talks about the little girl who will soon be turning seven, something eases in his chest, and he finds himself opening up in ways he never has, with anyone. Ras seems both genuinely interested and truly touched by the story of Sierra's first steps, her first tooth, her first word. Nate talks until his throat is dry—unaccustomed to holding conversations that last for more than a few moments. Ras puts an arm around his shoulders as he talks, and somehow, that seems fine, seems safe, despite the danger those hands represent to the rest of the world. He doesn't need to wonder what it means, the physical affection he drinks in like he's dying of thirst. These moments, suspended in the sky with the city sprawled all around them, are like time out of time, unconnected to anything he's lived before.

JUDE #4, SERIES. 2001

Acrylic on paper

Nate is alone in the empty house, the old windows rattling as the winter winds sweep by. Troy is on one of his trips to California, and this time, he decided to leave Nate behind with no dope, no money, and instructions not to "fuckin' go anywhere." Now, Nate sits in the small circle of light cast by an overhead lamp in their shabby living room, trying to draw. He's not withdrawing yet— Troy hasn't been gone that long—but he knows it will start soon. But even worse than that is the crushing sensation of being abandoned. He knows Troy is coming back in a few days, and everything will go back to normal. But a little voice in the back of his head keeps taunting: what if, what if, what if.

He wonders if he's done something wrong, if that's why Troy took off. Or maybe Troy realized, as every foster family eventually did, that Nate isn't worth the trouble.

A knock on the door startles him out of his thoughts, and he gets up and approaches the door. "Troy ain't here," he calls out. Usually, that's enough to make whoever it is leave.

"I know," comes the voice from the other side, low and just a little bit husky. "Can I come in?"

Nate pulls open the door. Jude de Haven is standing on the stoop with a small smile on his face.

"Hey," he says as Nate lets him into the apartment and shuts the door behind him. "Troy asked me to come check in on you. And give you this."

Jude pulls a little baggie out of his pocket, and it's all Nate can do not to snatch it from him. It's the good stuff, too, with a little silver stamp in the corner that means it's a syndicate product, a mark guaranteeing quality.

"Thanks, man," Nate says.

Jude smiles, sinking onto the worn futon with effortless grace like he intends to hang around for a while. Nate wonders if Troy asked him to, if Troy knew how lonely Nate would get. Nate doesn't know Jude, not really, but the syndicate enforcer comes around sometimes to meet with Troy. He's basically Troy's boss when Troy sells for the syndicate, an enforcer for the shadowy criminal organization. But Troy once told Nate that Jude has a notoriously soft heart, that he's never killed someone or even broken a knee. The syndicate gets someone else to do that when it needs to be done.

"Go ahead," Jude says, nodding at the drugs. "I don't mind."

He watches curiously, but without judgment, as Nate goes through the familiar ritual. His hands, so unsteady holding a pencil, don't shake at all as he holds the spoon over the flame of his lighter. He always has clean, fresh needles—Troy takes care of him like that and in a thousand other ways—but that hasn't stopped him from developing track marks along the inside of his left arm. Jude doesn't look away as the shining needle sinks into his skin, and Nate leans his head back and closes his eyes. The sweetness rushes through him, smooth and sparkling through every nerve all the way to his fingers and toes.

He feels the warm press of fingertips on the side of his neck, over his pulse, and he opens his eyes. Jude gives him a shy smile and pulls his hand away.

"Just checking. I've seen someone OD."

Nate smiles back at him. Jude is so kind to him, so gentle.

"What's it like to get high?" Jude asks.

Nate has to think for a moment. Words would be utterly inadequate, but he still tries. "It's nice. It's like...everything that was broken inside me is fixed and beautiful. Like a painting."

Jude nods thoughtfully.

"Ain't you ever been high?" Nate asks.

"No." Jude looks down at his long, slender fingers, frowning. "I don't trust myself enough to lose control like that."

"I trust you." Nate takes one of Jude's hands in his own, lacing their fingers together. He wants to be touched—not in a sexual way—but just like this. Just easy, just gentle.

"Nate..." Jude says, but Nate is already pulling him closer, tugging Jude's arm around his shoulders and lying down on the futon.

Jude moves with him fluidly, and they lie together on the futon's wide base, Jude curled around Nate like a shell, his arm thrown over Nate's chest. In this moment, Nate feels perfectly content, like the world could shatter beneath him and he wouldn't even care. He pretends the warmth filling his chest didn't come from a needle, but rather from a man like Jude, a good man who loved him, who Nate loved back.

ALLEY CAT. 2005

Acrylic on canvas

Nate wakes with a start, the blankets falling off his chest as he sits up. The morning sun shines through the big windows, and it takes him a moment to remember why he's in this room full of light and not his dark, dingy apartment in Bayside.

Jude.

He looks around. A man about his age is sitting at the kitchen table, writing in a notebook. The man looks up, curly black hair falling over his forehead, and gives Nate a friendly smile. "Good morning."

"Hey," Nate grunts, shoving the blankets off, feeling more and more vulnerable as the grogginess fades.

The man gets up. He's wearing all black, a tank top, and tight jeans. Leather bands of varying widths cover his left wrist and forearm, and a black collar circles his neck. He has tan skin and very dark eyes, and he doesn't look like a thug at all. Nate wonders what the hell he's doing here.

"I'm Ash," he says with a friendly smile.

Nate gives him a brusque nod. "Nate."

"You know, we have a guest bedroom. I don't know why Ras made you sleep out here."

"He didn't make me," Nate mumbles. "We were talking, and I...just fell asleep, I guess."

He looks away, remembering how exactly he'd fallen asleep, sitting on the floor, his head on Ras's shoulder, the crime boss threading his fingers gently through Nate's hair as they talked. There hadn't been any sex, or even any kissing. Just...affection that, for once, didn't feel like it came with a price tag. Ras must have picked him up after he fell asleep and put him on the couch, tucked a pillow under his head and pulled a blanket over him. Nate feels an odd, wistful twinge in his chest, thinking of it.

"Well, next time, you can stay in the guest room," Ash says.

Nate nods, his eyes catching on the deep purple hue Ash has painted his nails. "Are you, like, Ras's assistant or something?"

Ash laughs, settling into the easy chair opposite Nate. "I'm his boyfriend."

Heat flushes Nate's neck and chest and face. "I don't.... I mean...Ras is gay?" He stumbles over the words for reasons he refuses to let himself understand.

Ash's smile fades. "He's pansexual. I thought you knew."

Something in Nate's chest is suddenly shuttered like a window before a storm. "No," he says, and his voice is too loud, abrasive to his own ears. "I didn't know. Why would I know?"

"Is it going to be a problem?" Ash crosses his arms, his open, easy demeanor becoming guarded and aloof. "Because Ras shot the last guy who called him a fag."

Nate's prickly anger subsides somewhat. He doesn't want Ras to think he's one of those guys, not when he's spent his entire life trying to avoid them.

"Not like that," he mutters, staring down at his restless hands. The blue smudges on the thumb and forefinger remind him of the unfinished painting on his easel at home, the one he wants to put away so he can pull out a fresh canvas and immediately start on a portrait of Ras.

"Not like that," Ash says skeptically. "Then what? What's the problem?"

Nate kicks at the carpet, unable to meet Ash's eyes. "It's stupid."

"I won't think it's stupid."

Nate looks up. Ash's face is gentle, open. Nonjudgmental.

"It was kinda like a date, okay?" Nate struggles to get the words out. "Last night. I thought we were friends, but maybe he thought something else. Didn't know he had a boyfriend either."

"So Ras wants to date you, and you're freaking out because you're not into that. You can relax. Just tell him you're straight, and he'll leave you alone."

"I'm not straight." Nate raises his head to glare at Ash, even though none of this is Ash's fault and most of it is probably pretty upsetting to him. "I'm not anything. I'm not letting someone do that to me ever again. I just wanna be left the fuck alone."

Ash nods, and it's not sympathy in his eyes, but an acknowledgment of Nate's suffering that feels both kind and objective. "That's fine, Nate," he says carefully. "No one's going to make you do anything you don't want to do."

"Sorry," Nate mumbles. "Didn't mean to..."

"Don't worry about it." Ash folds his long legs underneath himself and smiles. Oddly enough, he doesn't seem the slightest bit upset or jealous. "Just tell him you're not interested. He'll be fine. He's got an ego the size of this city."

"Who does?" Ras walks through the doorway, covered in sweat, a towel over his shoulder. Nate lets his eyes travel over the muscles of Ras's bare arms, the contours of his torso through his tight black shirt, then bows his head and tries not to blush when he realizes what he was doing.

"You." Ash gets up and crosses the room to give Ras a kiss. "Of course."

When Ras looks at Ash, it's like no one else in the world exists, for a few seconds. He presses his thumb against Ash's chin and smiles, and Nate realizes he would give almost anything for someone to look at him with such tenderness, to give him a smile like that.

*

Ras pulls up in front of Nate's apartment complex. "Nate." He leans back against the seat and smiles. "I had fun with you last night. Can I take you to dinner again?"

Nate stares at the paint stains that never seem to wash off his hands, torn between wanting and caution. He's been here before, about to trust, about to find out the kindness he's so drawn to is only an illusion, a shellac veneer. This tenderness is dangerous; this yearning will only lead to ruin.

Ras is not the same person, the same man who helped Nate climb out of the pit of his own despair. But he's close enough that Nate has to force himself to stay aware of the difference.

"It was real nice," he begins, without looking at Ras. "Thanks. But I...I don't really think it's a good idea. Sorry."

Ras seems disappointed, but he still smiles. The unofficial king of the city probably doesn't get rejected often.

"Okay. I'll probably see you around the gallery, when you have your first show."

Nate realizes with an odd lurch to his stomach that he's going to look forward to it.

SIERRA WITH BIRTHDAY CAKE. 2005

Colored pencil on paper

Sierra sticks seven candles in the little chocolate cake with lopsided white frosting that her mom made in the microwave because they don't have an oven. Her mom is sleeping now, passed out before they could celebrate.

She doesn't have anything to light the candles with, so she sits on the rickety wooden chair and pretends they are lit, casting a warm glow over the room. Just as she's about to blow the imaginary flames out, the cell phone on the couch rings, and she runs to answer it before it can disturb her mother's rest.

There's silence on the other end of the line for a long moment, and then a familiar voice says, "Hey, Sierra."

She draws her knees to her chest and picks at invisible lint on her pants, her heart leaping against her ribcage. "Hi, Nate."

"Happy birthday."

She smiles into the tiny kitchen, at the sad little cake huddled on the table. Nate doesn't call often, and she never knows when it will be, but he remembered her birthday, and that sends a warm contentment through her to the tips of her toes. She remembers his face, the big hands that would tie her shoes and zip up her coat in the winter. But it's been years since she's seen him, and she's gotten used to the idea that all she'll ever have of him is a phone call two or three times a year. It makes her angry, and she doesn't understand it, but she has come to learn that the hurtful whims of adults will never make any sense.

"Is there a brown paper bag somewhere in your apartment?" he asks. "It has a picture of a cat on it."

She gets off the chair and hunts through the junk discarded by the door until she finds it, a bag with the logo for a local market on it, the top taped closed. "Can I open it?" she asks, her heart racing.

"Go ahead."

She rips open the brown paper with her free hand, her other clutching the phone to her ear. Inside is a stuffed shark, blue and fuzzy and the perfect size to hold in her arms. "How did you know I love sharks?" she asks, hugging it tightly against her chest.

"Just a guess."

"He's going to be my new best friend," she says, staring into the shark's beady black eyes. "What do you think his name is?"

"I dunno." Nate's voice is rough over the phone, like he's been coughing or has a cold. "Sharky?"

She giggles. "That's the worst name ever."

"You name him, then."

"Fine. I—" She stops abruptly as the door swings open and her uncle Troy steps in, bringing the winter cold with him.

"Who are you talking to?" Troy asks, crossing the tiny room with his usual swagger. Water has collected on the shoulders of his gray coat and in his hair, and he carelessly brushes it away.

"I love you, Sierra." Nate speaks quickly, frantically, and then a soft click lets her know he's gone.

Sierra throws the phone at Troy, missing him by a foot and hitting the wall. "You ruin everything!"

"Jesus fuckin' Christ, kiddo," he says, spreading his arms. "You talkin' to your boyfriend or somethin'? Ain't you a little young for that?"

Sierra curls up into a ball on the couch, sandwiching her shark between her knees and chest, and buries her face in its blue fuzz. "I hate you. Go away."

Troy heaves a heavy sigh, running a finger alongside the edge of her cake and then licking off the frosting. "What's the cake for?"

"It's my birthday, you asshole," Sierra mutters.

Something like kindness crosses Troy's face, and he sits beside her on the couch. "I forgot. I'm sorry."

Still curled into herself, Sierra shrugs.

"Shit, I remember the day you were born like it was yesterday. Your mom screamed like she was dyin' the whole time." Troy chuckles softly. "I had to go take care of some business, but Nate wanted to stay the whole time. He wouldn't fuckin' leave for a minute. When I got back, he was in the room with your mom, and he was holdin' on to you like you were the only thing in his world. Like he already knew you and already loved you." Troy's laugh is bitter this time. "He never looked at me like that, that's for damn sure."

The story makes Sierra feel warm, like she's loved, even from all this distance. "Do you think he could be my real dad?" she asks in a tiny voice.

"He ain't your dad." Sierra's mother is standing in the doorway to the only bedroom, hands on her hips. "You know that, honey."

"Yeah," Sierra mumbles, looking down at her shark. "I know."

"Your daddy lives in the Rise, in one of those big houses with ten bedrooms and a pool. Someday, he's gonna come for us, and we'll live there too. We'll have a wedding and a happy ever after," Traci reminds her.

Sierra doesn't look up from her shark. It's a promise she's heard before, one she's tired of. She doesn't know if it's true, and she doesn't care. She wants Nate to be her dad, and she wants him to come back, and she knows neither of those things will ever happen.

STILL LIFE OF LILIES. 2005

Acrylic on canvas

Through the windows of the elevated train, the city blurs by, streaks of bright lights in the gray, drizzling dusk. Ras doesn't look up from his phone as the train jostles to a stop, a pleasant female voice announcing the neighborhood. He's absorbed in a file his information broker put together detailing the documented aspects of Nate's life, records which are spotty at best, particularly after he turned sixteen and ran away from his foster family.

Ras prefers the train to the slog of traffic when he's traveling in and out of the denser regions of the city. His destination is in the Warrens, a once regal district of stone buildings and brick-paved streets. Now, it's the worst part of the city, its crime-infested dark heart. Ras got his start there, dealing drugs for the syndicate and working his way up until he commanded every street corner and seedy back alley. Now, he's the second in command of the entire operation, a criminal empire run like a ruthless corporation, bringing in massive profits. Working beside Scarlett, Ras has already more than doubled his father's not inconsiderable fortune. He's the boss's knife in the dark when a show of force is necessary, and her representative on the streets when diplomacy is enough.

Someone slumps into a seat near him, heaving an exhausted sigh. Her heavy bag slides across the seat as the train lurches forward, crushing the bouquet of calla lilies next to Ras.

"Oh shit," she says, reaching for it. "I didn't mean to—"

Ras looks up from his phone, and the woman draws in a sharp breath.

"Oh god. I didn't—I didn't know it was you. I'm sorry. I—"

Ras tilts his head, studying her face. It's not familiar to him, but then, he knows a lot of people. And there are those like Nate, who he simply doesn't remember. People that one half of his mind kept secret from the other when he was a teenager, and therefore, only hints of them remain in his memory.

"We haven't met," she says. "I just...seen you around."

"Well, then you have me at a disadvantage," he says, smiling pleasantly.

"Tallie." She's still clutching the heavy bag to her chest, but she seems to be calming down considerably.

"It's a pleasure to meet you, Tallie."

"Wow. You really are just like they say. A real gentleman."

"That's what they say about me?" Admittedly, Ras is going to be a little disappointed if that's all the rumor mill has to offer him.

"Well, the *Daily* ran a story that you used to be an assassin for the government until you met a beautiful woman you couldn't bring yourself to kill, and then you turned to a life of crime."

Ras grins at her. That's more like it. He used to have to bribe the tabloids to print stories about the syndicate, spreading its influence across the city, but now they do it because it sells papers.

"Look, I'm real sorry about your flowers," Tallie continues. "You going to a funeral or something?"

Ras glances at the crushed lilies. "A funeral?"

"Yeah. Calla lilies are funeral flowers. It's bad luck to bring them to anything else, you know."

Ras picks up the mangled blossoms. "I'm going to kill that florist," he says amiably enough.

Tallie gives an awkward half laugh and looks away.

"I'm kidding," he reassures her.

"Sure," she says, but she sounds uneasy. "I know that."

"And you know about flowers?"

"You bet. I love flowers. I always wanted to be a florist. I used to read those flower dictionaries, you know, that had all the different meanings. Look, if you get off with me at Lispard, I'll take you to someone who can make a better bouquet than that."

"I'd appreciate it." Lispard is his stop anyway, and now that the lilies are mangled, he will need something else. Maybe that's for the best. He glances at the broken white blossoms. *Funeral flowers*. That's certainly not the message he intended.

He picks up his phone again and resumes reading the file that had him so absorbed before Tallie got on. He's halfway through the report from Child Protective Services about ten-year-old Nate, detailing the reasons he was removed from his mother's care, when the pleasant feminine voice chimes through the car.

"Lispard Street Stop. Please exit to the right."

Ras helps Tallie with her heavy bag, carrying it for her as she leads him to a flower shop crammed into a tiny sliver of a storefront. She helps him choose a better bouquet, pale orange roses and a bird of paradise in the center.

Tallie bows her head over the bouquet, breathing in the fragrance, then grins, handing it to Ras. "Whoever this is for is a lucky lady."

It turns out Tallie is going the same direction, so they walk together through the wet streets. The rain falls softly, more of a drizzle than a downpour, and little droplets of water collect on the curved petals of the roses. Ras stops in front of a long, squat stretch of apartments, three stories high with dreary gray siding.

"Oh, hey," Tallie says, ambling up beside him. "I live here too. What's your girlfriend's name? Maybe I know her."

"Not a girl. And he's not exactly dating me. Yet." Ras doesn't advertise his sexuality, but he doesn't go out of his way to hide it either.

"Holy shit," Tallie gasps. "You're gay? That's the one rumor I always figured couldn't be true."

Ras turns to her and raises an eyebrow. "Why would that be so hard to believe?"

"'Cause there's always a woman in the stories about you. The syndicate boss, right? The story goes you love her so much you'd die for her."

"I would," Ras says as they reach the end of the hall, approaching the door marked 202. "These things are not mutually exclusive. I'm pansexual. And capable of loving more than one person at once."

"But you work with criminals. Gang members. Tough guys. They fuckin' hate people like you."

"A few men have made an issue of it." Ras turns and gives her a vicious grin. "Where do you think they are now?"

Her eyes get wide, and she swallows, forcing a smile back onto her face. "Well, I guess they're gettin' what's comin' to them."

"Yes." Ras approaches the familiar door and knocks hard on it.

"Oh," Tallie says from behind him, clapping her hands together in excitement. "I know Nate. We're real good friends. He's painted me, like, five times now. He ain't here right now though. He's off visiting his sister."

Ras hands her the flowers and turns to the door again, rummaging in his pocket. "Tell me about him."

"Well, he's a good guy. About as good as they come, really. He ain't got nothing, but he shares what he's got. He's the one guy I know will come get me when I'm too fucked up to get home by myself. And—hey, what are you doing?"

Ras presses just so with his lockpick and the door makes that satisfying click he loves to hear. He turns the handle and steps into the apartment.

"You can't just go in there," Tallie says. "Nate's not home."

Ras takes the flowers and gives her his most charming smile. "I want to surprise him. I've done it before—I'm sure he won't mind."

Tallie looks worried but nods reluctantly and says goodnight. It's not as though she could stop him even if she tried.

By the time Nate opens the door, Ras has found a tall plastic cup to put the flowers in and arranged them on the tiny dining table among the pastels and sheets of thick white paper. He's on Nate's sofa, reclining with his feet up on the armrest, reading over the rest of Nate's file on his phone. It paints a bleak picture of a man who's been mistreated all his life, and Ras wishes he could remember how they knew each other. Nate isn't the only gap in his memory from those years, and he's mostly gotten used to the idea that those parts of himself may be gone for good, part of the price he had to pay to make his mind whole again.

"You're in my apartment." Nate sounds more resigned than surprised, standing in the doorway with a heavy book tucked under one arm.

"I wanted to see you." That much should be obvious.

"And...you brought flowers?" Nate sounds puzzled.

"Don't you like them?" Ras asks, sitting up.

Nate glances uneasily at the bouquet, then finally steps into the apartment and shuts the door behind him. "You, uh, you're supposed to bring flowers for girls."

"It doesn't seem fair they should have all the fun. I thought you might like to paint these. That's all."

Nate sighs, setting the thick black book on the table by the couch. Ras peers at it.

"A bible?"

"I already got four." Nate gives him a weary shrug. "I went to go see my sister. They're pretty religious. I think giving me this makes them feel better."

"Can I make you dinner? As a friend," Ras adds before Nate can make a predictable protest.

Nate crosses his arms over his chest with a suspicious frown. "Why?"

"Because we're going to be working together, and I'd like to get to know you." It sounds very convincing, Ras thinks. And it's not entirely a lie.

But more than that, he can't get it out of his head, that moment when Nate stood in the doorway to the restaurant's back room, his shoulders high and chin raised like some kind of knight from a bygone era as he said the words that would save someone's life. His surly, suspicious persona had fallen away, revealing a shining nobility. Ras can't for the life of him figure out why he finds it so compelling. Nate is a hero, and Ras is a lifelong villain, and he should find heroism antagonistic, or at least boring, but when it comes to Nate, he doesn't. He's fascinated by the light within Nate, and he's not about to let it slip out of his grasp.

"Just friends," Nate says. "I guess so."

Ras grins at him. He wonders if the fire inside Nate can be tamed, if it can be owned. It's a challenge he'll certainly enjoy.

JUDE #5, SERIES. 2001

Graphite on paper

Jude glances through the narrow doorway into the next room where Nate and a little girl sit together on the sofa, high, squeaky cartoon voices coming from the TV they're watching. Nate nods at him, more guarded than the last time they were together, but of course, he's probably not high right now. Jude has learned how much of a difference that makes.

"In here, Jude," Troy says, leading him farther into the house to a bedroom with rumpled sheets on the bed and enough drugs spread across a worn dresser to make a DEA agent's career. "Look, I ain't got it all today, okay? I gotta take care a Nate now, and that little girl until her mom gets back. Shit's expensive."

Jude hesitates, running his fingers along the edge of the dresser. "I'll talk about it with Ras. But he won't be happy."

"Come on, Jude," Troy whines. "I ever been late before? Ever? Just cut me a little slack. No need to bring the big guy in on it."

Jude suppresses his annoyance. He and Ras are exactly the same size, but everyone thinks of Ras as somehow larger than life, and Jude as strictly ordinary. No one knows they wear the same face and reside in the same body.

"If you're having cash-flow problems, we can talk about it."

"Nate's an addict," Troy says, sighing heavily. "I use sometimes, sure, but he's a fuckin' mess about it. It ain't cheap keepin' him in dope."

It's not that expensive, either, not for a drug dealer who moves as much product as Troy. Jude knows very well how much a dose of heroin costs, and how much profit Troy should expect to keep after the syndicate takes its cut. He does the math without thinking about it, in the back of his mind, while the rest is occupied with wondering what exactly he should do with Troy. Extend his loan a few more days, or make an example of him?

"Look, I gotta take care of Nate first, all right?" Troy says. "Cut me a little fuckin' slack, man."

It's rare to find a drug dealer who is openly gay, but Troy makes no secret of it. He shows off Nate—more than ten years younger and handsome—the way other high-level dealers display the beautiful young women drawn to their wealth and power. Jude admires that, and secretly envies it.

He picks up a bag of dope on the dresser—low quality black tar. No syndicate stamp of approval in the corner of the bag. "You give him this shit? Or do you sell it along with our product?"

"I don't sell nothin' but what you give me," Troy says, his face red. He knows the rules of their arrangement are unbreakable. "Swear it."

"So you give it to Nate?"

"What choice do I got?" Troy throws his hands up. "You sure as shit ain't gonna cut me any slack."

Jude studies the heroin in the light. He's as familiar with illicit drugs as anyone who has never used them can be—though Ras has tried almost everything at least once. "Do you really care about Nate?"

"'Course I do." Troy sounds offended. "Nate can be a pain in the ass, but I love him. If you got a problem with that, I—"

"I don't." Jude sets the drugs down. "I have a problem with not being paid on time."

Troy sighs, shaking his head, then goes to the closet and pushes aside a pile of clothes to reveal a floor safe. "Fine, fine," he mutters. "Romance is fuckin' dead; I get it."

There are no decorations on the walls of the bedroom, except one large drawing tacked to the wall above the bed. It's recognizable as a portrait of Troy, but there is a nobility and kindness to his features Jude has never seen before. He moves closer to examine the pencil strokes, the block letters in the bottom right that say NATE R.

"How did you know you were gay?" Jude didn't intend to voice his thoughts but was unable to hold them back.

"I dunno," Troy says, still rummaging around in the safe. "Guess I kinda always knew. Why? You havin' an identity crisis?"

Jude doesn't answer, because the truth, to some degree, is yes. He's been around heroin users enough to know that the desire for physical contact is a part of the high, nothing more, but he hasn't forgotten what it felt like to hold Nate in his arms.

Troy snorts laughter, straightening and turning to hand Jude a pile of cash. "Tell you what. Spend some time with Nate and see what it does for ya." He winks extravagantly, making his meaning clear. "He ain't cheap, but he's worth it."

Jude looks quickly away, trying to hide the sudden surge of anger. It's a little unusual—he's no stranger to *pragmatism, and a large part of his job is managing the prostitutes who work for the syndicate. Still, it bothers him. Nate is different, and he doesn't belong in a place like this, with a man like Troy. If Nate were his, Jude would give him everything he wanted, before he could even think to ask. He would never have to earn it.*

Jude counts the money quickly, the way he's been trained to from the time he was a little boy, and raises an eyebrow at Troy.

"If you try to cheat me one more time, I will have Ras pay you a visit." He's tired of people assuming that because he's seventeen and quiet, they can cheat him with impunity. He's only been in this position for a month or so—before it, he was just another dealer—and he's constantly having to exert his authority.

"Shit," Troy mutters, pulling a few more hundred dollar bills out of his wallet. "There. Happy?"

Jude nods and tucks the cash away.

"Look, kiddo. You wanna piece of advice? Just do what makes you happy. If you don't feel guilty about sendin' Ras to carve people up, don't feel guilty about bein' whatever you are. It ain't hurtin' nobody."

Jude smiles then. He reaches into his pocket and takes out a baggie containing several little balloons of heroin, stamped in the corner with the syndicate mark.

"For Nate," he says, handing them over.

Troy grins, wide and sly. "He's a fuckin' prize, ain't he? Light of my fuckin' life."

On the way out, Nate glances up at Jude, gives him a shy smile. He really is handsome, with a nobility that doesn't seem to fit in this dark, smoke-smelling apartment. The little girl keeps her eyes firmly on the TV, as though trying to pretend no one else is there.

As he makes his way down the sidewalk, Jude turns Troy's words over and over in his mind. He doesn't think about where he's walking until he finds himself in front of a familiar blue door with scratched paint, one of many in a long row. He's been here before, of course, but only to drop off drugs for the man who lives inside.

Jude knocks on the door, his heart beating hard against his ribcage. After a few moments, Ash opens it. He smiles and leans against the doorframe, his gangly body at ease and open. He's wearing a shirt that's too big for him, with the logo for a local restaurant on it, and tight, torn black jeans. His nails are painted black to match. There are always dark circles beneath his eyes, but the ashen cast to his skin is absent, and his eyes are bright and clear. That means it's a good day.

"I wanted to let you know..." Jude's been going around the Warrens, telling all of his former clients he won't be dealing anymore, and hooking them up with other syndicate operatives to continue the distribution. But when he stops bringing Ash his pills, he'll have no excuse to see him again.

"You got promoted? Yeah. Your buddy told me. It's cool, Jude. Just give me the number of whoever I should call."

Jude takes a deep breath. He feels like his whole life has been leading up to this moment, the sunlight filtering through the clouds above them, Ash's curly dark hair and his golden skin, his strong features and night-black eyes.

"Did you have dinner yet?" Jude asks. "I know a good Thai place just down the street. I'll buy."

When Ash smiles, Jude thinks of that breathless magical moment when his mother flips the switch in the living room and the hundreds of little lights on the giant Christmas tree and along the windows come on all at once.

Jude doesn't have the courage to take his hand under the table as they sit together in a booth in the back of a dark, smoky bar, or, later, to kiss him goodnight, standing just inside Ash's apartment saying a reluctant goodbye. But he thinks maybe someday he will.

LEO THINKS ABOUT HIS GIRL. 2005

Watercolor on paper

Leo sighs heavily, sitting in the back room of an upscale jewelry store, looking over the array of obscenely expensive diamond necklaces the obsequious clerk has laid out for them. A twenty-thousand-dollar diamond necklace just isn't going to be good enough. Crown jewels wouldn't be good enough.

"What do you think?" he asks Nate, perfectly still beside him, like he's afraid to so much as breathe on the expensive gemstones. "Do you think she'd like any of them?"

"I dunno," Nate says. "What are you asking me for? I never even met her."

A fair point, but Leo doesn't really have anybody else to ask. He's relatively new to the city, drawn by the promise of notoriety and fortune, and he hasn't made many friends yet. But he's glad to have stumbled upon Nate, a diamond in the rough and his newest project. There are few things Leo enjoys more than being the first one to discover talent and setting that artist on their way to success. Nate has talent, no question. Oodles of it, and literally no confidence to back it up.

"This is for...a girlfriend?" the clerk asks. "A wife?"

"A girlfriend. She's gorgeous. Here." Leo pulls his phone out of his pocket and brings up a picture to show the clerk, who squints at it and then sits up straighter.

"That's Scarlett Bancroft," the clerk says.

Nate takes the phone and studies the photo, frowning. "Bancroft, huh?"

"You know her?" Leo asks.

Nate sets the phone down. "Everybody knows the fuckin' Bancrofts, man. They run this city. Ain't you heard of the Bancroft Bridge? Bancroft Tower?"

"Hey, I'm new here," Leo says.

"Scarlett is a difficult woman to buy jewelry for," the clerk says, setting his fingertips on the velvet surface of the table. "But I knew her when she was younger. I'm sure I can recommend something."

"Sure." Leo watches the clerk's hands as they flutter around the diamonds, without making it obvious he's watching. He's not planning to buy or steal anything—none of it seems right—but it can't hurt to know their procedures should he ever get itchy fingers and choose this store as a target.

"You should get her something more personal," Nate suggests when they're back out on the street. He seems to breathe easier, not surrounded by polished and expensive things.

Leo sighs. "This is impossible. No matter what I get for her, Ras will get her something a hundred times better."

It's cute, or...something, the way Nate startles at the very mention of Ras's name. Poor guy—Ras must have him pretty spooked. It doesn't seem like real fear though. Ras is scary as fuck, but only if you give him a good reason to be, and as far as Leo knows, Nate hasn't. He's no expert but he can read people pretty well, and the brief conversations he's had with Ras tell him Nate isn't in any real danger of anything except maybe getting laid—if he's into that. Nate seems like a good guy, though, too good to be getting mixed up with someone like Ras. If asked for advice, Leo's going to tell him to stay the hell away.

"What's Ras got to do with it?" Nate asks, and Leo's eyes widen because he realizes Nate doesn't know. Which is really kind of shitty, that Ras would try to seduce Nate and not even bother to explain his weird situation.

"He's dating Scarlett. Fuck, but Leo hates saying that out loud. There's no way he would touch something like this with a ten-foot pole except that a woman like Scarlett only comes by once in a lifetime. "They have a polyamorous relationship. Ras, his boyfriend, and her."

"Polyamorous. The fuck's that mean?"

"It means they fuck whoever they want, I guess. It's fine for them, but I just know that Scarlett's gonna want to settle down soon. Ras is never gonna change, but I'll be there when she wants something different."

"That's your master plan?" Nate glances skeptically at Leo. "Just hope she outgrows it?"

"Look, you've never met Scarlett, so you can't possibly understand. She's like a fucking queen, man. She pretty much runs this whole city. She's smart and cutthroat and drop-dead gorgeous." *Sometimes literally.*

"She runs the city? Because she's a Bancroft, you mean?"

"Nah, man." Leo lowers his voice. Years of practice have taught him exactly what level is audible to a companion but impossible for a passerby to overhear. "Because she's the syndicate boss."

"Oh," Nate sighs. "I guess that makes sense. Everybody in this whole fuckin' city is crooked."

Nate's got that right. For Leo, it's part of the appeal. He doesn't go in for violence, and he would never steal from someone who really needed the money, but when you come right down to it, he's still a crook.

They spend the clear, cold December day wandering through jewelry stores and clothing boutiques, looking at scarves and more expensive necklaces, but Leo clucks his tongue and shakes his head at every suggestion the salespeople make.

"Nothing I get her is going to be as great as the Goya painting," he says as they step out of the seventh store. He had to get her attention somehow, and only a masterpiece would be grand enough to woo the syndicate boss. But he wishes he hadn't had to lead with the best gift he'll ever give her.

"What about a book?" Nate asks, gesturing to a bookstore. Leo shrugs—he loves bookstores, but they don't exactly scream expensive, extravagant love—and leads Nate inside anyway, into a hushed space with thick carpets and aisles lined with towering wooden shelves. Leo breathes in the musty smell of pages as he wanders the aisles, picking up various books and leafing through them, murmuring to himself.

Nate stops in front of a display of rare books, safely ensconced in a glass case.

"Aha," Leo joins him. "There it is." He points to a book bound in red leather with intricate gold embellishments. "The perfect gift for the woman who has everything."

"*The Prince*?" Nate asks, reading the title.

"By Niccolò Machiavelli." Leo grins and waves at the shopkeeper down at the other end of the store. "It's perfect."

Nate glances dubiously at the price tag. "It's a thousand dollars for a book."

"It's a very old, very rare first edition," the shopkeeper says, looking at Nate disapprovingly over her thick glasses. "A thousand dollars is a bargain for a book like this."

"It's worth it," Leo pays for the book with ten fresh, pressed, hundred-dollar bills. The shopkeeper purses her lips in suspicion but says nothing.

"Thought you were going to steal it, man," Nate says when they're back out on the street. Leo has been swiping stuff all day, mostly worthless trinkets, quickly hidden in the many pockets of his coat. Nate gives him a disapproving look each time but hasn't said anything until now.

"I don't steal books." Leo's offended Nate would even think that, though maybe it's a reasonable assumption given his general appetite for larceny. "I'm not a monster. Besides, I have too much cash right now. I need to get rid of some of it. Anyway, now that I've finally got something for her, we need to get your gift."

"Me?" Nate asks, startled.

"Yeah. You're going to the opening of your very first art show tomorrow night. I'm guessing you don't have anything to wear."

"I gotta dress up?" Nate scowls, scuffing his feet. "I fuckin' hate dressing up." And Leo is sure he doesn't own a stitch of appropriate clothing.

*

Nate doesn't like shopping for clothes and, as a rule, avoids it as long as he can until the hems of his shirts fray and holes appear. He mutters complaints as he changes into the suit Leo picked out. They're in a ritzy store where you don't even pick stuff off the rack, but rather wait for the salesperson to bring it to you. The obvious luxury makes Nate uneasy, like he's inconveniencing the salespeople with his inexperience and lack of wealth.

He stands in front of the mirror in a posh dressing room that could be in a movie, arms crossed tight against his chest. He barely recognizes himself in the new clothes. A pressed shirt, suit jacket, slacks, and vest all complimentary shades of tan and blue, tailored to fit snugly but not uncomfortably. They're something you might see on a men's magazine next to advice about how to seduce a woman or choose the right wine, and he's afraid to move for fear of ruining the illusion.

Leo sits on a bench nearby, flipping casually through the ridiculously expensive book he just bought, while the staff measure Nate and force him to stand unreasonably still so they can put pins in everything.

"What's the book about?" Nate asks.

Leo shuts it and looks up at him thoughtfully. "Well, let's see... It's a treatise on how the ends justify the means. And the delicate art of ruling through fear. If I ever knew a person who pulled off the term "Machiavellian," it would be Scarlett. I'm sure she's read it—hell, she could have written it—but I doubt she has it in such a rare edition."

"Machiavellian?"

"Charming, manipulative, and very ambitious," says the man hemming Nate's pants, speaking around the pins in his mouth. "Also, pragmatic and cold and willing to do whatever it takes."

Nate glances at Leo. "And you like this about her?"

Leo shifts uncomfortably and tucks the book back in the bag. "I don't like some of the things she's done. But no one's perfect. And there's so much more to her than just that. She's strong, and she's smarter than anyone I've ever met. She's as dangerous as she is beautiful, and when I'm with her, I just feel like..." He trails off with a soft laugh. "I'm a goddamn idiot for her, is what it is."

"If she makes you happy," Nate says, "then it's all good, I guess."

"And I'm not the only one with delusions. Ras might be a pussycat with you, but he's a fuckin' monster most of the time."

"I know that." But the truth is, Ras's charm and bright smile makes it easy to forget.

HANDS. 2005

Colored pencil and graphite on paper

Nate is holed up in the back of the gallery, which is adorned with fairy lights and glistening silver decorations. He's been hiding out, trying to tame the fierce anxiety coursing through him because the show is about to have its grand opening, with music and distinguished guests and flutes of champagne, and then the people are all going to look at his art.

From the front room, the murmur of voices, just two, a man and a woman, and then a slow, sweet love song begins playing. He peeks out from the storeroom. Ras and a beautiful woman are standing in the center of the gallery, slow dancing. Ras murmurs something in her ear as they move across the wood floor. With his grace and her elegant bearing, they make Nate think of a pair of dancers in those old black-and-white movies Becky always used to watch. The woman wears a shimmering white dress, and her high heels click softly against the floor.

Nate stands frozen in the doorway. He didn't think it possible to love a person as completely and recklessly as Ras seems to love Ash, then turn around and give your heart again to someone else. Nate can't imagine letting a single person own that much of him, let alone more than one. But when Ras and the woman part, he presses a kiss to her lips and pulls away with a smile that makes it seem like she is a close bright star, and he is blind to anything else. Nate ducks sheepishly back into the storeroom. He probably just intruded on something personal and precious, a moment Scarlett and Ras probably didn't mean to share.

The tabloids haven't pieced that part of the puzzle together—that the syndicate boss and the woman they say Ras would kill for and die for are the same person. But it makes sense to Nate that it would be as much about love as violence.

He waits among the paints and canvases until more guests arrive, their voices filling the open gallery space. Only then does he venture out, awkward in the fancy suit Leo bought for him.

Leo throws an arm around his shoulders and guides him around the room, introducing him to more people than he can keep track of, who all tell him he's talented and that they love his art. It's surreal enough to be a dream.

"These are the real art critics," Leo murmurs, leading him across the room. "Not the fake buyers Ras has lined up to launder money. If they want a piece, it's the real deal. I worked it out with the boss."

"Ras said it's okay?"

"He probably would, but it's not up to him. This gallery belongs to the syndicate boss, not her guard dog."

"She won't mind?"

"She likes your stuff. But anyway, I— Shit, shit, that's no good." He's glancing across the room at two people who seem to be in a heated argument. "I'd better break that up. Excuse me, Nate."

Nate finds himself alone in the room of people he doesn't know, adrift on a sea of strangers. He wanders around, looking at the other artists' work. They've made such beautiful things he's awed to think he's in the same show as them, if not in the same league.

"Nate."

Ras's voice is cheerful and melodic, and Nate turns to see him smiling his jack-o'-lantern smile, Scarlett on his arm. There's something cold about her, despite the full red lips and big, soft brown eyes. She holds herself a little aloof, a little distantly.

"Hey." Nate shifts uneasily and shoves his hands into his pockets. "Ras. Hi."

"This is Scarlett Bancroft." Ras puts his arm around the woman and squeezes. "One of the loves of my life." She smiles at him indulgently, like someone might smile at an overenthusiastic child, and holds out her hand to Nate.

"Pleased to meet you." Nate takes her hand and thinks of everything Leo has told him about her. "Uh, I hope you're enjoying the show."

"I am." Her jazz singer's voice, low and husky, cuts through the din of people with the ease of someone always in command. "Your portraits are beautiful. I'm buying the one of the sex worker standing under the streetlight."

"Uh, thanks," Nate says, fidgeting the way he does every time someone compliments his work. He's a little shocked that a woman who owns a Goya painting would stoop so low as to buy one of his.

"A lot of artists paint sex workers," she says. "But you do it with humility, and without judgment. There aren't many who have such a keen perspective."

Nate swallows. Her eyes, fixed on his face, seem so perceptive he worries she might intuit exactly why he understands the prostitutes he paints so well. That's a piece of his history he's glad Ras has forgotten.

"There you are," Leo says to Scarlett, joining them. "Hey, beautiful." He reaches into his jacket pocket and hands her a small metallic rose, carefully shaped, the petals thin and lovely, the stem studded with tiny, dull thorns.

She smiles and gives him a kiss. "Thank you."

Nate keeps his eyes on Ras, who doesn't seem to mind the exchange at all, despite the adoration with which he gazed at Scarlett when they were slow dancing. He's looking at the painting behind Nate, the one of Sierra perched anxiously on a swing set, staring up out of the canvas at the viewer.

"This is your little girl?" Ras asks, and Nate nods. "I can see your love for her in the way you made it."

"Thanks," Nate manages through a suddenly tight throat. "I, uh..."

He catches a glimpse of Becky in the crowd. She's wearing a conservative, pastel-colored dress, out of place among the sophisticated cocktail dresses the other women wear. She looks around, wide-eyed and oddly vulnerable.

"That's my sister," Nate says. "I better go show her around."

Becky greets him with a hug and a kiss on the cheek.

"Nate," she whispers. "This is like a real art show. I'm so impressed. I thought it would be... Well, never mind what I thought. This is wonderful."

Nate swallows the lump of resentment in his throat.

"Show me which ones are yours," she says.

Nate guides her around the room, points out the one of Sierra and another of a tabby cat in a back alley, stepping proudly among the trash and broken glass.

"That looks like Jeremiah," Becky murmurs as she studies the cat. "Do you remember him?"

"'Course I do. He used to sleep on my bed every night. What ever happened to him?"

Becky gives him an odd sideways glance. "Mom never told you?"

Nate shakes his head.

"She put him to sleep after you left us. He reminded her of you, and it made her too sad."

"You never have to go back there again." The social worker puts a gentle hand on Nate's arm. Even the gentle touch makes him flinch. "You never have to see or talk to your mom again if you don't want to."

Eleven-year-old Nate is crying. Tears of sorrow and tears of relief.

Twenty-four-year-old Nate stands in a softly lit room with his sister, among people celebrating his finest accomplishments, feeling the loss of a cat who died more than ten years ago like a punch to the gut.

"Nate," Becky says, soft but urgent, an insistent hand tugging at his the way she used to when they were kids and she was taking him somewhere to play. "It was a long time ago. You're here now—don't let it take you back there."

Her gentle tone pulls him into the present, to the crowded room and his sister looking up at him, the warm, diffuse light highlighting the narrow tip of her chin, the roundness to her eyes and nose. She's a woman people would call cute but never beautiful, and Nate has drawn her more times than he can count.

With their hands still intertwined, Nate leads her across the room to show her the portrait he's done. It's smaller than most of the other pieces, an intimate rendition of her face that fills the canvas.

"Oh," she says, pressing her hands to her mouth in delight. "It's lovely, Nate."

"Thanks," he says, cheeks flushed with a slight glow from her praise. From the time when he would render her in thick crayon, wide circles for eyes and an upturned crescent of a mouth, she had always encouraged him, cherishing what he made. As a teenager, she hid the pictures he drew for her from their mother's vigilant, disapproving eye, but never got rid of them.

"I wanna paint the girls sometime," he continues, emboldened by her smile. "If...if you'd let me."

"I'd love that." Her smile stays steady, but the light fades from her eyes. "But you know Aaron would..."

Nate doesn't need her to finish. "Yeah. I know."

"I'll talk to him." She puts a hand on his arm. "I can't promise anything, but I'll try."

Nate sometimes wonders if she's as much a victim of their childhood as he is, held captive by a man who is the same kind of tyrant their mother once was. He hates his mother, and still fears her, but Becky loves her, and maybe that's worse.

When Becky leaves, Nate slips away, too, keeps his head down as he makes his way through the gallery to the back, and ducks into the storeroom again. He sits on a little bench, the smell of paint and turpentine in the air, canvases stacked around him.

After a little while, a slender, graceful form fills the doorway.

"Hey," Ras says as he joins Nate on the bench. "I brought you a drink. It's nonalcoholic."

Nate takes the glass of sparkling grape juice gratefully. His throat is dry and sandpapery.

"Not fair you don't hafta wear a suit," he grumbles, tugging at his tie. He glances at Ras's white button-up shirt and black slacks with envy. He looks like a waiter, but his arrogant bearing makes it clear he's not serving drinks.

"No, I suppose it isn't. Here." Ras reaches out and deftly loosens Nate's tie. His fingers brush the skin of Nate's throat as he unbuttons the top button of the ridiculous formal shirt. "Better?"

Nate swallows his disappointment and relief as Ras pulls his hands away.

"Yeah," he says gruffly. "Thanks."

They sit in silence for a few moments, staring up at the giant canvas one of Nate's friends is working on.

"Did your sister like the show?" Ras asks.

Nate hunches his shoulders. "Yeah. She liked it okay."

Ras glances at him, and Nate feels that gentle scrutiny cut through him like a knife.

"Ain't any of your fuckin' business," he says, looking away.

Silence settles between them for a few moments, but Ras doesn't seem offended, just thoughtful.

"You really have a gift," he says finally. "You paint the things I see every day, but I've never seen them so beautiful before."

Nate smiles, a pleased blush heating his neck and face.

"I want you to do some portraits for me," Ras says. "I want a portrait of Scarlett and a portrait of Ash. And maybe one of my mother."

Nate thinks back to Scarlett's imperious, beautiful face, Ash's mess of curls and narrow nose. Neither of them will be a hardship to paint. They're both interesting in their own way.

"Do you really love them both?" *Is that even possible?*

"Yes," Ras says with the giddy grin of a man enamored. "Of course. We have an open relationship, but that doesn't mean they are any less important to me."

"Oh," Nate says softly. "Yeah. I kinda...I kinda had one like that too."

It was open in the sense that Troy was Nate's pimp as well as his boyfriend. But Ras seems so deeply in love with both of his lovers, not at all like Nate reluctantly turning tricks to bring money home for Troy.

"But it wasn't a good thing for you?" Ras asks.

Nate shrugs. "I dunno. It was okay. He didn't love me the way you love them."

"Nate." Ras looks into his eyes, that green he could drown in. "You deserve someone who loves you passionately. You deserve someone who thinks the sun rises and sets on your smile."

When Ras looks at him like that, like there's no one else in the world, maybe Ras could be that person, if he wasn't so, so wrong about Nate deserving it. Of course Scarlett and Ash would agree to their arrangement, would rather share Ras than lose him. It's impossible not to respond to such reckless devotion, like a flower turning toward the sun.

"You know, they put up the lights and the big tree in the park last night," Ras says. "I haven't had a chance to see them yet. If you're done mingling, would you walk with me?"

*

The night air brushes against Nate's cheeks with the distinct cool tingle that means it will probably snow. Beneath the starless sky, a soft mist makes the air sparkle around the streetlamps and Christmas lights, wrapping them together in an intimate shroud.

They walk to the giant tree in the park and stand there looking at it. Well, Ras looks at it, and Nate looks at him, the way he seems to blend into the darkness between the circles of light cast by each streetlamp, the play of shadows on the angles of his face.

Silence drifts over them, and Nate thinks: *I want to hold his hand.*

He almost laughs to himself at the absurdity, that the man someone once fucked behind a dumpster is now standing in the mist and the chill air, looking at Ras's pale skin in the dim light and wondering what it would be like to twine their fingers together and just hold hands.

He can easily recite all the reasons this is a terrible fucking idea. But he can't get it out of his head. And in the dark and the mist, it's easy to believe they are the only two people left in the world.

Nate takes Ras's arm, tugging him just slightly closer, and reaches for his hand. His actions are furtive, stealing this affection, a thief in the night. He knows—Ras has made it clear—he could have it and more, but the act of asking is utterly terrifying, the jumping off a cliff to the cool blue water far below.

He doesn't dare look at Ras as he laces their fingers together and presses his palm to Ras's. For a fragment of a moment, they're completely still, linked together. Nate doesn't even have time to breathe, but when he meets Ras's eyes the moment seems to linger and last. The first tender green leaves of summer, even in this winter night.

And then Ras closes his fingers around Nate's, holding him securely, and even though it's just this stupid little thing, it makes Nate's insides fizz softly, like the golden bubbles in champagne.

They walk together, gently intertwined, through the empty park, and then back to the gallery. Ras talks about nothing in particular, and Nate nods along, enjoying the melodic sound of his voice. He used to imagine, all those years ago, that he could be with Jude like this, that Jude would want him in this way. And the man he has now isn't Jude, but in gentle moments like this, seems close enough.

SELF-PORTRAIT. 2005

Graphite on paper

Ash enjoys his last class of the day. It's a small seminar course which he holds in his office. The space is ridiculously large to belong to a professor as new as he is, but Ash has distinguished himself in the academic world as well as the literary one, publishing in prestigious journals and winning awards for his first chapbook of poetry. Though, it may have more to do with his connections to Scarlett Bancroft, scion of one of the most influential and wealthy families in the city. She recently appointed Ash to the board of directors for the Bancroft Foundation, her pet charity project, and it was around that time that Ash got a bigger office and a promotion from assistant professor to the real thing. Ash isn't about to donate any proceeds from the foundation to the exclusive and wealthy private college, but he doesn't feel the need to tell anyone that.

The office is beautiful, with long, narrow windows that let in the golden afternoon sunlight. It reminds Ash of a church, but with a very different kind of reverence. The five students hold their dog-eared copies of *What Belongs to You*, and the discussion flows fluidly among them. Ash listens to the way they talk about Mitko, the prostitute—some with compassion, some with slight contempt—and wonders what they'd think if they knew where he came from and the kind of person he used to be.

He reads a passage from the novel, a moving, surreal moment on a train, and when he finishes and looks up, Ras is standing in the doorway. He's holding a large bouquet of red roses in a slender glass vase.

"Class is in session," Ash says, but he can't help the smile that stretches across his face.

Ras grins back, steps into the office without invitation, and sets the roses on Ash's massive oak desk. "I'll be quiet." He sits on the couch beside one of the students. "Promise."

Ash is acutely aware that all the students are trying to keep their curious glances at Ras to a minimum and failing.

Ash knows he's something of a mystery in the English and literature department, and Vintir is a small college where everyone knows everyone else and has since the time they were kids playing on the same exclusive private beaches together. Sometimes, Ash feels like an outsider, an impostor. Any minute now, they might see through his disguise and send him back to the Warrens.

Vintir is very much old money and old values. Ash is the only openly gay person on the faculty, and he's gotten several memos addressing his "lack of professional attire," by which they probably mean the tight black clothes, the leather collar around his neck, and his fingernails, painted a sparkling purple right now. But with the overt backing of the Bancroft family and the rumors that swirl around about his syndicate ties, he's untouchable, so he deletes the memos without answering them. Those don't bother him as much as the suggestions by other literature faculty members that his curriculum is "too...alternative." By which they mean "too queer."

"Okay," Ash says, gathering his thoughts. "So, we're in this moment on the train..."

He steps back into his lecture, trying to get the swing of it again, but having Ras there, watching him, makes him feel curiously exposed to this man he has no secrets from except the dark whisperings of his own heart. They first met when Ash was addicted to painkillers, when he lived on the streets, when he sold his body to pay for his drugs. Ras had seen him at his worst, and fell in love with him, even then.

"I think most of that went over my head," Ras admits as the students file out when the seminar is done, casting a few last glances at him before they're out the door.

Ash feels some slight anxiety. It's unlikely anyone in this ivory tower would recognize the king of the criminal underworld, but there's always a chance. "You should have done the required reading." Ash shuts the door behind the last student.

"I suppose so. Come here." Ras holds out his hand and Ash takes it, lets himself be pulled onto Ras's lap. "I missed you."

Ash laughs. "It's only been two days, baby."

Ras stays at Scarlett's on Tuesday, Wednesday, and Sunday nights in an arrangement that feels oddly like shared custody and works better than Ash initially thought it would. The truth is, while he loves being with Ras, he also needs his moments of solitude, and he suspects Scarlett is the same way. No one loves the way Ras does, ardently, passionately, like someone out of a story. But what the stories never say is how it is both wonderful and exhausting to be the object of that kind of love. And Ash likes Scarlett, prickly and aloof as she is. The three of them, bound together by Ras's exuberant capacity for love, have started to become a family. He doesn't care much that Ras has added a third person to his life. It's happened before and will happen again, but Ash knows Ras will always belong to him.

Ras trails kisses along the line of Ash's jaw, and Ash is reminded vividly of the first time they kissed. How Ras—Jude, he was only Jude back then—had traced the contour of Ash's jawline with a fingertip, looking at him with eyes the green of a coiled jungle snake, filled with a desperation Ash assumed was lust and only later understood as love.

"How was your day, professor?" Ras murmurs against his neck, between kisses.

"It was good. I finished the cobra poem. I think it's actually done this time."

Ras pulls away to grin at him. "The one about me?"

"It's going to be a collection of love poems. Most of them are about you."

"Can I read them when it's done?"

Ash had forbidden him from reading his first book of poetry, *Needful*, the chronicle of addiction that won him a major literary prize. That book, reviewers had called a "harrowing triumph," and an "intimate portrait of despair." There's a lot of pressure to make this new book equally as good.

"No," Ash says, holding back a smile. "But I'll read one of them to you. The best one." He already knows which one it will be.

*

Nate feels wildly out of place on a college campus, the students rushing by him on their way to class with books clutched to their chests or bent under heavy backpacks.

He imagines all of them must be so much smarter than he is.

He gets lost trying to find the correct building, wandering hopelessly around the beautiful campus, its wide lawns covered in pristine white snow beneath bare, regal trees. Finally, he steps into a building with no signs and walks up to the reception desk.

"Hey," he says timidly. "I'm, uh, I'm looking for where they teach literature classes."

She arches a perfectly plucked brow at him. "Are you a student?"

"No," he says, his face growing hot under her scrutiny. "I'm trying to find someone. A professor. His name is, uh, Dr. Greendale."

She narrows her eyes at Nate, examining him suspiciously. "I should have guessed. He's the last door on the left."

"Thanks." The sound of Nate's feet on the wood floor echoes through the quiet building as he approaches Ash's office.

Nate nods at Ash, shoving his hands in his pockets. He scuffs his foot against the floor just outside the doorway, waiting for permission to enter. Ash is at his desk, a stack of papers on one side and a large vase of red roses on the other. They must be from Ras. Nate has a similar bouquet on his own kitchen table, but white rather than red.

"Hey." Ash gives him a warm smile. "Nate. Come in. You just missed Ras. He had to go take care of something."

Nate steps awkwardly into the office and looks around. "Nice office. You must be some kinda big shot."

Ash laughs and gets up to shut the door behind Nate. "They know I've got an in with the heir to the Bancroft fortune."

"You mean Scarlett?"

"Yeah. She's my best friend."

"Huh." Nate's a little surprised there wouldn't be more jealousy between Ash and Scarlett, more competition.

He runs his fingers restlessly over the spines of the books on the shelves lining the walls. Some of them are in a foreign language with strange, angular letters. "These all your books?"

"Yeah. Ras likes to buy them for me, even though the next building over is Vintir's library."

Nate can picture it, Ras eagerly giving gifts to his lover. Ash must be really smart; beside him, Nate feels like a Neanderthal. Scarlett is beautiful and commanding, a queen of the dark city, and Ash is brilliant, his intellect and sensitivity like a beacon in darkness. Next to the two of them, what could Nate possibly have to offer?

Nate glances at the ground, trying to push his dark thoughts away. "Ras wants me to do your portrait. You want it here? With the bookshelves in the background?"

Ash is quiet for a moment. "Do you know the Warrens very well? There aren't many green spaces, but near the center, just north of Bancroft Square, there's a little park with a big grassy hill and trails through it."

"Sure. Quarry Park. I been there." Nate used to take Sierra to that very playground, even though some of the equipment was rusted and unusable, and he had to check for broken glass before letting her toddle across the dirt.

"When I was a teenager I'd sleep there sometimes. There's a little underpass, or if the weather's nice, you can just stretch out on the grass. Ras had a family and a home, but he hung around. Selling drugs and doing whatever else. One night, he stayed out with me until the sun came up. We weren't dating or anything, but we laid down together on the grass and talked for hours. Back then, I was addicted to drugs, and I was hustling to pay for it. I was a mess and he knew it, but he didn't care. He still fell in love with me."

Nate nods along, his fingers itching for a pencil. He can already see the painting take shape, Ras and Ash lying back on a vibrant green blanket of grass, their faces filling the frame as they look up out of the canvas at the viewer.

"It's not gonna be easy," he says when Ash looks at him expectantly. "'Cause you're gonna need Ras to be in the painting too. And he can't sit still."

"It's funny. You don't seem jealous at all." Ash sounds pleased by this, giving him a slight smile. "Most people struggle with it at least a little."

Nate shrugs. He's hesitant to claim Ras for his own in any meaningful way. They haven't even had sex yet. Ras's advances toward him have stopped at good-night kisses and an affectionate arm around him when they sit on the couch together watching movies. Once, Ras had put a hand on Nate's thigh as they cuddled on the couch, sliding it upward, but the fear that gripped Nate at the gentle touch must have been evident, because Ras pulled his hand away, resting his head on Nate's shoulder instead.

Without sex, Nate's not sure what keeps drawing Ras back to him, but each time they say goodbye, he's half convinced it will be the last time, and he's always bitterly disappointed and slightly relieved.

"It's a good thing," Ash says. "Because you're not going to change him. Sometimes people think that, but they're always wrong."

"Do you have another boyfriend?" Nate asks. "Girlfriend?"

Ash laughs. "No. Of course not. The only time I ever tried to date someone else, he almost broke the guy's jaw. He might be okay with Scarlett's boyfriends, but he's stupidly jealous when it comes to me."

"That's kind of shitty. He gets to fuck around, but you don't."

"Sure." Ash shrugs. "But he's Ras. You have to take him as he is, or not at all, because he's never going to change."

Nate doesn't argue, but something stubborn and tenacious in him refuses to believe that. Ras used to be a different person, and he could be that person again.

"It means he cares," Ash says, looking at Nate as though daring him to disagree. "It helps me not be insecure when he brings home some gorgeous artist without any warning."

It takes Nate a moment to realize Ash must be talking about him.

Ash laughs then, a warm, pleasant sound. "Don't you ever do self-portraits? You must have some idea what you look like."

Nate shakes his head. He's never done a self-portrait, and aside from the time he spends shaving each morning, he never looks in the mirror for more than a few seconds.

"Can I do some sketches of you?" he asks, mostly to change the subject. "It helps, when I do the painting."

Ash agrees, and Nate shows him how to pose, then sits down with his sketchbook to trace the distinctive lines of Ash's face, his proud, regal nose, his full lips, his dark, curly hair. Unlike Ras, Ash is perfectly still the whole time, his eyes gazing off into the distance like he's thinking of something far away.

*

But Ash's words never really leave Nate's mind, and when he's home in the late night, he takes out one of the most worn books from his small shelf. It's a collection of van Gogh's work, large glossy pages with the colorful paintings printed across them. Nate traces a sunflower with his fingertip, imagining he can feel the contours of the paint he knows must be on the original canvas.

He turns the page to a self-portrait, van Gogh staring resolutely up at him from the book. It seems like all of the great artists do self-portraits. They don't flatter themselves with the paint, but neither are they afraid of what they will see.

Ras compliments him frequently, but Nate knows better than to trust in those words. Although he knows deep down that he's an ugly creature, he wonders if maybe drawing himself is still worthwhile. It wouldn't be a work of beauty, but it would be honest and come from his heart.

He goes into the bathroom, where the only mirror in his apartment is, and sets his sketchbook beside the sink. He studies his face for a few moments with a detached curiosity, wondering what it is Ras sees in that countenance to care so deeply about. To him, it's just a collection of features—eyes, ears, nose, mouth—with no particular significance.

He looks deeply into his own eyes, and it takes him back, and back, to his mother screaming in the kitchen that his sins were written on his face, to the other kids at church who averted their eyes when he went by with his strange family, to Troy, who called him handsome and kissed him before he was ready—how afraid he'd been, and how desperate for love—to the anonymous men he fucked, who told him he was pretty before they told him what he had to do.

He looks down to see he's drawn himself, and it's the distorted drawing of a child, a simple oval for the face, rough approximations of eyes and nose and mouth. He might be more startled, but this isn't the first time he's been pulled away from himself and returned to find a child's drawing in his sketchbook, like the frightened creature inside him woke—just a little boy in a dark closet—and made himself heard.

Frozen Lake. 2005

Watercolor on paper

Nate has never been in a place like this quiet little town, the shopfronts with colorful awnings, a grocery store named after the owner, an old-fashioned movie theater with a fading sign, and only one stoplight.

They're in the mountains outside the city, driving through gently falling snow with a Christmas tree affixed to the top of Ras's car, because Ras had insisted on the importance of going to a "real" tree farm and cutting down a "real" tree for themselves. He said he had some business outside of the city anyway and wanted to bring Nate out to help him choose.

It was strange and surreal to see Ras laugh with the ruddy cheeked, robust couple who sold the trees, like he was just a normal person. He could walk into a black tie affair at the mayor's house in the cargo pants he always wears and no one would think twice, but he seems out of place in the countryside, slick and sharp like his sheer glass and metal building, while the townsfolk are warm and homey like the little cottages that fill the town.

Instead of taking the main road back to the city, they drive toward the mountain on a steep dirt road, winding through groves of trees holding heavy branchfuls of snow.

Ras pulls the car into a campground, reaching past Nate to take a gun from the glove compartment as casually as he might grab a map or a book of matches. "This should take ten or fifteen minutes. Keep the car running so you don't freeze. I'll be right back."

"You gonna shoot someone?" Nate fights to keep his voice steady.

Ras raises an eyebrow at him, tilting his head. "Do you really want to know?"

Before Nate can work out an honest answer to that, Ras is gone. The car door slams behind him, and he walks off, black coat and black hair striking against the snowy backdrop. Nate watches him disappear into the gray distance, his heart racing. Ras is going to hurt someone. Nate just knows someone is going to get hurt.

"What did I tell you about makeup?" Nate's mother smacks a sharp-edged ruler against her palm, advancing slowly. Sixteen-year-old Becky shrinks back, her eyes wide and white with fear. She's not used to being hit—whatever devil is in Nate is absent in her. But every once in a while, she'll do something rebellious, like buy the bright red lipstick their mother found hidden under the sink.

The ruler swings through the air and lands with a hard smack—not on Becky's face but on Nate's palm.

"It was me," he says, though he knows the punishment for a boy with lipstick will be far beyond anything their mother would dream up for Becky. "I bought it. For me."

Becky protests, tugging hard at their mother's sleeve. "Nate's lying! It was mine!"

But their mother doesn't hear a word. She's incandescent with rage, blinded by it, and Nate knows Becky is safe now. It doesn't hurt as much—it doesn't scare him as much—when there's a reason for the pain. Protecting someone gives him a purpose—and for that he can endure anything.

Nate pulls his scarf around his neck, tugs on his gloves, and steps out into the snow. He might or might not be able to protect whoever Ras is out to get, but he's here, and it's just him, and that means he has to try. Even if it will break everything between them.

He finds Ras standing in a little clearing at the edge of a lake and hides behind a big shrub to watch. Tall, leafless trees form a checkered canopy above him, snowflakes collecting on his hair and shoulders. The lake is frozen over, a blue spread of ice with a jagged white crust on the shore. Everything is muffled by the snow.

After a few minutes, a scruffy guy in jeans and a skullcap swaggers into the clearing, long strides on short legs. At his side is a very skinny woman with stringy blonde hair falling in clumps around her face. They're both armed, holsters at their hips.

"You made it." Ras grins at them and spreads his arms. Nate thought he might be different when he's working. But even here, he's the same cheerful, vaguely sinister person who haunts Nate's thoughts in the best way.

"Wasn't easy." The man spits in the snow by his feet. "But we got what you wanted."

"Nice work. Where is it?"

"Usual spot," says the woman. "So pay up. This one was a bitch."

"Of course."

Ras pulls an envelope out of his pocket. It slips out of his hand, flutters on the wind, and lands at the woman's feet. Nate relaxes, because it looks like Ras is just here to make a deal, not to hurt anyone. He closes his eyes for a moment, letting the relief wash over him, and when he looks back up, Ras has somehow crossed the small clearing and is standing between the man and the woman. He pulls the gun out of the woman's holster and shoves her back, while the man falls forward and hits the snow with a solid whump.

Nate wants to jerk away, he wants to run, but he's rooted to the spot.

The woman sobs, scrambling furiously to her feet. She lunges at Ras, who knocks her backward and down. He pushes the corpse over with his foot and pulls a knife out of the man's neck, flicking it so the blood flies off and spatters in a red arc across the snow.

"You killed him," the woman shrieks. "You killed him!"

"I'm not sure how you didn't see this coming." Ras is totally cool, glass so dark and reflective it's impossible to know what's behind it, if anything.

"Fuck you! You killed him."

"Lenore." He's gently chiding. "You're better than this. Did you really think I wouldn't find out?"

Breathless terror replaces the anguish. "We did nothing."

"Is that so?"

"We had no choice, Ras. It was him or us."

"You got greedy." Now his voice is bitterly cold, like the ice that stretches across the lake, and just as dangerous. "You ignored the boss's instructions. And now one of our best people is in a Mexican prison because you disobeyed her."

"You didn't have to kill him."

"That's true. I could have killed you first. A little late now though."

"What are you going to do to me?" Her voice is hoarse with fear.

"I'm going to kill you. Slowly or quickly, that's up to you. You know what I want."

Nate's heart races as he hears those words—a promise, not a threat. His legs tremble, and it takes a few seconds before he can stand. When he does, he's rewarded with a flash of hot anger in Ras's eyes. It was only a second, but definitely there.

Nate raises his chin defiantly. He may be shaking all the way through from the cold and the fear, but he's not going to let that show, not in front of this monster.

"Don't hurt her," he says.

"Nate." Ras's voice is as harsh as cracking ice, absent of its usual melody. "Go back to the car. Now."

Nate walks toward Ras, his hands open, palms empty. He has no weapons, but he can't just stand by while someone gets hurt. Maybe this woman is a criminal, and maybe she deserves to be behind bars, but he doesn't think she deserves to die. And he doesn't want to see Ras kill, ever again. Maybe if he can stop this one act, he can pretend it will all stop, that Ras's violence can be tamed with enough courage and determination.

Nate stands between Ras and the woman, so the gun is pointed squarely at his chest. "Let her go. I'm not gonna let you hurt her."

"You're fucking insane," the woman says breathlessly. "Thank you." Behind him, Nate hears the scuff of her feet on the rocky trail as she starts running, smart enough not to take any chances. But he stands still and straight, meeting Ras's gaze, unafraid.

"You really are a hero, aren't you?" Ras stalks closer. He reaches up and, with a gentleness that's shocking after such violence, he places his right hand on Nate's cheek. "But you should know that in this city, heroes never win."

With a fluid sweep, he lifts Nate and throws him over his shoulder. Nate struggles, but Ras holds him easily, moving fluidly with every attempt of Nate's to get away.

"Put me the fuck down," Nate growls, but gets no answer until Ras sets him gently at the base of a large tree, its branches stretching around and above him.

Ras takes something out of his pocket—a length of thin black cord, and Nate tries to back away but bumps into the solid trunk of the tree behind him.

"Hold still," Ras murmurs, pinning him against the tree while he ties one end the rope around Nate's wrist and the other to one of the thick tree branches by his side.

Nate struggles, but Ras moves faster than he thought anyone could move, evading easily when Nate tries to shove him out of the way, smiling grimly at Nate's attempts to knock him off his feet. With one hand pressing Nate's body back against the tree, Ras grabs his chin with unforgiving fingers and gives him a very dark look.

"We're going to talk about this, baby."

And then he's off, running down the trail after that woman.

When Nate starts after him, the snug rope around his left wrist jerks him back. He tugs on it, but the thick, knotted wood of the branch keeps the loop of rope from slipping off. His cold fingers scrabble at the knot, but he can't figure out how to untie it. He wishes for a pocketknife or even a lighter, but he carries neither.

He waits for what seems like a very long time, in the cold and the snow, until he hears the woman scream, just once. He wonders if Ras is going to leave him there, but a little while later he appears in the clearing. He pulls off his gloves and tosses them carelessly into the snow as he advances, stalking towards Nate. The trunk of the tree is solid against Nate's back, but the rest of the world is spinning beneath him as Ras pins him there with a firm hand on his shoulder and something darkly burning in his eyes.

"My hero." He tugs away Nate's scarf so his fingers can trace cold trails over Nate's throat. And Nate realizes he's misread the darkness in Ras's eyes. Not anger—lust.

"You killed her."

"Yes." Ras's lips are hot and insistent on the skin of Nate's neck. "I give you an A for effort though."

It's savagely intoxicating, Ras's rainwater scent, his rough hands sliding underneath Nate's clothes, his thigh pressed between Nate's legs. Nate feels as if the cold has eaten all the way through him, except for the points of searing heat where their bodies touch.

"You're so fucked up," Nate says, but he doesn't pull away. He can't pull away, and not because he's tied to the tree and trapped by Ras's hard, slender body. "You just killed two people, and you wanna fuck me?"

"Yes," Ras purrs. "Can I?"

"No!" Nate's surprised at the force of his outburst. "You fuckin' monster. This ain't okay, Ras. Maybe everybody else in your life thinks it's okay, but it ain't."

Ras pulls away, startled.

"Lemme go," Nate says, and he's suddenly weary with grief for what might have been between them if he could just let this one thing go. If he could look the other way and pretend he never saw that bloody body hit the snow. "I wanna go home."

*

For the whole drive back, they don't speak, and Nate sneaks furtive glances at Ras, trying to gauge if he's angry.

The entire time, he has to stamp down the urge to say, "I'm sorry," to tell Ras it doesn't matter, to mend the thing he broke in that field of snow. But, instead, Ras parks outside his apartment, and Nate turns and looks his lover in the eye.

"I don't wanna see you again," he says, and each word is bitter on his tongue. But he knows if he doesn't make it clear, he will see Ras again. And he might not be as strong the next time.

"I don't understand," Ras protests.

"Yeah. You don't. That's why." He gets out and shuts the door. He doesn't look back, and Ras doesn't follow him, and eventually, the car pulls off into the night.

The next day, Nate quits his job at the gallery, leaving a note with another of the artists so he won't have to speak to Leo directly and explain how fucked everything got.

Ras once called him a hero, but in the end, he wasn't able to save anyone—not the people Ras killed, not Ras himself.

"I don't want to talk to you," he says into the phone the first time Ras calls. The second, third, and fourth times, he doesn't answer.

After a few weeks, Ras stops calling and texting, and Leo gives up, too, and it's so easy to withdraw from everything, curling in on himself like a lonely snail in a hollow shell.

JUDE #6, SERIES. 2001

Charcoal on paper

A year ago, six months ago, Nate would never have kept anything for himself. He gave Troy every penny he made, like he was supposed to, like Troy expected. Then Troy took care of shelter, food, dope, and anything else that mattered. It was easy that way. Nate didn't have to think; he didn't have to worry. Someone loved him, and so it was okay. Anything Troy did was okay because Troy loved him.

That's how it was months ago. Now, Nate feels nothing but despair. His desperate hunger for love, that protectiveness he feels for Troy's sweet little niece, the desire to paint and draw and make beautiful things—all blunted by the overwhelming despair. Only the craving remains as powerful as ever.

Nate wants to go somewhere where nothing will hurt, and the dope can't take him there any longer.

When he gets back home, Troy is in the front yard talking to Jude de Haven, who is leaning against the fence with such graceful self-assurance Nate feels twinges of both envy and admiration. Jude has always been kind to Nate in the few interactions they've had. And now, he's Nate's only hope.

"There you are," Troy says, grabbing Nate's arm. "Took you long enough. You got the money?"

Nate answers with a vague shrug. He pulls the cash out of his pocket, and hands it to Troy. Troy counts it twice, then frowns intently at him.

"Nate, this is half," he says.

"Sierra needed a jacket." It's the honest truth, or at least part of it. The little girl needs someone to look out for her. Once, Nate thought it could be him, but now he knows better. He's no good for her or anyone.

"So, you ask me," Troy growls, his fist flying out to strike Nate on the cheek. Even that, Nate barely feels. Jude flinches more than Nate does. "You don't just take my shit."

"I did ask," Nate says in the low monotone his voice has recently acquired. "You said no."

"Jesus fuckin' Christ." Troy runs his hands through his hair.

"Don't hit him," Jude says.

"Did I fuckin' ask?" Troy snaps.

Nate shakes his head wearily at Jude, trying to tell him not to bother. Soon it won't matter anyway.

"Lemme get some cash for you, Jude, since Nate decided to spend what he owes me." Troy casts a baleful glance at Nate. "Don't you fuckin' go anywhere, babe."

As soon as Troy steps in the house, Nate grabs the syndicate enforcer by the arm and frantically digs in his pocket for the money he's been saving up.

"I need something," he says, brandishing the cash like a weapon. "Please, you gotta help me. You can have all of this, and I'll do anything you want, anything, I'll—"

"Nate." Jude puts his graceful hands on Nate's shoulders. "Slow down and tell me what you need."

"I want drugs. I don't care what kind. Just—enough to put me to sleep and make it so I don't ever wake up again."

Jude releases Nate's shoulders and steps back. "You want me to help you kill yourself?"

Nate shrugs. If Jude refuses to help him, he'll have to figure out something else. "You always been kind to me. Troy watches how much I take, so I need you to help me. I'll do anything you want."

He presses his palm to the front of Jude's jeans to make his offer clear. This is no great sacrifice; he's given his body away for much less.

Jude grabs his hand and pulls it away. Nate sags helplessly. He has nothing else to offer.

"I want you to do two things for me." Jude gently squeezes his hand. "I want you to get sober, and I want you to leave Troy. After that, if you still want to die, I'll help you."

Nate shakes his head slowly. "I can't. I can't."

"You can. I know you can." Jude still hasn't let go of Nate's hand, and that firm grip steadies the world spinning under Nate's feet. Nate wonders what it would be like to just hold hands with Jude, in a world with less darkness. In a world full of brilliant sunrises, instead of this endless night.

"Is there anyone in the city who can help you?" Jude asks.

Nate thinks of Becky in her floral apron, her mixing spoon in her hand and tears in her eyes as she told him she would never give him money again, and that as long as he was an addict, he wasn't welcome in her house.

"I got a sister," he says quietly. "In River's Heart."

"I'll help you pack your things. You're not coming back here ever again."

Troy tries to stop him, but after a few quiet words from Jude—words Nate couldn't quite overhear—he backs down for good, sitting surly in the corner while Nate packs up his sketchbooks and his few items of clothing. Nate feels some relief because Sierra isn't there to say goodbye. It would have broken what little is left of his heart. She'll cry, and she'll miss him, but the truth is that this is for the best. What can a broken-down, worn-out junkie offer a fatherless four-year-old anyway? She's better off without him.

Jude takes him to River's Heart, to Becky's doorstep, and helps Nate carry the one box that holds all of his possessions. He lingers long enough to be sure Becky is going to let Nate in, then leaves with a shy smile and murmured goodbye.

Nate thinks he'll probably never see Jude again.

BECKY GREETS THE CONGREGATION.

2005

Acrylic on paper

Nate sits in the back pew of the church, the bright sunlight falling in through high, narrow windows. At the altar, Aaron is finishing a fiery sermon about the impending perils of Hell and how they might be avoided, but Nate doesn't pay much attention. It's so much like the church he grew up in he wonders how Becky can possibly bear it every Sunday. It's been a long time since he believed in anything at all, but he has a standing invitation to her Sunday dinners if he attends the service first. He doesn't take her up on it often, but he's been unbelievably lonely in the month since he told Ras to get out of his life.

Becky catches sight of him in the congregation after the service is over and waves from near the front. She looks delighted that he came, like she always does, but she quickly gets caught up greeting the faithful churchgoers, as is the duty of a pastor's wife.

Nate takes out the little pocket sketchbook he carries with him and draws her outline as she gives hugs and clasps hands, smiling sweetly with a soft, demure laugh until his nieces spot him and join him, clamoring for him to draw pictures of them. He draws them both, cartoony caricatures that he tears out of the sketchbook so they can show their friends.

"Thanks for waiting, Nate," Becky says, joining him in the pew. "How have you been?"

"I'm fine." Nate clears his throat. "Fine."

"Well, good." Becky gives him her warm, open smile. "Are you staying for dinner?"

Nate studies her patient face, wondering why he came, why he could possibly think he could lean on her shoulder and spill all of his troubles. Pansexual, polyamorous Ras would have no place in her understanding of the world—she would only condemn. She would think Nate a fool for falling for it in the first place.

"Nah," he says, looking away. "I just wanted to hear the sermon. I gotta go now."

"Well." She brushes his arm with her fingertips. "The girls will be disappointed."

"Next time," he promises.

She gives him a hug, which he returns stiffly, trying to stifle the resentment blooming bitterly in his chest.

*

Nate lingers in the store's large toy aisle, looking over Barbies and toy cars, plush stuffed animals with big eyes and dolls with tidy hair. He wonders if Sierra has changed in the time they've been apart and, if so, what kind of toys she would like now. Would she like to brush the hair of one of the dolls and tug little shiny shoes onto its feet? Probably not. She's changed, but not that much.

Farther down, he finds art supplies and buys paint in bright primary colors, brushes, and a book of thick, high-quality paper.

He makes his way to the clothing section next. Tallie told him the last time she was there, Sierra was running barefoot around the cold stretch of dirt in front of their apartment complex, complaining that her shoes were too tight.

"Her clothes are just awful," Tallie had said. "They don't fit her at all, and her shirt had holes in the armpits. Poor girl. If she has to go to school like that, the kids are all gonna make fun of her."

"She won't," Nate promised, a little surprised to hear about this problem. Traci loves clothes, and usually Sierra has plenty of things to wear. But Tallie's sporadic reports have been of a woman slipping deeper and deeper into addiction. Maybe Traci just doesn't care anymore.

He finds himself in the little girls' clothing section, bewildered by what feels like miles of pink fabric and cute pictures of flowers and unicorns. Sierra would never wear any of this.

He tries the boys' section instead, picking up cargo pants because he knows she loves to put all sorts of things in her pockets, T-shirts with bright cartoon characters on them, a warm winter jacket, and three pairs of shoes. Tallie gave him some guidance on the sizes, and he hopes they'll fit.

It's a lot of money—probably more than he should spend now that he's trying to live off the little he makes teaching his drawing class and what he's got saved. It wasn't much to begin with. The gallery paid him a small salary and took most of the commission he made on any paintings he sold. When he worked up the nerve to bring it up, Ras had looked startled by the complaint.

"I will buy you anything you want," he told Nate, and that was the end of the discussion.

Now, Nate's not even sure where to start looking for employment, with no work history he can talk about and no references to speak of. As his money dwindles, it feels like he's starting to drown, and it's hard to bring himself to care.

And this is worth it. Sierra is worth it.

As he sits on the train with his bags in the seat beside him, he imagines her face when she opens them and sees the gifts inside. He pictures her running around a park with warm clothes and good shoes or setting the paints out on the table to make something beautiful.

She's not his daughter, he reminds himself constantly. But he changed her diapers and fed her bottles, was the only one to see her first steps and hear her enthusiastic first word. It feels like they were meant for each other in a way that goes much deeper than blood.

*

Nate makes his way through the strip club, the bass pulsing heavily around him, the room dark and filled with cigarette smoke. Neon lights wind their way around the base of the stages, and above them, the dancers gyrate and pose.

He sits at a small table and pulls out the pocket-sized sketchbook he always carries with him, tracing the shapes of Tallie's bare legs with his pencil while he waits for her to finish the dance. He gets lost in it, as he often does, moving fluidly onto the form of the dancer after her, until a touch on his shoulder startles him into reality.

"You wanna lap dance, big guy?" Tallie says, winking. She takes Nate's hand and leads him into one of the private back rooms.

"How'd it go?" she asks as soon as the door closes behind them. "Did they like my painting?"

"Yeah," Nate says, settling on one of the small couches around the raised center stage. "The syndicate boss bought it."

"Holy shit," Tallie squeaks. "For real?"

Nate nods. "I brought some stuff for Sierra too." He sets the bags of clothes and brightly wrapped gifts on the floor.

"Oh." Tallie presses her hand to her heart. "You are such a good guy, Nate."

Nate just shrugs because she's so wrong about that.

"If only you weren't gay," she says, sighing, and grins at him. "I'd snap you up in a heartbeat."

"How is Sierra?"

Tallie crosses her arms uneasily. "She's okay. But her mom's in danger. Traci begged me for cash, said Charlie B's collecting his debt, and she got nothin' for him."

"How much?" Nate asks, his heart sinking. He still owes this month's rent.

"A grand. But, hey, Ras is gonna help you with it, right? That's like chump change to him. I know you broke up, but I bet he'd still help you. He seemed like that kinda guy when I met him."

Nate shakes his head. "I got someone else I can ask."

There is one person he can turn to for help, one resource he hasn't entirely drained. The thought of going to see her fills him with heavy dread, but he'd rather face down this demon than grovel at Ras's feet.

ANGEL. 2005

Crayon on paper

"Your room is all made up," Nate's mother says in her soft, flowing voice. The voice he still remembers, the way it made Bible passages seem haunting and unearthly as she read them over and over. Her dull brown hair, streaked with gray, is pulled back in a long ponytail, and her willowy form sways as she reaches for Nate.

"I always knew you'd come back," she murmurs, holding him in a tight embrace.

Although Nate once walked into his own death and fought for his life like a cornered wolf, he stands still and defenseless against her affectionate onslaught, wearing the wide-eyed panic of a deer in bright lights. He'd stood outside the house for an indeterminate, fuzzy amount of time, trying to force himself to step across the threshold before she noticed him and called him in, just like she was calling him to supper and he'd only been absent for an afternoon.

"My Nathaniel," she says. "I've missed you so much."

Nathaniel—no, he doesn't want to be Nathaniel. He can't. Nathaniel is a scared child, cowering in a darkened pantry and praying she won't find him. Nathaniel is a sinner, Nathaniel is the devil's spawn, and Nathaniel needs to be punished.

"I'm not coming back," Nate says, pulling out of her embrace. "I'm not...coming back."

She peers at him through her perfectly circular glasses, the thick lenses slightly distorting her eyes. "What do you mean, sweetie?"

"I just need to ask you something." Nate's voice, the high pitch he's hated since he was a boy, seems feeble in the still, dusty air. The house has been dark for as long as he can remember, shutters drawn, curtains closed so the claustrophobic interiors are cast in dull shadows where the wan yellow light doesn't reach. Knickknacks line the shelves, angels and Jesus figurines among teddy bears and ceramic cats.

"I'll make you some tea," she says, bustling into the kitchen. "You're tired, honey. You need to rest. Some tea will have you feeling all better in no time."

"I don't need tea, Mom," Nate says but follows helplessly anyway. "I just wanna ask you for something."

"Ask me what?" She turns to face him, clearly puzzled. "Be specific, honey, or people will never understand what you're saying."

"I...I need to borrow some money," he finally manages.

"You have always been a difficult child," she says, sighing sadly. "I did my best. It broke my heart when they took you away from me. I knew without me, you would lose your way. And you have, haven't you? You've lost your way?"

What could Nate say to that? He hangs his head with shame because he knows it to be true. He doesn't know how to put it into words, what she did to him. He's still not even sure it was her fault.

"It's good you've come home," she says, setting the kettle on the stovetop and reaching for the dial. "There's so much evil in your heart. You need me to show you the way."

"You are the last thing he needs."

The familiar voice with its harsh chord of anger breaks the silence, and Nate startles so violently he knocks over a teacup on the counter. It shatters on the floor, and he shrinks back from it, but his mother's attention is focused solely on the intruder standing in the doorway to the kitchen. Numbly, Nate wonders how Ras got here, and why he came.

"There is one thing you should say to him," Ras growls. "And that should be—I'm so fucking sorry. And then you should have the fucking decency to get out of his life."

"Who are you?" Nate's mother hisses. "Get out of my house."

"I will," Ras says, "but I'm taking Nate with me."

"Nathaniel wants to stay with me. He needs me."

They both look to Nate, but from very far away. The room has stretched to impossible proportions, and all Nate can do is stare dumbly back at them, helplessly trapped within his own fears.

"He's coming with me," Ras says. "If I have to drag him over your corpse."

"I see what this is," she says in the sharp whisper she uses when she's really furious. "You want to use him for your twisted—"

Ras cuts her off. "I love him."

Any other time, hearing that would have given Nate an incredible rush, but he's beginning to realize none of this is real. He's slipping away from the world, little by little, bits of himself fading into a static background. Until he finds that faraway place beyond the pain and the anger and the fear, where everything just floats, like balloons let loose in the wide sky.

Ras would be a green balloon, Nate thinks in a detached, nonsensical way as their distant argument rushes by him without touching him. Maybe Nate would be an ocher or a blue, and their balloons might gently bump together once, then the momentum would send them off on different drifting paths to the sun.

This is the place where nothing is real, where all the colors are bright and false, mechanical. And in this facade-world Nate is eight years old again, the grown-up parts of him dissolved away like a sugar coating over something ugly.

Eight-year-old Nate knows when he's been bad. He knows he's been bad when his mother's face turns pinched and ugly, and she uses that hoarse whisper to scold him, and she hits him or locks him in a closet or simply refuses to speak to or acknowledge him, until the loneliness becomes so overwhelming he falls at her feet and begs for forgiveness. One time, when she was really angry with him, when she assured him God was really angry with him, she taught him to make amends. She showed how pain and fire and suffering were the only way to atone for the bad things he had done, the only way to purify his rotten insides.

And when the doctors came and took him away, he let them blame her for the scars and the burns because he knew he needed to escape, or he would die. But he would always know the truth. How could he forget? It is written on his skin.

Behind him, his mother and Ras are yelling, but Nate's not afraid. They're both angry, but that doesn't matter, because Nate knows how to fix it. How to draw that poison out.

The teakettle is hot. The water inside is bubbling frantically against the inner surface, but it hasn't begun to whistle yet. Nate carefully moves it off the burner and reaches for the glowing red coil with the palm of his right hand. Eight-year-old Nate does what he has to, to survive. He does what he's been taught.

But strong fingers close around his wrist and pull his hand back before it can reach the heated metal. He jerks away in a desperate panic because this is not how the story goes, and change is always dangerous and ends in suffering. But his attacker holds his wrist firmly with one hand, pulling him away from the stove with his other arm across Nate's chest, stifling him in something like an embrace. And he says Nate's name, a melody played out across a single syllable.

Nate stops fighting as the world rushes in around him so quickly he might faint. He becomes aware of the dull pain in his wrist, the fingers holding him so tightly it will probably leave a bruise. The press of a warm body against his back and the arm wrapped across his chest, holding him gently.

"Nate," Ras says without letting go. "What were you doing?"

"I dunno," Nate mumbles, clumsy again in his adult body. Dimly, he wonders where his mother has gone. He has no sense of how much time has passed since he left the world. It could have been five minutes or a day.

"Your mother took a walk," Ras says, and there's a kind of venom in his voice Nate has never heard before. "Let's get you out of here before she gets back."

*

Nate wakes in his bedroom in the late evening. He has only the barest memories of getting back from his mother's house, and in his imagination, Ras tucked him in and kissed him on the forehead like he was a child, letting his fingers brush Nate's cheek as he said goodnight. It's a good fantasy, and it feels almost real, and Nate will hold it close to his heart.

He gets up. He feels refreshed, returned to himself, fully back in his adult body.

Ras is in the kitchen, humming while he kneads bread dough. Nate wonders what he's still doing here.

"I hope you like black bread," Ras says without turning around. "It's my mother's recipe. One of the many she brought over from Russia."

"Your mom's from Russia?"

"I am too." Ras washes the flour from his hands. "I came to the city when I was very young."

"So you got dual citizenship?"

"I do." Ras gives him a wry smile. "Though I think if I were to go back, the Bratva would shoot me on sight. I've made some enemies over the years."

"Guess so." Nate's a little startled by the nonchalance with which Ras mentions he's a marked man. "Ain't you worried?"

"This is my city. They're not going to risk venturing into my territory."

"Must be nice," Nate murmurs, hardly aware of what he's saying. "Having a place that's safe."

"It's not so easy when the demons are all in your head, is it? You can talk to me, Nate. I might understand better than you think."

"How'd you know where I was?" Nate asks.

"Well…" Ras leans back against the kitchen counters and gives him a sheepish glance. "I track your phone." He holds up his hands in response to Nate's angry glare. "I do it to everyone who's close to me. Scarlett, Ash, my mother, my secretary. It's very unlikely you will ever encounter any danger because of me, but I like to have that safeguard just in case. And today, I'm glad I did."

Nate isn't sure whether he should be angry or feel that funny warm feeling that comes from being told he's someone "close to" Ras. That feeling that comes from being rescued. He's only felt like that a few times in his life. Once, when the police and doctors came and took him away from his mom, and once, when Troy took him in off the streets and gave him a warm place to sleep and smiled at him like he really mattered. He should have known better than to trust the system, which bounced him from foster home to foster home until he ran away, and he should have known better than to trust Troy.

Or maybe it was you, that insidious voice inside him whispers. *You ruined your chance at every home they put you in. You made Troy hit you. You asked for the dope, that first time. And then he made you fuck for money because you weren't good enough to do anything else.*

Ras takes Nate's hand, and Nate startles at the warmth of his fingertips but doesn't pull away. Ras kisses the back of it, the scar in the shape of two thick concentric circles that matches the burner at his mother's house perfectly. A gallant gesture, but he's no knight in shining armor. If this is any kind of fable or fairy tale, he's surely the villain. And yet, would it be so bad to forget that, just for a little while?

"Why'd you come?" Nate asks.

"Did you really think I wouldn't?" Ras frowns. "I care about you, Nate. If you send me a text like that, I'm going to come running."

Nate crosses his arms tight against his chest. "I didn't send you nothin'."

Ras takes his phone out of his pocket and unlocks it. He hands it to Nate, who looks down at the text messages displayed on it with growing dread.

I'm sorry. I was bad. I will be good now promise please don't

It ends there, cut off, and Nate stares at it. He has no memory at all of sending it. The words are familiar, though, the litany eight-year-old Nate knew by heart.

"I didn't mean to send it," Nate says and swallows hard, shaky with embarrassment and shame. "Sorry."

"Don't be sorry." Ras's fingertips brush his arm. "I'm glad you did."

"Ras..." Nate takes a deep breath. He has to ask, he *has* to, even if it will ruin this moment, this little cocoon. "I went to my mom's because I need money. Sierra—that little girl I told you about—her mom's in bad trouble. She needs a thousand bucks tomorrow or else her dealer's gonna fuck her up. I don't...I don't got anyone else I can ask."

Ras shakes his head. "I don't lend money to anyone I'm not willing to kill to get it back."

Nate's heart sinks. "I'll pay it back. Or do anything you want. If you want me to get down on my knees and—"

"Nate. I won't lend you the money. But I will settle this debt. Where can I find Traci?"

Nate laughs with relief, and then, to his utter embarrassment, finds himself on the verge of tears. "Thank you," he manages.

"Anything for you, love." Ras runs his thumb over Nate's cheekbone and smiles, gentle, fond, and pleased as a cat with a dish of cream.

SIERRA, PORTRAIT. 2005

Charcoal and graphite on paper

There is a soft popping noise, and the weak yellow light illuminating the dirty, dingy one-room apartment goes out. Sierra sits up in the sudden darkness, clutching her stuffed shark to her chest.

"Mom?" she says, her voice tentative, wavering. She knows her mother isn't home and probably won't be for hours.

Plucking up all of her courage, she crosses the room, her shark in one arm and the other stretched out in front of her. The heavy curtains block the light from the only window—her mom prefers the darkness in the mornings when the sun peeks in from the east—and the apartment is pitch-black. Sierra runs into the wall sooner than she expected and feels along it for the light switch. It takes a long time, but her fingers finally land on it, and she breathes a soft half sob of relief.

She presses it and nothing happens. She tries again, and again, but the dark remains. She curls up on the floor, her back to the wall, and clings to her stuffed animal as the darkness grows thick and menacing around her. She can't help it. She starts to cry.

A knock sounds on the door, and she startles upright but doesn't answer it. She knows better than to talk to strangers, here, in this dangerous neighborhood.

"Hello?" A man calls from the other side of the door. "Can I come in?"

She shrinks away from the sound and waits for him to leave. But instead, she hears a soft click, and the door opens. A dark silhouette stands in the doorway, rainwater dripping off of a black trench coat. In the dim light that falls in from the streetlamp outside, she can see well enough to scurry across the room and under the bed.

The man glances around, and then he reaches for the light switch too. It clicks but doesn't turn on any light. "Well," he says, companionably enough, "that's a problem, don't you think?"

Under the bed, Sierra buries her face in the fuzz of her stuffed shark and doesn't answer. She knows if it were a real shark, she would have to touch it just the right way or tear the skin of her hand. She knows a hundred shark facts, and in her terror, they run senselessly through her head as she huddles under the bed and waits for the man to go away.

But he doesn't. Instead, he sits on the floor, facing her. She can barely make out angular features and dark hair in the light from the open door behind him. She considers running out into the street, but he's blocking the way.

"Are you Sierra?"

She squeezes her eyes shut and refuses to answer.

"My name is Ras."

She has heard grown-ups murmur that name before, but she doesn't know who he is, or what it means. "Go away," she manages, her voice thick with tears.

"Nate sent me. He wanted me to see if you were okay."

"Go away," she says again through hiccupping sobs. If Nate cared, he would come himself, and men will say anything to get you to do what they want. She has seen them do it to her mother enough times to be wary.

"I want to help you."

"Leave me alone!" She curls around her stuffed shark, trembling and crying. She doesn't know what he wants, only that men are dangerous; they say cruel, dirty things to Sierra and hit her when she gets in the way. Usually, her mom is there to protect her, but now she's all alone, in the dark, with a stranger.

Ras is quiet for a moment. "Where is your mother?"

Sierra burrows farther under the bed and doesn't answer.

"I'm going to find someone who can help you." He gets up and leaves, shutting the door behind him, and Sierra breathes a long sigh of relief. Now it's just her and the darkness. She scoots out from under the bed, climbs on top of it, and wraps herself around her shark, trembling from the remains of spent adrenaline.

She doesn't know how long she waits, only that it feels like forever when the door opens again. The man has returned, and this time, someone is with him. Sierra doesn't have time to dart back under the bed, so she shrinks against the wall and bites on her fist, watching them come closer.

"Are you Sierra?" The woman has a low, husky voice, and she sounds kind. "My name is Scarlett. I'm a friend of Nate's."

"Nate doesn't care," Sierra says, drawing her legs to her chest. Behind the woman, Ras looks around the apartment in the pale light from outside the open door, something bulky in his arms.

"It must have been scary to be all alone in the dark," Scarlett says.

Sierra sniffles, watching her carefully. "Yeah."

Something makes a clicking sound, and warm yellow light fills the apartment from a table lamp Ras has set on the messy counter next to some empty plastic baggies and paper plates stained with food.

"That's better, isn't it?" Scarlett says. She perches on the very edge of the bed, all beauty and elegance like a storybook princess come to visit this humble peasant's home. Or so Sierra could pretend, if she tried hard enough.

Sierra nods, keeping one wary eye on Ras, who leans on the counter, giving them space.

"Do you know where your mom is?" Scarlett asks.

Sierra's lip trembles and tears sting at her eyes. "No."

"I used to live here, you know," Scarlett says. "Just a few blocks down the street. Do you know where those blue buildings are? That's where I lived when I was a little girl."

"Really?" Sierra stares up at her. She can't imagine a person further removed from the gutter where she lives than this beautiful angel.

"Really. I know how scary it is to be all alone."

Sierra scoots forward, a little closer to Scarlett. She really does sound like she understands, like she really cares. "Will you stay a little while?" she asks, her voice tiny.

"I'll stay until your mom comes home," Scarlett promises. "After that, we're going to see about finding you a better place to live. You're a good girl, and you deserve better than this."

Sierra sniffles again, then scoots forward until she can lean her head cautiously against Scarlett's shoulder. She's worried Scarlett will get angry, like her mom sometimes does, and brush her off. But she's also desperately lonely, and no one has ever been so kind.

Scarlett puts her arm around Sierra and pulls her close until Sierra is in her lap, resting her head against Scarlett's soft chest and crying all over again. Scarlett murmurs gentle, comforting words into her hair, rocking slightly until the soothing sounds and movement overcome Sierra, and she relaxes into the embrace.

STUDY IN GREEN. 2005

Acrylic on canvas

Nate sits on his bed, flipping through his sketchbook. He should feel some anxiety about Sierra's situation, but he doesn't. Ras might be a monster, but he would never harm a child. Nate knows instinctively that Ras will always protect him and the people he cares about, and he feels an odd contentment and peace as he waits for Ras to return and tell him Sierra is safe.

Most of the drawings filling the sketchbook are of Ras, cooking in the kitchen, sprawled on the couch, any time Nate can catch him sitting still for a few seconds. A black cat wanders across the pages, catching mice and bringing them forward like little offerings. Sometimes he has a rose in his mouth or is playing with a tabby with a torn ear.

Nate moves to tear one of the more romantic drawings from the book, but he can't bring himself to do it. He pictures Ras's tender eyes, imagining the brush of Ras's fingers against his burning hand, and the yearning in Nate crashes like waves rising higher and higher along the line of a crumbling cliff.

He slams the book shut. He doesn't know what to do or think or how to weather the stormy sea inside him. So he turns to the only thing he trusts, the only thing he believes in, and when he holds the palette in his hand, he feels stronger, safer.

He spends a long time studying his array of acrylic paints, and then he reaches for them, one by one.

If he stole the inky black and gave the night sky a color, it would be the deep rich blue he draws into the center of the palette. He adds to it a brushful of a yellow warm enough to end winter, soft as the reaching petal of a sunflower turned up to mirror the sun.

Next is a careful single dab of black, a hint of darkness on the very end of the silky strands of his paintbrush.

It's still too much, so he brings in a tip full of white, brilliant and pure like the blinding glare of sunlight, the day's truest color.

It takes him a long time, and there's paint on his shirt and pants because he was so eager to dive into these colors he didn't even put on a smock. He throws three palettes down on the drop cloth and leaves them there because they are so wrong, but finally, on the fourth one, he gets it right. He takes a big brush and slides a thick stroke of it across the canvas.

It sounds crazy to think a color could be so meaningful, but in that moment, Nate feels like he's been looking his whole life for this exact combination of pigments. Finding it seems like such sheer luck and such momentous grace that he can barely speak.

It's beautiful, a symphony in a single tone, but it's also melancholy, because he already knows nothing this precious can last. And it's so compelling that if he had to mix his blood in with the paint to make this color, he'd do it to fill this canvas.

"I like it," says that warm, soft, melodic voice, and Nate startles, almost drops the palette, blushing like he's hiding a secret too delicate and precious to share with anyone else.

"It's nothin' really."

"You have a color." Ras glances at the palettes on the floor and the one in Nate's hand.

"Yeah, but I dunno what shape goes with it."

"Hmm." Ras gazes at the canvas with its single fat brushstroke, like he's really thinking about it.

Nate looks down at his palette and dips a finger in the paint. It's cool against his skin and rich as silt when he rubs his thumb and finger together.

He steps forward, assertive and unashamed as he brushes his finger along the line of Ras's cheekbone so he can see the color against his skin. Nate stops breathing entirely once he does. He might never breathe again because the color is so right, and because for once, he is touching Ras, rather than just letting Ras touch him.

Ras looks down at the palette, tilting his head and thinking, and then he picks that blue, that twine-along-the-stars blue, dips his finger in it and looks at it in the light. He runs that finger along the curve of Nate's cheek in the same way, and it's like the moment freezes for a second and hangs in the air because it's too perfect to shatter right away and fall into the past.

Sometimes, Nate draws Ras as an evil sorcerer, standing atop a tower weaving black magic. And right now, it really does seem like he's casting a spell, because Nate can't look away from his eyes and the green on his cheek that fits him so perfectly. He has Nate enthralled, his insides trembling like a strummed guitar string because the color has always been his, and so has Nate.

And then Ras smiles, wide and playful. He pokes Nate on the nose very gently. "Forgive me?"

"Just like that?" Nate's voice comes out rough and desperate. "You're a fuckin' monster." He says it more to remind himself than to reprimand Ras, who is beyond reprimand anyway.

"I know," Ras says carelessly. "But I love you. Surely that redeems me, at least a little bit?"

PHOENIX #4, AWAKE. 2005

Acrylic on canvas

Ethan is not the kind of person to make a fool of himself for a handsome face. After all, he's a grown man, a lawyer with a 401K and a closet full of sensible, well-tailored suits. Outside of his work, his life is simple and quiet, and he doesn't mind too much the fact that he's past thirty and still single. He's been in love, had his heart broken, and is content to settle for a loyal German Shepard as the significant man in his life. He goes to bed on time, wakes at six to run before work, and likes to think he has some small effect on the city's mostly indifferent justice system.

But there he was just last week, attending the fourth session of a weekly figure drawing class even though his circles look more like mangoes and his lines wobble and wander, so that he can watch the teacher's steady, confident hands conjure wondrous images out of white paper and graphite. Okay, so maybe he's a little besotted. But that's a harmless enough pastime. What he's doing right now is slightly crossing the boundary into stalker territory. He doesn't mean it that way; really, he doesn't. He just wants to know a little more about the enigmatic Nate Redfield, who smiles and banters with him after every class but rarely reveals anything about himself.

So when Nate mentioned that his show just opened in a gallery downtown, Ethan knew he had to see it. A private investigator who owed him a favor figured out which gallery, and now here he is, standing in the threshold. Another step and he'll have to admit Nate's classes are the bright point in his ordinary, unremarkable life. It's a little ridiculous—he barely knows Nate at all.

But then Ethan walks inside and he sees the phoenix and he knows he has made no mistake.

The painting is at least four feet tall and almost as wide, and as Ethan stands before it, the canvas swallows him, the rest of the room fading into the distance. The bottom is gray-black, ashes collected in flakes that look like dirty crystal. Above it, a fire grows, red flames flickering and dancing in seductive curves, a perfect counterpoint to the angular ash. From the flames, a shimmering silver bird rises, each stroke of paint as fine as a feather, so vivid and real Ethan has to stop himself from reaching out and touching it. The silver phoenix shines in the light, soaring upward and upward, the movement captured so expertly by the painter it feels as though the bird is just about to burst free of the canvas and continue untethered up into the sky.

Ethan doesn't need to look at the little card beneath it to know Nate painted it. The card also informs him it is worth ten grand, and it's already sold. He feels a jolt of disappointment, even though ten grand is not a trivial amount of money for him. He's not poor, but he's not the kind of lawyer that gets rich.

"You like it?"

Ethan turns, startled. His heart races like he just got caught doing something much more illicit than admiring art. Nate gives him a shy smile, tucking his hands into paint-stained jeans. He acts like he doesn't know how attractive he is, like he doesn't notice the heads that turn when he walks by, his own face tilted to the ground.

"Yeah," Ethan says. "I love it. God, it's so beautiful. How did you come up with it?"

Nate shrugs, but he looks pleased. "Dunno. I just got a head full of things like that, I guess."

"I'd buy it if I could," Ethan says wistfully.

"It ain't worth ten grand." Nate glances balefully at the card. "I told them."

"It's worth at least that much. Maybe more."

"You always flatter me." Nate rocks back on his heels, a suspicious glint in his eye.

"I don't flatter anyone." It's largely the truth. "I—"

The door to the backroom swings open, and a man scuttles out, his face bright red and blood dripping from his nose. He sprints past Ethan and out the door. Another man follows him, slender with dark hair and eerily familiar, and he moves with the easy grace of a predator. Ethan steps a little closer to Nate, his hand hovering near the concealed pistol he's carried in a hip holster ever since he successfully sent a gang member to prison on a domestic violence charge and the rest of the gang threatened retaliation. The man gives him a dismissive once over, then ignores him entirely.

"Do you gotta be so cold?" Nate asks, so softly it hurts to hear.

The man gives him an icy glance but quickly relents. "I'm sorry, love. It's just business. Nothing to do with you."

He wipes blood off his knuckles with a black cloth as he crosses the room, and with a cold shock Ethan feels all the way down to his bones, he realizes who the man standing before him is. Really, he should have figured it out sooner. There's a picture of this guy tacked to the wall in the district attorney's office that the DA and her deputy sometimes throw darts at when they're drunk, cursing the latest batch of botched evidence, the witnesses who go missing, and the judges bribed to turn cases away.

That picture isn't one taken from the tabloids, which print gossip about Ras like he's just another celebrity behaving badly and not the cancer eating their city from the inside out. It was taken by an investigative reporter—a serious journalist hellbent on uncovering corruption. In it, Ras has a wide, mocking smile, captured as he was telling him what would happen if he continued to write his story. The journalist fled the city the next day, leaving his camera and everything else behind.

Ras is smiling now, but it's different, kinder. He presses his lips to Nate's, and Ethan looks away. It's hard to watch, and not only because he's infatuated with Nate, but also because he knows Ras is bad news—about the worst you can get.

"Here." Ras tucks some money into Nate's front pocket, ignoring Nate's protests. "Take a cab home. I have to go deal with something. I'll see you tomorrow."

"Sure," Nate bows his head.

"Nate." Ras puts his fingers beneath Nate's chin and tilting Nate's face upward. "I love you."

He sounds like he really means it, but Ethan has prosecuted enough abusive spouses and parents to know love isn't always enough to keep them safe, and certainly not from a man like Ras.

After he leaves, Nate slumps against the gallery wall, sighing. "I just wish he wouldn't do it here. This is my good place."

He's not really talking to Ethan, but Ethan follows anyway as Nate walks into the back office where the altercation must have taken place. The office is a mess, two chairs knocked on their sides, papers strewn everywhere. Ethan isn't sure how he and Nate didn't hear anything.

Nate sighs again and goes to right one of the chairs. Ethan takes the other one, and between the two of them, they silently put the office back in order. Ethan's eyes linger on the paperwork as he picks it up off the floor, even though there's not much he could do with any evidence he found. No judge in the city will hear a case against anyone who matters in the syndicate, much less the king himself.

"Why did you come here?" Nate asks, and Ethan realizes he's still staring at the paper in his hand.

He sets it carefully on the desk and turns to Nate. He wants to shake Nate by the shoulders and tell him what kind of man he's mixed up with. He wants to ask if Nate is okay, if he needs help getting free. There's a strange mix of shame and defiance in the way Nate holds his head, like he knows he's guilty but he's daring Ethan to judge him. Ethan knows if he makes the slightest aggressive move, Nate will startle like a bird and fly away, and that will be the last they ever see of each other.

"I wanted to see what kind of art you made," he says.

Nate crosses his arms skeptically. "You said you were a lawyer. A prosecutor."

"I am. But I didn't come here to investigate a case. I came here because..." Ethan hesitates. "I wanted to get to know you better."

"Now you know."

"Now I know a little more," Ethan says gently. "But not everything. Will you tell me about the phoenix? I've never had a painting take my breath away like that."

Nate gives him the slightest hint of a smile, like the soft curve of a rose petal. "It's kinda a long story."

"I have time." Ethan blocked out the entire afternoon for this venture, in fact. "One of my favorite places to get coffee is just around the corner. Let me buy you a cup, and you can tell me about it."

He holds his breath while he waits for Nate to answer, even though this very clearly isn't a date, even though Nate is very clearly taken by someone who would think nothing of breaking Ethan's legs to prove his ownership. But his heart still does a little somersault when Nate says yes.

*

At a funky coffee shop a block away from the gallery, Nate sits across from Ethan at a table so tiny their knees brush together beneath it. For some reason, it doesn't make Nate uncomfortable, though he usually avoids contact or proximity with people he doesn't know very well.

"I know I'm unteachable," Ethan says with a sheepish smile. "But you really are a great teacher. I love your class."

"Thanks," Nate says. Ethan really sounds genuine, like it isn't flattery at all.

"So tell me about the phoenix."

Nate hesitates, wrapping his hands around the white paper cup of coffee Ethan bought him. "I was addicted to heroin for a long time. Quitting was the hardest thing I ever did. When I was going through withdrawal and in the program, I drew that phoenix every day. At first, my hands were shaking so bad you could barely see what it was, but by the time I recovered, it came out right."

"Wow," Ethan murmurs, eyes wide and gentle. "That's amazing, Nate."

Nate gives him a shaky smile. Whenever he speaks those words—addicted to heroin—he holds himself alert and on guard, ready for the inevitable judgment and dismissal.

"I have the same design tattooed on my back." He brushes his finger along the feather on his neck. "This is the tip of the wing."

"Oh," Ethan says softly, reverently. "I'd love to see it. I mean—" He corrects himself quickly, blushing. "I mean, I'm sure it's beautiful."

"Thanks." Nate's not sure how to respond. Ethan's shy smile fills him with a strange contentment, an unusual but not unwelcome peace.

"I'm not hitting on you. I promise. After all, I just met your boyfriend."

"Yeah." Nate's smile fades as he thinks of where Ras probably is right now, what he's probably doing. Nate wonders what the manager of the gallery did to get on Ras's bad side, but realizes he'd probably rather know as little about it as possible.

"Do..." Ethan hesitates, choosing his words with great care. "Do you know who he is?"

Nate looks away and nods.

"If you ever need to get away," Ethan says in that careful way, "I would help you."

Nate looks back at him, flushed with ugly anger. "I can take care of myself."

"I know." Ethan doesn't seem bothered by Nate's reaction, looking back at him with a casual unflappability. "You're strong. It's one of the reasons I want to know you better." He gives a soft, self-conscious laugh. "If it sounds like I'm hitting on you, again, I promise I don't mean anything by it. I think you're someone I'd like to know."

Nate isn't sure what to make of Ethan's quiet confidence, his calm, steadying presence. But he likes it. He likes how it makes him feel just to be around him.

"I wanna know you too," Nate says, and it comes out more eager than he'd meant it to. "Tell me about you. What kind of prosecutor are you?"

"I work for the district attorney's office. I specialize in family crimes, abusive parents, intimate partner violence, that kind of thing."

Nate thinks back to the lawyer he talked to briefly when they took him from his mom's house. He'd refused to speak in court, of course. He's still not sure if what she did to him really was abuse.

"That must be hard, man. No kid would ever say their parents abused them."

Ethan gives him a thoughtful look, and Nate averts his gaze. "It depends on the kid, and on who the abuser was, how severe the abuse was, and how long it went on."

Nate nods, mulling this over, and when he realizes Ethan is looking at the scar on the back of his right hand, he quickly slips it under the table. "You don't seem like a lawyer."

Ethan laughs. "I get that a lot. But I'm a different person when I'm in the courtroom. I believe in what I do. I want to protect those people however I can, even when it seems like nothing I do makes much of a difference."

Nate studies him, the righteous shine in his eyes, the steady confidence to his posture. He pictures Ethan—a knight in a gray business suit and tie, charging into the courtroom to put something wrong to rights.

*

After coffee, Nate sequesters himself in the gallery loft. He's so absorbed in his sketching he barely notices when closing time comes. It doesn't matter to him, really. He's got nowhere better to be. So he lets his pencil take him where it will, while the hours slink past, unnoticed.

"Hey, Nate," Ras says gently, and Nate's not at all surprised he let himself in and crept silently up to the loft. It's barely even sneaking when Ras does it—he's so used to walking silently it would probably take more effort to make a sound.

"Hey," Nate replies gruffly without looking away from the painting he's examining for flaws. "What're you doin' here?"

Ras's hands land gently on his shoulders. "I wanted to see you. Is that a crime?"

"What you did before is a fuckin' crime," Nate mutters, but the accusation lacks heat. "Do you gotta do it here? I like this place."

"Oh," Ras says softly. "You want me to keep my work separate from yours. I can do that, Nate. Next time, I'll be more careful. I'm sorry I didn't think of that before."

Nate turns to face him, furious words on the tip of his tongue. He doesn't want there to be a next time; he doesn't want it to happen ever again.

But he knows that's unrealistic, and the tenderness in Ras's eyes and the apology on his lips disarm him, snuffing out his righteous anger.

"You have paint on your neck." Ras brushes his fingertips just below Nate's chin. Nate stops breathing for a moment.

He and Ras haven't done anything even a little sexual, but he wants to. Sometimes he wants it so desperately he's dizzy with it, but the fear always holds him back. It's not an emotion he fully understands; he's had a lot of sex in his life, most of it an exchange of one sort or another, and he's used to the mechanics of it by now, and the way his mind separates from his body, the pleasure a distant, shameful sensation. With Ras it might be different, or it might be exactly the same. Nate is afraid to find out.

"And this," Ras says, his finger moving to the feather tattooed on the side of Nate's neck, an elegant blue curve that starts below his ear and disappears beneath the collar of his shirt. "Does this go to something?"

"Yeah." Nate swallows, and for a moment, the wanting overcomes the fear. "Wanna see?"

"Yes."

Nate has never backed down from a challenge, from the edge of a cliff, no matter how far the drop. He's not about to start now. He pulls off his sweater, a thick blue one made of a fine, soft material Ras bought for him a week ago, and then his shirt.

He stands there, exposed. His many tattoos don't cover the constellation of scars—different shapes, sizes, and origins—that mar his body. On his left arm, a dead tree grows along his bicep, the roots twining around the marks left by burns and cuts that line his forearm. The biggest design covers the entirety of his unmarred back.

Ras looks Nate over, and Nate struggles to stay still, to not hunch over and cross his arms and hide his body from the scrutiny. Now that he stands there, exposed in a way he hasn't been to anyone in years, he realizes the sight of his body is more likely to inspire revulsion than passion.

"Nate," Ras murmurs softly, awed. "You're gorgeous."

And Nate realizes the nature of the gaze sweeping over his body. It's not condemnation darkening those green eyes, but lust.

The realization sends blood rushing through Nate, the surface of his skin heating and the rhythm of his heart accelerating. When Ras puts his finger just below Nate's elbow and traces one of the tree roots inked into his skin, then slides that point of heat up along the crooked trunk on his bicep, Nate draws in a sharp breath. Ras is kind enough to pretend not to notice, and Nate is both relieved and disappointed when Ras pulls his fingers away from Nate's shoulder and doesn't trace the jagged tangle of dead branches that juts out across his shoulder, to where a crow perches above his heart.

"A crow?"

"Doesn't mean anything," Nate says defensively. But that isn't true. The dark bird is a symbol of death watching over Nate, summoned by the many times he has wanted to die. "It's just a picture I liked."

"Hmm." Ras runs his finger along the feather on Nate's neck. "What about this one?"

Nate opens his mouth, but between the fear that makes his throat dry and the hot desire that makes his pants too tight and stifling, he can't think of a single thing to say. He turns around so Ras can see that the feather is the tip of a wing. The wing, gracefully unfolding upwards, belongs to a phoenix that covers Nate's entire back, all sweeping lines and elaborate feathers. The asymmetrical curves of the wings rise above a blazing fire, the flames dancing in unpredictable patterns like they keep twisting up above his shoulders and into the sky. It's a twin to the painted phoenix on the wall downstairs.

Nate stops breathing for a moment when Ras's fingertips press gently to his back and trace the lines of the tattoo. It's been so long since anyone has touched Nate, and he can't remember anyone ever touching him like this, in a way that makes him tremble and ache and want to beg for more.

"This is beautiful," Ras says. Warm hands close around Nate's shoulders, hot breath in his ear. "You are beautiful."

He wraps his arms around Nate and holds him close. Nate closes his eyes and lets himself drift in the embrace, trying to stretch out each second as long as he can. This is what he's always wanted from a man—not just sex, but this tenderness, a salve on his wounded soul.

"Is this okay?" Ras asks.

Nate has never felt so torn, scared, and wanting at the same time. Like he's a starving stray cat, and Ras is holding out food, but he's been beaten enough times to be wary. He knows he can trust the fear. The fear has kept him alive. Still, he says nothing, hoping Ras will make the decision for him, that Ras will either embrace him or reject him, and all he will have to do is follow.

"Nate." Ras's hands land on his shoulders again. "Look at me, love."

Nate turns slowly.

"I like you," Ras says, looking him in the eye, sincerity written across his face. "I want to be with you. Whether that means we're friends or something more is up to you."

Nate swallows, hard. He doesn't understand what's happening to him, the heat flushing his body and the desperate fear that accompanies it. Half of him exists as he is now, twenty-five years old, strong, stable, and yearning for intimacy with the one man who's ever cared even a little about him. The other half is sixteen years old, in Troy's shitty apartment, doing something he doesn't fully understand, something that scares him, so that Troy will hold him for a moment afterward, and then get him high.

"You don't remember," he says, his words rushing desperately from his lips. "You don't remember how I was back then. I used to be an addict. I used to fuck for money and dope. I used to—"

Ras presses his fingers gently to Nate's lips, cutting short his ugly confession. Nate feels hot with shame and self-loathing. They taught him a lot of things in rehab, but not how to handle this moment, where he feels like a water glass overfilled with emotion, and still, Ras pours more in with the tender way he tucks a lock of Nate's hair behind his ear.

"I don't care about any of that," Ras says. "If you don't want this, that's okay. If you're afraid, that's okay. But don't ever think you don't deserve it." Ras's gaze doesn't waver, and his green eyes look remarkably sincere.

Nate realizes he might never get another chance like this. In his twenty-five years, this is the first time he can remember being touched with such tenderness. It may never happen again.

"I'm scared," he whispers. "But I want to."

"You have nothing to be afraid of," Ras murmurs. "I'll take care of you."

SIERRA AMONG GIFTS. 2005

Pastel on paper

On Christmas morning, Nate wakes in the darkness to the buzzing of his phone. It vibrates three separate times before he finally rolls over and reaches for it.

Ras: can I come in?

Ras: I'm coming in

Ras: get up I'm making you coffee

Nate sits up, noting the bar of light beneath the door. He glances at the clock. Five fucking thirty. Ever since he let Ras back into his life it's been like this, extravagant displays of devotion that leave him helpless.

"You're fucking insane," he calls through the door.

"I know," Ras says on the other side. "Can I come in? I made coffee."

"Yeah." Nate runs his hand through his messy hair. "I guess. Better be really fucking good coffee."

The door opens, and Ras steps in with a smile warm enough to make Nate ignore the fact that he just let himself into Nate's apartment in the wee hours of Christmas morning to wake Nate up.

"This is not morning," Nate grumbles.

"There are lots of little kids who are getting up right now to see what Santa brought," Ras says, grinning. "Aren't you curious what you got?"

Nate rolls his eyes, to hide the ache in his heart, never healed. "Santa never brought me shit. Not even when I was a little kid."

"Never?"

Out of all the terrible things Nate has let slip about his childhood, this one seems to shock Ras the most.

"Santa only comes for good kids," Nate explains.

"Not true. Santa came for me every year. And I was a terrible child. I used to get in fights at school, steal, sell drugs, set fires..." Ras has a nostalgic smile, like those are happy memories. "All that and I still got a pony when I was ten years old."

Nate laughs. "The rules don't apply to you."

"No. I suppose not." Ras hands him a mug of coffee. "Merry Christmas, love."

Nate bows his head to hide his big, goofy smile. "Yeah. Merry Christmas."

"Do you want to know what I bought you?" Ras is way too bright and eager for five thirty in the morning, acting like a child about to receive a gift rather than an adult about to give one. "Well?"

Nate sips his coffee. "I guess." He pretends reluctance to tease Ras and draw the moment out. No one has ever been so excited to give him a gift before.

"I got you"—Ras spreads his arms extravagantly—"a house. It's a cozy three bedroom in a suburb in River's Heart, across the street from a park with a little playground, in a very good school district."

Nate blinks at him, confused. It's too early in the morning, and he's really not sure what he would do with a house like that, or why the school district would matter.

"It's for your daughter. She and her mother have already moved in. If you like, we can go see them. Sierra is probably just about to wake up and go to see what Santa brought."

"Ras," Nate murmurs, his voice trembling. "This is too much, this is—"

"Nothing is too much for you," Ras says.

*

River's Heart is a quiet suburb nestled at the crook where the river that bisects the city splits into two offshoots. Cozy houses line streets with grand old oak trees planted along the sidewalk, bare limbs against the starless sky. Ras pulls the car into the driveway of a green house with a yellow door. He gets out and approaches the house. Nate hesitates in the car, feeling oddly anxious, before hurrying to join him.

Ras knocks on the door, and it opens barely a second later. Sierra is by herself in the doorway, tall enough now to reach a doorknob. She freezes, mouth open in a soft little O, dark eyes shimmering in the light that spills in from the porch.

"Hey," Nate says, and the word comes out strained and weak.

Ras pulls on his arm, and he stumbles into the warm, lighted living room. It's the kind of house he always wished Sierra might have, with comfortable furniture and not worn and broken, a large Christmas tree wearing a plethora of mismatched decorations in one corner.

"Hi, Nate." Sierra's expression is set and surly. "I didn't think you were gonna come back."

"I missed you," Nate tries to pour as much sincerity into those words as he can.

"I don't need you anymore," Sierra shouts, standing on her tiptoes to yell at him more effectively. "I hate you. I didn't want you to come back."

Nate steps backward, hit by the force of her anger. "I'm so—"

"I don't care." She starts to cry, shimmering tears making trails over her cheeks. "I hate you." She runs off down the hall before Nate can think of anything to say.

Nate sits heavily on the couch. The shock of her anger has broken his heart neatly in two. This is all his fault because he wasn't brave enough all these years to risk seeing Troy again. Because he isn't strong enough to say no, if Troy offers to get him high.

"I guess I should just...go," he says.

Ras sits beside him on the sofa and puts an arm around him. "She's just like you. You realize this is exactly what you would have done in her place?"

"Maybe." That doesn't make it any easier to bear.

"She's just angry because you left. She doesn't hate you. Let me talk to her. You unload the trunk." He hands Nate his car key.

Cold guilt washes over Nate as he makes his way to the car. He opens the trunk, but even the sight of more than a dozen brightly wrapped gifts isn't enough to cheer him. As he carries them into the house and arranges them beneath the tree beside the ones he sent with Tallie a few days ago, he wonders if Sierra will ever forgive him. If he was in her shoes, he probably wouldn't.

*

After all the presents are in place, Nate waits as long as he possibly can, but the seconds stretch like hours. Eventually, he walks down the hall and peers through an open doorway. It's clearly a child's room, but tidy, decorated in gentle pale greens, giraffes on the wall and patterned on the sheets. Nate wonders if this is Ras's doing, or if Traci really has pulled her shit together enough to make this place a home. He feels a solid, tangible sense of relief because Sierra is in a good place, a happy place, perhaps the best he can hope for without somehow taking her away from her mother. Even if those fierce words, hurled like glass and shattered against his chest, are never taken back, he'll take solace in knowing she's safe and taken care of.

She and Ras are sitting on the edge of the bed about a foot apart, which is closer than Nate's ever seen her voluntarily get to any man other than himself. Watching them together, hearing the tenderness in Ras's voice as he talks to her, makes Nate think that whatever else Ras might be—monster, murderer—he is this too. And maybe that could be enough. All Nate wants is to sit with them, let Ras put his arms around them both, and pretend for as long as he can that they are a family.

"I thought you would want to see Nate." Ras doesn't try to touch Sierra, careful of her boundaries. Instead he reaches for a tissue and offers it to her.

"He's going to leave again." She sniffles. "He probably already did."

"He's not going to leave this time."

"He forgot about me," Sierra murmurs, hunching her shoulders.

"He never forgot about you. He draws pictures of you all the time. I saw one he made of you fighting a big scary dragon, just the other day."

Sierra is quiet for a moment. "He remembered I like dragons?"

"Yes. Of course. He sent me to find you and take care of you, because he knew he wouldn't be able to for a while."

"Because he's scared of Uncle Troy," she says, matter-of-factly, and Nate winces.

"Who is Uncle Troy?" Ras asks.

"He's my uncle. Nate was his boyfriend, but Uncle Troy was mean to him and hit him. Uncle Troy said if Nate ever comes back, he better watch out."

"I see." Ras's voice is noticeably colder.

"Hey." Nate steps clumsily into the room. He wants to stop Sierra before she can say more. "I, uh…"

"Hi, Nate," Sierra says, her gaze downcast and shy. "Sorry I yelled."

"Think I deserved it. I'm really sorry I left you for so long. It's okay if you're mad."

"I'll let you two talk." Ras slips past Nate and out the door, pausing only to kiss Nate on the cheek before he leaves.

Sierra scuffs her foot on the carpet, frowning intently. "Are you gonna leave again?"

"No," Nate says, vehemently, before he can think about it. He'll just have to be stronger because he can't possibly leave her a second time.

Sierra nods, her face turned up to him, but he knows it will take time to earn back the trust he broke.

"I love you," Nate says, getting down on his knees. "I missed you so much."

"Did you tell Ras to come find me?"

"Yeah," he says, his voice gruff. "I told him you needed help."

She nods thoughtfully.

"Okay," she says finally, as though coming to some weighty decision. "You can be my dad again."

Something warm and tender floods Nate's chest, and he has to brace himself so he won't cry. He should remind her he's not her dad, not really, but this moment feels too perfect to spoil with facts. And anyway, she knows that well enough. It's just a game they play, a pretty thing to pretend.

"Can I hug you?" he asks, forcing his voice to be steady.

She hums while she thinks about it. "Not yet. Maybe later."

"Okay." He gives her an easy smile. He never wants to push physical affection on her and wants to make sure she knows she can always refuse. "Do you wanna go see what presents Ras brought for you?"

She sits up straight, and her eyes light up. "I got more presents?"

"You sure did." He gets up and follows her as she darts into the living room.

Ras and Sierra have a short discussion about the best order to open the gifts, which she immediately disregards, tearing into them and strewing wrapping paper everywhere. When she's finished, she runs into her room and returns with two items—a painting she made and something else, something she clearly wrapped herself in plain white paper with crayon scribbles across it.

She glances sheepishly at Nate. "I didn't know you were coming, so I don't have a present."

"That's okay," Nate says. "Seeing you is the best present I could get."

She gives him a shy smile and presents the gifts to Ras.

"This is for you," she says, gesturing to the wrapped object. "And this"—she points at the painting— "is for Lady Scarlett."

Ras opens the present carefully, while Nate glances at Sierra's artwork. It's done in acrylics and shows a woman wearing a red dress with a golden crown.

"I love it." Ras holds up the lumpy mug with his name on it in glittering letters. "And Scarlett is going to love this drawing. She's going to hang it in her room."

"Lady Scarlett," Sierra corrects him, hands on her hips, but she has a radiant smile.

Nate glances at the painting again, feeling worry creep through him. How does Sierra know Scarlett? The syndicate's ice queen would be an even worse role model than Ras.

"Lady Scarlett is going to love this," Ras says. "Thank you, Sierra."

She gives him a wide smile, then turns and begins to rummage through her absurdly large pile of presents.

"Let's fight." She grabs the two foam swords and handing one to Ras, who takes it with delight.

"Not in the house," Nate says, feeling for a moment like the only adult in the room.

"Fine." Sierra heaves a melodramatic sigh. "Let's go in the backyard."

*

Dawn slowly turns the sky from black to pale pink. Sierra and Ras run around the huge backyard with their toy swords, the little girl squealing in delight as Ras chases her, growling and stomping with a comical clumsiness so unlike his usual effortless grace. Nate leans against the trunk of the large oak tree at the far edge and watches, aching with fondness and wanting. It's surreal to see the most dangerous man in the city playing, just like a kid. How does he find such innocence in the depths of his black heart?

Nate, despite himself, begins to make wishes as tiny and fragile as the snowflakes drifting down around him.

A wish that Ras might love the little girl, that he might love Nate too. A wish for a different place, a different path, a different life. If the gently falling snow could wipe everything clean, Nate would open his eyes in a yellow house with a big kitchen and a swing set in the backyard, with a lover who has traded his gun for a briefcase, the seedy back alleys for a corner office.

Nate closes his eyes. *I wish. I wish. I wish I wish I—*

"Jesus Christ," says a wry voice, and Nate smells a familiar mix of weed, cigarette smoke, and cheap cologne. "You came back, babe."

Nate has to struggle not to flinch when he meets Troy's stark, severe gaze. Of course he would be here to see his sister and his niece. He has no other family to visit on Christmas.

"And holy fuck, did you find the biggest sugar daddy in the whole city." Troy puts an unlit cigarette in his mouth and searches in his pocket until he comes up with a lighter. He's pissed, and for a long time that meant Nate was going to pay, one way or another. "Nice work."

Nate steps back, swallowing down the hot shame. He should have known people are going to assume that's what this is—Nate has nothing else to offer, and Ras has everything to give.

"He cares about me," Nate says.

"I can tell." Troy gestures expansively. "He bought your baby girl a fuckin' house. You must have gotten a lot better in bed since the last time I fucked you."

Nate crosses his arms tight over his chest. "It's not like that. It's not a...a trade. It's a relationship."

"That's sweet." Troy's cold mockery is as familiar as the worn futon Nate woke up on every day for years, as familiar as the lines on the face of the man who was always beside him. "Do you tell him that when he gets you high?"

"I don't get high. I'm sober now."

"Babe." Troy levels a matter-of-fact gaze at him, arms crossed. "You might not be high, sometimes, but you are never gonna be sober." He sounds so certain, like a doctor giving a diagnosis, that it makes Nate wonder if he might be right.

"Fuck you," Nate growls, taking another step back until he bumps against the wide trunk of the tree behind him. Troy presses his advantage, trapping him.

"I'm just being honest," Troy says, and Nate knows this tone as well, the soothing contrition that always used to calm him, that he mistook for love. "I miss you. When that rich asshole is done with you, come back home, huh?"

"No." Nate's surprised by the vehemence in his voice. "That rich asshole is a way better man than you."

"Ras?" Troy snorts. "You've gotta be fuckin' kiddin' me. Ras is a fuckin' monster. And anyway, you love me. You told me once you'd always love me, Nate."

He reaches into his pocket again and takes out something very familiar. The dope is tied up in a glossy green balloon, which Troy takes out of the little baggie and taps gently against Nate's nose, the way he used to tap Nate with his finger when he was feeling playful. And Nate feels something that goes beyond hunger, a craving deep in his bones, a wanting like a torrent of water straining a dam.

"Whaddya say?" Troy stands close enough to kiss. "I've got the gear on me. We could do it right now. All you gotta do is get on your knees and ask for it."

Nate's eyes linger on the drugs as memories rise like floodwaters and threaten to overwhelm him.

"I'll count to ten." It was Troy's favorite trick, a surefire way to get Nate to do just about anything—if he reached ten, which he rarely did, he wouldn't let Nate get high. Hearing the numbers trickle down brings back a flood of memories, moments Nate had wanted only to forget.

"Ten." *Twenty-two-year-old Nate is handing over all the tips he made at his short-term bussing job because Troy handles all the money, no matter the source.*

"Nine." *Twenty-year-old Nate is letting someone film him, as much as he hates the idea, because Troy thinks they can put up the video online and make a little money.*

"Eight." *Seventeen-year-old Nate is putting back the box of colored pencils and the pad of paper he placed in Troy's shopping cart because they don't have money for that shit.*

"Seven." *Sixteen-year-old Nate is giving his first blowjob because Troy told him to, and told him what to do.*

"Six." Troy hesitates. "Hold up. Here comes daddy now."

"Uncle Troy!" Sierra runs toward him, Ras in tow. "Don't be mean to Nate."

"Troy," Ras says softly, and Nate can see the exact moment when he remembers. He glances at Nate, eyebrows raised, and Nate winces, ducking his head down. He had hoped Ras would never recall that moment—the worst and most pathetic of his life.

"Jude." Troy's tone is not at all friendly. "Jude fuckin' de Haven. They said you was dead, man."

Ras's fist flies out so fast Nate doesn't follow the movement, and he's startled by the heavy smack it makes as it connects with Troy's face. Troy stumbles backward, and Ras advances on him, perfectly calm but deadly cold, like his eyes are lovely green lagoons, suddenly frozen over.

"My name is Ras. And you should know better than to fuck with my lover."

Troy shakes his head wildly, his hand pressed to his bloody nose. "Swear to god I—"

Ras hits him again, and he falls to the ground. Sierra gasps sharply as she grips his hand so tightly her little fingernails dig into his skin.

"Stop," Nate says, jerking on Ras's arm. "Sierra is here."

Ras looks her over with a thoughtful frown. "You're right. I was a little older the first time I saw my father work someone over. You should go inside and close the curtains. I'll be there in a minute."

"No," Nate says, his voice strained and desperate. "I don't want you to hurt people 'cause of me."

"Why not? It's not like I'm going to kill him." Ras seems genuinely confused, and for a moment, it's like the cold brush of the show and the chill air wake Nate, just enough to make him wonder what he's doing with a monster like this.

"What are you going to do?" Sierra asks, a little tremor in her voice.

At the sound of it, something about Ras shifts. Not just his expression, but something deep beneath. The pulling on of a hood, or the throwing back of a shroud, the ice melting, the spring thaw and those green eyes are the warmth of summer again.

"Nothing." He grins at her, and she smiles back as charmed as Nate is by the snake himself. "Troy and I were just having a grown-up talk. But I know where he lives, if we need to talk more later."

Troy gets as pale as the snow, hearing that. Sierra stands over him, little hands on her hips. "Don't be mean to Nate. Or Ras will hit you."

"Nobody is gonna hit nobody." Nate steps forward. He desperately wants to keep her from learning this poisonous lesson. "That's not how we deal with our problems. Right, guys?"

"That's right." Ras sounds sincere, even though Nate knows he's anything but.

JUDE #7, SERIES. 2005

Graphite and watercolor on paper

"I'm glad you found her again," Ethan says, and he sounds like he genuinely means it. He gives Nate a warm smile across the little cafe table where they're sitting together. "I'll bet she was glad to see you."

Nate looks away sheepishly. "Yeah. Think she's still pissed at me for leavin' her, but we're startin' to get back to how it used to be."

"Trust takes time." Ethan hesitates, looking self-conscious for a moment. It's an odd look on him; he's always so quietly self-assured. "I got you a gift. Just a small thing, but I hope you'll like it."

He takes a small box out of his messenger bag and slides it across the table toward Nate, who studies it guiltily.

"I didn't get you nothin."

"That's okay," Ethan reassures him. "I'm just glad to spend time with you."

"I didn't get presents for anybody but Sierra. I just...I dunno what to get. The whole thing seems kind of weird. My mom wasn't big on presents, and I guess I just never learned how." Gifts were for Becky, or for the "poor, unfortunate souls" who the church delivered charity to, but never for Nate. Even as a child, he was undeserving.

"Don't worry about it," Ethan says with an easy smile. "Sierra's presents are the important ones."

Nate shrugs. He still feels a little guilty. "It's just... what would you want? I don't even know where to start."

"Honestly?" Ethan thinks for a second. "I'd love it if you drew something for me."

Nate gives a surprised laugh. "That's all?"

"You're a very good artist. I love seeing what you make."

Ethan's words make Nate feel warm, embers glowing in his chest. He pushes his empty plate aside and takes out the sketchbook and pencil he always keeps in his pocket, so he can sketch the strong lines of Ethan's face, the set of his chin and the weariness around his eyes.

"You have an interesting profile," Nate says, reaching out without thinking to turn Ethan's head to the side. "This line here." He traces the curve of Ethan's jaw down to his chin.

"Right." Ethan's voice sounds a little strained, and he forces a laugh. "That's what all the men tell me. That I'm interesting-looking."

"That's not what I meant," Nate says, flustered. "I just mean...it's like this." He holds up his drawing for Ethan to examine.

"Huh." Ethan takes the tiny sketchbook from Nate to study the drawing more closely. "You make me look so noble."

Nate shrugs. It's rarely his conscious intention to convey character traits in his portraits. And yet they come across all the same, in every drawing. Ras with mischief and tenderness dancing in his eyes, Sierra's earnest desire to do better, to be better. And Ethan's quiet dignity, which Nate finds very compelling.

*

Nate leaves Ethan's gift unopened on the table for two days after he receives it. He likes seeing it there in its silver wrapping paper with blue ribbon, something someone took the trouble to pick out and wrap just for him. He's uneasy about the house Ras bought him, but the little box on the table is a comfortable size, and he enjoys guessing what might be inside.

When he finally opens it, he finds two tickets and a note. The tickets are for a movie at an indie theater downtown, a documentary about the life and work of a famous artist who was born and raised in the city. The note tells him to take whoever he wants along with him to the show. It's written nonchalantly, but when he calls Ethan to thank him and invite him to come along, Ethan sounds quietly thrilled, and that makes a tendril of excitement run through Nate as well.

Over the next few days, Nate spends some of his time with Sierra, slowly building back the trust he'd broken by disappearing from her life without a word of goodbye, and much of the rest brooding on how immense and ridiculous Ras's gift is—a house that probably cost more than he could earn in ten years.

So when Ras shows up unannounced on his doorstep, three days after Christmas, Nate's elated but also deeply uneasy. And Ras picks up on it right away.

"Is something wrong?" he asks, stepping into the apartment before Nate can think to invite him in, greeting Nate with a frown and raised eyebrow instead of his usual dramatic kiss.

Nate shrugs. "Nah. It's nothing."

"Clearly, it's something. You don't look at all happy to see me."

Nate shakes his head and turns away. Ras's scrutiny makes him feel wildly self-conscious.

"Did I do something wrong?" Ras asks.

"It's not that," Nate says, studying his shoes. "It's just...you spent way too much money on that house. It's weird, you know?"

"No." Ras sounds oddly hurt by Nate's reluctance. "I don't know. I honestly thought you would like it."

"I do." Nate feels hot and flustered. He gets up and crosses the tiny kitchen to fiddle with the coffeemaker so he'll have something to do with his hands. So he can look away from Ras's sincere, shining eyes and try to think. "It's...it's a lot. For someone like me."

"That's ridiculous. You deserve the world, Nate, and I intend to give it to you."

Nate opens the container of coffee grounds and breathes in the rich, heady scent. "It feels like...if you do something so big for me, then you own me, kinda."

"And would that be so bad?" Ras's hands are on Nate's hips, and Ras's lips brush the top of Nate's ear. "Would it be so terrible to lay down your sword and shield for a few moments and let someone else take care of you?"

It's a seductive idea, and Nate can't help but lean into it, just a little, just for a second. Ras's body is warm against his, firm through the layers of their clothes.

"Let me love you," Ras murmurs, hot breath against Nate's ear that makes him weak in the knees. "You deserve all this and more."

How could this be the same man who ruthlessly advanced on Troy's prone form, a tiger leisurely moving in for the kill? How could two such different entities live beneath the same skin?

Nate leans his head back when Ras's lips move to the side of his neck, along the contours of the phoenix feather tattooed there. Every nerve ending is alight, shining like the lights of the city at night. He turns and meets Ras's eager kisses with his own, his hands moving of their own volition over Ras's body.

"Jude," he murmurs when he's lost to the pleasure, and Ras is watching him with green eyes dark with lust. "Please, Jude. Please."

"Anything for you," Ras murmurs, sinking to his knees, and is it Nate's imagination, or is his voice lower, huskier, the way it used to be all those years ago. "I've always wanted to be with you. From the first moment we met."

And Nate could swear it's Jude who looks up at him with shining green eyes, bright with adoration before he wipes away every one of Nate's thoughts with a pleasure he's never known before. Without fear to give it a sharp edge, without heroin to dull it away, every sensation is hot and heady, and Nate gives himself over to it, to a love that makes the rest of the world fade away.

*

"You're cuddly," Nate says with a soft huff of laughter. He invited Ras to stay the night and didn't realize it would mean such close proximity—Ras curled around him, an arm over his chest and their legs intertwined in the darkness.

"I am." There's slight edge to Ras's voice. "What of it?"

"Nothing," Nate says quickly. He remembers being a teenager, in an actual bed with someone for the first time. Troy turned away from him, told Nate to "give him some fuckin' space," and Nate did.

But this moment, right here right now, is almost perfect, and he doesn't need to let the past intrude on it.

Instead, he thinks about the way Ras had *changed* during the sex that really felt like making love. His features took on the quiet intensity Nate remembers from years ago, and his eyes were more solemn, lacking their usual playful glint. Maybe Nate was imagining things—but maybe not. Maybe Jude is still there, still at the heart of him, despite all the layers of smiling armor he's accumulated since.

"Tell me about Troy," Ras says.

He seems to know this is the best time to ask such questions. In the darkness, unable to turn and see the expression on Ras's face, it's easier for Nate to talk about the things that haunt him. In Ras's arms, he feels safe. But even that comes with a degree of uncertainty. Nate recognizes he's becoming more and more dependent on Ras for support and comfort, when a year ago he relied on no one but himself. He's also very aware that while Ras is everything to him, he is only one of three lovers in Ras's orbit.

"You remembered him," Nate says with an edge of annoyance. It bothers him a little that just the sight of Troy brought back memories, but Nate's face never did. "You remembered him even though you forgot me."

"To be fair, you didn't recognize me when we first met."

"You're not the same person anymore. I mean, I like you now and everything, but Jude was..." Nate searches for the right words to explain how he used to lie awake at night, imagining Jude would take him far away from that seedy house in the Warrens, to somewhere warm and welcoming where they could fall in love and be a family. Jude didn't have Ras's cold sharp edges, and he didn't have two other lovers to divide his time.

"I think maybe you idolized him a little bit," Ras says. "The person I was back then...he was weak. He let his big heart make him helpless, and it almost killed us."

"What I mean is, you weren't always Ras. And you don't always have to be. You could change—you could do anything."

Ras is quiet for a moment. "Do you think because I'm a violent person in my work I will treat you like Troy did? Is that why you're worried?"

It's so far off base Nate wants to laugh, but the reminder of his relationship with Troy, and the sinking realization that Ras now remembers it, makes him sick to his stomach.

"I would never hit you," Ras murmurs in the darkness. "I would never make you do anything you didn't want to do. I'd like to make him pay for what he did to—"

"No." It comes out ferociously. "Don't hurt anyone because of me. Please, Ras."

"If that's what you want." Ras gently strokes Nate's hair. "But if you change your mind, let me know."

"I won't," Nate mutters, curling in on himself. The darkness has changed. No longer a sanctuary, now it feels like it's stifling him. It's a long time before he gets to sleep.

THE SCHOOLYARD. 2006

Woodblock print

Nate walks through the elementary school, sick with anxiety. He remembers parent-teacher conferences from when he was a kid in foster care, the disapproving frowns of his teachers and his foster parents because he was too dumb to learn the material and too filled with anger to play nicely with the other kids. Now, he's somehow on the other side of it, filling in for Traci who had some engagement she couldn't miss. Or more likely, she just didn't want to go, and knew Nate would think it was important enough to do it for her.

He meets Sierra outside the classroom, and her eyes are filled with worry as they wait for the teacher to get to them.

At first, he's summoned without Sierra, who has to wait in the hallway with the other kids. She squeezes his hand and hangs her head before letting him step into the classroom.

"I'm Amber." The teacher has frizzled auburn hair on a very round face, and she studies him, unsmiling. "I was expecting Sierra's mother."

Nate has spent a lot of time thinking about how to answer the unspoken question before him.

"Yeah. Hi. I'm Nate. I'm Sierra's dad." The lie comes easily to him because it feels like the truth.

Amber gives him a slight smile, but he can see suspicion in her eyes.

"It's good to meet you." She gestures for him to take a seat in one of the plastic school chairs and sits facing him. "I have some concerns about Sierra. She's a very sweet child, but she struggles to focus on her schoolwork. And there have been a few incidents on the playground that concern me. She's gotten into three physical altercations in the past few months. Each time I've spoken to her mother, but this is the first I've actually seen of either of you, despite my repeated requests that you come in for a meeting."

Nate bows his head at her chastising tone. "Yeah. Sorry. Didn't know about that."

"I don't believe Sierra started the fights, but she's the one who escalated them to physical confrontations. She has some anger issues."

Nate can picture exactly what happened—someone insulted her, and she responded instantly and furiously, screaming and hitting and kicking. He knows because that's how he used to be too.

"Okay. I'll talk to her."

"And then there's the matter of her schoolwork. When she can focus, she's a very bright student. But often, she zones out and doesn't participate at all."

Nate understands that intimately as well.

"Does she get a good breakfast before coming in to school?" Amber asks. "Do you read to her and help her with her projects? A little more engagement from you and her mother could make a big difference."

"I dunno," Nate admits. "I don't live with her. But I'll fix this. I swear I will."

*

The navigation app on his phone leads Nate to a neighborhood of tree-lined streets and well-maintained old houses, each with a unique character and coloring. The yards reflect the whims of the owners—some are neatly landscaped stretches of unadorned grass, others overflow with flowers or are stretches of ornamental rock.

The address he has written on a little scrap of sketchbook paper directs him to a modest but lovely yellow house with a large porch and tidy shrubs out front. He knocks on the door, wondering why he feels such trepidation.

When Ethan opens it and smiles at him, most of the anxiety washes away, because if Ethan is anything at all, he's a soothing presence, as relaxing to be around as a smooth sandy shore and the gentle sea that meets it.

It's a strange feeling to have for someone Nate doesn't know all that well. He and Ethan have a standing coffee date every week, and text frequently outside of that, but Nate is slow to make friends and slower to trust. It's just—something about Ethan makes it a little easier.

Still, Nate's not accustomed to asking for help. He does everything he can to avoid it, no matter the consequences. He's not sure why he sent a text to Ethan after that parent-teacher conference, asking if they could talk right away about something important. It's not something he can ask Ras about; *his* solution would probably involve bribing or intimidating the teacher into overlooking Sierra's problems. But Nate needs someone to tell him what to do, what a normal person would do. His own experience is as far removed from normal or healthy as Ras's.

Ethan invites him in, and they end up seated at a little table in a sunny kitchen, a steaming cup of coffee for each of them. Ethan makes small talk with a friendly smile, waiting patiently until Nate feels comfortable enough to bring up the reason for his visit.

"I went to Sierra's parent-teacher conference today," Nate says and hesitates. "It's—her mom couldn't go. But someone had to."

Ethan looks slightly puzzled. "And the teacher was willing to talk to you?"

"Legally...I'm kinda her dad."

Nate tells Ethan the story of Sierra's birth, the desperation in Traci's eyes when she looked at the lopsided birth certificate, only half the parentage filled out. Traci might tell Sierra her father is a rich man who will someday come to take them to a better place, but Nate knows the truth. Traci isn't sure who Sierra's father is, and no one in her life was willing to take responsibility when she found out she was pregnant. No one except Nate. He was sixteen at the time, an addict without a dollar of his own to his name, but he knew what he had to do. He made a promise that day, and now that he's fought off his own demons, he intends to keep it.

Ethan is quiet for a moment when Nate finishes his story, thoughtful.

"It's really something," he finally says. "Sometimes when it seems like nothing is going right for a kid, someone steps forward to change their life. It makes all the difference in the world."

Nate bows his head to hide his smile. The words warm him, breathing life into the embers that burn inside him. He knows he can make a difference for Sierra if he can only figure out how.

"What did the teacher say when she talked to you?" Ethan asks.

Nate looks away with an odd sense of shame, as though Sierra's struggles are his fault. Maybe they are—a result of his long absence. "She's havin' a hard time focusing on her work. And she gets into a lot of fights."

Ethan nods, his brow furrowed as he considers this. Nate has told him a little about Sierra's situation, enough to understand that her home life is far from ideal.

"The teacher said she needs a good breakfast in the morning before school, and someone should help her with her homework and make sure she goes to bed at a good time. But I don't—I mean, her mom ain't gonna do that."

Ethan is quiet for a moment.

"I have a suggestion," he says carefully. "But you should keep in mind that I don't know everything about the situation. So take my advice with a grain of salt, okay?"

Nate nods.

"If you want those things to happen, you're going to have to do them yourself. If I understand right, no one else is going to step up for her. It has to be you. And it's a big commitment. No one would think less of you if it's more than you can do."

Nate looks away, through the big window into the long stretch of backyard. "I dunno. I'm not really the best influence for her."

"I disagree. You're a successful artist, you overcame an addiction, and you genuinely care about her. You're stronger than you think, Nate."

Nate searches Ethan's expression for artifice or flattery but finds only a calm sincerity. "I...I don't really know how."

"I'm not a parent, so my experience is limited," Ethan says with a hint of a self-deprecating smile. "But I'm pretty sure it doesn't come with a manual. Let your love for her guide you, and you'll figure out the rest."

Nate opens his mouth to remind Ethan he isn't Sierra's parent, then closes it. The generational legacy written in her DNA is not important to him, not compared to the pull he feels in his soul whenever he thinks of her, as inexorable and inevitable as gravity. What matters is they found each other. And if they're separated, he knows deep down they will find each other again, and again, because his love for her will always lead him back.

*

Traci is in the living room with her feet up on the coffee table, flipping through channels on the TV. She doesn't look high, and Nate takes that as a good sign.

"Hey, Sierra." He glances at the little girl drawing at the kitchen table. "I wanna talk to your mom. You think you could wait in your room for a minute?"

"Is this about school?" she asks, hanging her head meekly. "I'm sorry I was bad."

"You didn't do anything bad," Nate promises. Traci's gaze flickers to her daughter for only a second before returning to the TV. "We just need to talk about grown-up stuff. I'll tell you about it after."

"Okay." Sierra gathers her drawing and gets up. She pauses in the hallway and scuffs her foot on the carpet. "You're not going to leave while I'm in my room, right?"

Nate shakes his head, with that familiar pang of guilt. "I promise to say goodbye to you before I leave."

Sierra nods and walks down the hallway.

"What do you want?" Traci asks.

Nate takes a deep breath and thinks of Ras for a moment. Ras wouldn't ask permission, he'd just say what he wanted, lay it out like it had already happened.

"I'm gonna stay here. In the spare bedroom. I'm gonna sleep here a couple nights a week so I can be here in the morning to make Sierra breakfast and help her with her homework after school."

"You think I'm a shitty mom." Traci leans back on the couch with a belligerent scowl. "You think I can't take care of my own daughter."

"I don't think that."

It's mostly the truth. Traci never hits Sierra; she's never locked her daughter out of the house on a cold night. She never tells Sierra she's bad or worthless. He has no other metric by which to judge mothering. All he knows is that Sierra needs more than her mom is able to give.

"You ain't her dad," Traci says, and Nate feels a familiar flash of anger. Traci has said that to him many times, and it never fails to get under his skin. "You're never gonna be her dad."

"Then where is her fuckin' dad?" Nate growls. "He's not here, but I am."

"Whatever," Traci stretches, yawning. Feigning disinterest, but Nate knows she still cares at least a little. "I give it a week. It's a shit ton of work taking care of her. You'll get sick of her before you know it."

"I won't," Nate vows, but her eyes are already back on the TV, and she's pretending she didn't hear him.

He sighs and walks off down the hallway to find Sierra. She's at the little desk in her room, pencil in hand, but she's not drawing. She just stares at the blank piece of paper—zoned out, like the teacher said. Nate knows what that's like, to leave your body behind and separate yourself from the world. Like the skin of an onion pulled back because it hurts too much to be present and aware.

"Hey." He waits the doorway for her permission to enter.

She blinks a few times and then turns toward him.

"I wanna ask you something. You're not in trouble, and nobody's angry. We just need to talk a little. Is that okay?"

She nods.

Nate sits on the bed and smooths the comforter with his hands. "You know I live by myself, right?"

"You don't live with Ras?"

Nate smiles wistfully. As though things could ever be that simple. As though he could ever trust a man that much again. "Nah. I'm by myself. And y'know, it gets real lonely sometimes."

"Oh. I get lonely too. When Mom is gone."

"And I saw there's an extra bedroom here. You think I could stay sometimes? Then I wouldn't be lonely by myself."

She smiles, and it's such a beautiful expression Nate longs for his sketchbook. "Okay. I don't want you to be lonely."

WOMAN IN WINDOW. 2006

Graphite on canvas

There is no reason for Scarlett to feel any trepidation, no reason for the nervous energy creeping up her spine as she stands on the stoop of a pleasant house in the suburb called River's Heart. She is the syndicate boss, the queen of the dark city, and whatever she says, whatever she wants, becomes the law of the land.

And yet, here she is. Holding a stack of children's books clutched to her chest like a schoolgirl, waiting impatiently for someone to open the door. After a few long moments, Nate opens it just a little and peers suspiciously at her through the crack.

"I…" She hesitates, wondering if she should be here at all. She is poison, she knows this, has always known it. And what does it matter if she poisons the city? But she doesn't want to bring harm to this little girl. "I brought these for Sierra." She holds out the books.

Nate opens the door a little wider, his gaze still steady and suspicious. "Why'd you—"

"Scarlett!" The little girl runs past Nate, deftly slipping out the door to wrap her skinny arms around Scarlett's legs. "Hi." She turns her face up to grin at Scarlett. "I knew you'd come back. I just knew it."

Scarlett smiles. She can't help it. The child has a sweetness and innocence that belies her circumstances. Not for a moment did she doubt that Scarlett had come to save her. That Scarlett was someone who would protect her.

Nate glances at the little girl clinging to Scarlett and frowns. But he steps aside to let them into the house. Inside, it's warm and homey, the rich smell of something baking in the air.

"How's she know you?" Nate asks Scarlett.

"When I was in the dark place, Scarlett saved me," Sierra says.

"The lightbulb in her apartment had burned out," Scarlett explains. "She was alone in the dark. Ras and I found her there."

"Scarlett protected me." Sierra holds tightly to Scarlett for a moment longer before reluctantly letting her go. "She's a superhero."

"I brought you some books." Scarlett sets her bundle on the coffee table.

"I don't really like to read," Sierra says. "I like pictures, not words."

"When you read, the pictures are in your head," Scarlett tells her. "Just try it, and trust me."

Sierra picks up one of the books, and turns it over in her hands, her brow furrowed thoughtfully. A timer beeps, and Nate hurries to the kitchen. Scarlett follows at a more measured pace and finds him gently settling a souffle onto a cooling rack.

"I didn't know you could cook," she says.

"I can't. Ras put that in the oven before he left. Just said to take it out for him." Nate clears his throat. "Hey, thanks for bringing books for Sierra. And for helping her."

"She's a sweet girl."

"I'm gonna read this one first!" Sierra bursts through the doorway, thrumming with energy. In her hand she has a book with a photograph of a deep-sea diver on the cover. "It's full of shark facts."

"Don't you already know every shark fact?" Nate asks, gently teasing.

"No," Sierra insists. "There are millions of them."

"I guess you'd better start reading, then."

"I will." Sierra stands at attention and nods. "But first, I need cake."

Nate surprises Scarlett by offering her a piece as well, and they sit together at the kitchen table to eat. Sierra wolfs hers in seconds and then gulps down a tall glass of milk.

"We have ladybugs here," she informs Scarlett, wiping crumbs from her mouth with her sleeve. "I'll go find one so I can show it to you."

Scarlett smiles. "I'd love that."

Sierra ignores Nate's recommendation that she put on shoes as she darts into the backyard. Scarlett watches her through the window as she stalks through the neatly mowed grass.

"How'd you..." Nate hesitates. "How'd you get her to trust you like that? Usually, she won't say a word to strangers."

"I don't know," Scarlett replies. "Only—we came from the same kinds of places."

"Yeah. I get it." Nate pushes his cake around with his fork, and Scarlett gets the sense something is bothering him. "So, how long did you know Ras?"

"Since he was a teenager."

Nate's eyes settle on her, clear and steady. "So you knew him when he went by Jude."

Yes, she knew Jude. She buried him and mourned him and sometimes still misses him. "I did."

"What happened? What happened to Jude—what changed him?"

She presses her lips together. "It's not my story to tell, Nate. I'm sorry."

"Jude was a good man." Nate speaks quietly but confidently. "I remember. I remember how he was."

"Jude is dead," she says as gently as she can. "That part of him...he'll never be the same. If you're hoping he'll change back into the boy you knew all those years ago, then I'm sorry. It's not going to happen."

Nate looks her in the eye and sets his jaw defiantly. "You don't know that for sure."

She doesn't want to argue with him about it, not when they've finally found some sort of understanding between them. She's not accustomed to having conversations like this with Ras's other lovers. Usually, they're too jealous of her to sit down and be civil for this long, but Nate doesn't seem as bothered by it.

The screen door clatters open, and Sierra runs in. "I found a ladybug and Ras," she announces.

"In the backyard?" Scarlett asks, raising an eyebrow at Ras, who doesn't look the slightest bit sheepish about spying on his newest lover.

"Checking the security system," he says.

Nate looks convinced by the lie, but Scarlett knows Ras better, will always know him better.

"Look at my ladybug." Sierra holds out her gently closed fist. She opens it gingerly to reveal a red spotted bug climbing across her palm.

"It's pretty," Scarlett says, and Sierra gives her a wide smile. When Scarlett looks up, Ras is watching them with an uncharacteristic solemnity.

"Okay." Nate puts his hands on Sierra's shoulders. "It's time to get ready for karate."

"But when am I gonna see Scarlett again?" Sierra asks, brow furrowed with worry. "I want to paint a picture of her."

"I'll come back soon," Scarlett promises. "Your dad and I can talk about it."

"Nate's not my dad," Sierra mumbles.

Nate winces slightly but says nothing to contradict her.

Sierra looks up at Scarlett with wide, pleading eyes. With her beautiful umber skin and dark eyes, she looks nothing like Nate or Traci, and Scarlett wonders if there's truth to what she's saying. "Please don't go. My class is short. You could stay here until I get back."

"That sounds perfect," Ras says without waiting for Nate to give permission. He's like this with all of his men—arrogant and domineering—and Scarlett wonders how they can possibly bear to put up with it. He's completely different with her, submissive in the bedroom and out of it.

Nate sighs, resigned, and ushers Sierra to her room so she can dress for the martial arts class. She reappears a few minutes later, a bouncing ball of energy in a white gi. She throws a few open-handed blows and kicks at Ras, who dodges good naturedly, then gives her tips on technique.

As soon as the door shuts behind Nate, Ras grabs Scarlett and pulls her into his arms, covering her neck with passionate kisses, his fingers sliding the hem of her skirt upward.

She laughs as his lips move to her bared shoulder. "It can't wait for tonight?"

"I liked seeing you with Sierra." He slides his hands under her thighs and lifts her. She wraps her legs around his waist and her arms around his neck. "You're good with her."

"You know, Sierra's mother is sleeping upstairs," Scarlett says. "And Nate's just dropping her off; he'll be home any minute."

"We'll be quiet." Ras carries her into the walk-in pantry and presses her up against the wall beside the cereal and crackers and cans of soup.

"You're never quiet." But her fingers move to undo his belt all the same.

As he holds her, kisses her, moves inside her, she thinks, not for the first time, of the possibilities the joining of their bodies could bring, if she was willing to take the risk. And then his hips thrust forward more quickly, and she thinks of nothing but him. She may have taken his family from him in their desperate struggle to win control of the syndicate—his father dead, his brother exiled—but together, they will make a new family, a new future.

"Do you ever think about kids?" she asks him in the still moments just after, as they hold each other in the dark pantry. "About kids of our own?"

Ras gives her a cautious, brief glance before he pulls away and turns his attention to righting his clothing. "Ash asked me that too. He didn't say why, but I think he was wondering how serious I am about Nate and Sierra."

Ras is wrong, of course. Ash and Scarlett have been talking, just the two of them, about the future. About the possibility of a child, a family. Ash only cares that it be Ras's child, and that Ash can raise it as his own. The three of them would be parents together—an unconventional family, maybe, but a strong one. Scarlett knows she and

Ras are too broken by their own childhoods to be parents without someone who can keep them stable. Ash would be the anchor they need.

"How serious are you, then?" she asks, playing along.

"I don't think I'm much of a father figure." His eyes sparkle with mischief. "I'm told I'm a bad influence."

"But is it something you'd want?" She presses on, even though she knows it's risky to reveal her own desires before she's ready to be so vulnerable. After so many years of scheming in the dark, secrecy for her has become a habit, a way of life.

"My father once told me being a parent meant you had to be selfless. Does that really seem like my style?" He gives her a cheeky wink and turns away, but not before she sees the melancholy in his eyes.

She's familiar with that look, that grief he carries with him all the time. It's old and weary and bone deep, and he sometimes still flinches when she reaches out to touch his face, like a little boy whose father hits him. Nate will never see this side of him, will never know these heart-kept secrets. Only she and Ash know him this well, only their love goes this deep.

STAIN. 2006

Ink on white carpet

Nate sits on the sofa in Traci's house, watching Sierra. She's seated at the coffee table with some paints and a big sheet of paper, working intently. He wonders if it's the escape for her that it's always been for him. She spends a lot of time on her art projects, intently focused on the colors and shapes. She likes to draw people most of all, and Nate has been explaining some basic techniques. He's been picking her up after school so she doesn't have to ride the bus, where kids tease and prod at her, and then staying overnight on weeknights so he can help her get ready in the morning. Ras has even adjusted his schedule—the meticulous way he splits his time between his three lovers—to accommodate this.

Traci's prediction hasn't come true, not even close. It is hard work taking care of Sierra—not her physical needs but her emotional ones. But Nate hadn't realized how lonely he'd been in his little apartment in Bayside. Even with the stress and strain, this is more fulfilling an existence than he could have hoped for.

A loud knock sounds on the door, then it's pushed open before Nate can get up to answer it. Troy steps in, the chill wind whipping around him. He glances at Nate from across the room.

"Daddy here?" he asks.

Nate's face flushes. *I have nothing to be ashamed of.* But he feels the shame anyway.

"No," he says, forcing his gravelly voice to come out even. Ras is with Scarlett tonight, and while Nate doesn't feel too much jealousy, most of the time, he does wish Ras weren't always so busy.

"Chill, babe." Troy shrugs out of his dripping coat and throws it over a chair. "I'm just looking for Traci."

"Mom's not here." Sierra casts a surly glance at Troy.

"She'll get here soon enough." Troy settles into an armchair and puts his wet boots up on the coffee table next to Sierra's drawing. She scowls at him, scooting her things away. In the process, she knocks over the little container of yellow paint. It pools on the table, staining her drawing and Troy's boots.

"Be careful," he growls, jerking his feet away.

Nate's heart constricts in his chest at the sight of the spilled paint. It takes him back, and back, to the dusty rooms of his mother's house, her hoarse, furious whisper and the darkness of the closets where he tried to hide.

"What the fuck, Sierra?" he yells, and when he hears his own furious voice, he's stunned into shamed silence. She bursts into tears and runs off down the hallway into her room.

"I don't know what the hell we're gonna do with her," Troy says, wiping the paint from his boots. He doesn't seem concerned about the table or Sierra's drawing, which is slowly being swallowed by the pool of yellow. "She's a pain in the ass, and Traci's pretty much checked out."

Nate stares down the hallway Sierra disappeared into. "I yelled at her," he whispers. "I made her cry."

"What doesn't make her cry these days?" Troy grumbles.

Nate barely hears him, sinking onto the couch and putting his face in his hands. He might cry himself. He certainly did enough of that on the cold night he spent curled up in the bushes that grew by the front porch. He would spend plenty of nights outside as a homeless teenager, but somehow it wasn't the same as sleeping on the porch beside the door his mother had locked against his return. And what she made him do before she let him back in, he only thinks of in the kind of panicky half-realized moments before he's fully awake, shutting the memory away as soon as his mind is alert and able.

"Ain't you gonna clean that up?" Troy asks. When Nate doesn't answer, he gives a heavy sigh and starts half-heartedly wiping at the table with some tissues. "This is just like I remember. The two of you are fuckin' space cadets."

"Fuck you," Nate says wearily. "You never did nothin' to help us."

"I took care of you for a long time, Nate. You were such a fuckin' mess when we met. Nobody else woulda taken you in, but I did. You never slept on the streets again, you always had what you needed." Troy crosses his arms, scowling. "A little fuckin' gratitude wouldn't hurt."

Nate bows his head because he knows Troy is right. "Sorry. I'm just in a bad mood."

"No fuckin' kidding," Troy says, pulling a pack of cigarettes out of his pocket.

"You can't smoke in here. Not around Sierra."

Troy deliberately flicks the lighter, his eyes on Nate. He lifts a cigarette to his lips, and Nate feels something in him come alive, hot and thrumming through his veins. He strides forward and grabs the cigarette and pack out of Troy's hands. He opens the front door and throws them into the snowy yard as hard as he can.

"Jesus," Troy mutters. "Chill, babe. I won't smoke around your precious baby if it's that big a deal."

Nate doesn't answer. He walks past Troy and down the hall to Sierra's room. He knocks softly on the door, and when he gets no answer, pushes it open.

She's lying on her bed, her face buried in her pillow, crying softly, and it breaks his heart.

"Sierra." He sits on the bed beside her and puts a gentle hand on her shoulder. "I'm sorry I yelled at you. It's not your fault. Please don't cry."

"You hate me," she says, her voice muffled by the pillow and thick with tears.

"I don't hate you. I did a mean thing, and I'm sorry. It doesn't mean I hate you."

She keeps her face buried in the pillow, but her sobs slow, then stop entirely. Nate rubs gentle circles onto her back, wondering how he could have possibly been so cruel, so thoughtless.

*

Nate is on one of the hardbacked chairs in Ras's living room, his attention on the drawing taking shape before him. Ras gave him a brush and ink set that probably cost more than Nate's daily paycheck, and insisted he try it out. Now, he's trying to concentrate on the project, and not think of the yellow pool of paint Sierra spilled onto the table, and the vicious way he yelled at her for it.

"You look worried." Ras is sprawled out on the couch with a comic book. He's a fan of Batman above all others and has shelves of the thin volumes in his bedroom.

"Nah." Nate forces a rough chuckle. "I'm fine."

"Are you sure?" Ras sits up. "Do you not like the gift? You don't have to use it."

"No," Nate says, fidgeting. His eyes linger on the half-full bowl of ink. "It's a good gift. I really like it. I just...you got such nice stuff. I don't wanna ruin it."

"It's just ink. I don't care if you spill it."

"Well, it's not just your apartment. Ash probably cares."

"You are more important than ink," Ras says.

Nate dips the tip of his brush into the ink and bows his head to his task, wondering at how easy it is for Ras to make him feel like he's unraveling, in a peculiar, pleasant way.

"It's just...I'm paranoid about stuff like that. My mom was real strict, and I think it just kinda stuck."

Ras sits up. "Did she hurt you?"

Nate shakes his head, flushing with shame, eyes on the drawing. "She locked me out of the house one time, for a whole night. That was the worst, I guess. And it's like I'm fucked up that way too. Sierra spilled some paint a couple days ago, and I made her cry. I didn't even think about it—it just kinda came out."

Ras gets up and makes his graceful way across the room to Nate. He puts one hand on Nate's shoulder and with the other, carefully moves the half-finished drawing to the other side of the table.

"I want you to spill this ink." He gestures to the little white bowl of very dark ink.

Nate glances warily at Ras. "You're fuckin' kidding."

"No." Ras takes Nate's hand in his own and guides it to the edge of the bowl of ink. "I want you to spill it. I want you to make the biggest fucking mess you can."

Nate knows there's no reason for the terror that rears in his chest, the tightness in his throat.

"We'll do it together." Ras guides their joined hands forward. "Okay?"

"No!" Nate tries to jerk back at the last second. In doing so, his hand knocks against the ink, so that the bowl tumbles to one side. The black liquid pools on the table, diving over the edge and spilling onto the carpet and Nate's pants. His heart thuds with dread. He's never seen a spill so devastating.

He looks up at Ras, filled with a familiar guilt. "I'm so fuckin' sorry."

Ras's mouth twists fondly. "Why are you apologizing?"

"It's never gonna come out. Never. It's totally ruined."

"Nothing is ruined," Ras promises. "The carpet is just going to be a little different now. That's all."

Nate shakes his head, his breath coming fast and shallow. He tries to mop up the ink with his hands, too frantic to even get out of his chair and look for paper towels.

Ras kneels between Nate's legs, careless of the pool of ink on the carpet, and catches Nate's stained hands between his own. He looks up at Nate and says his name. Even in this submissive posture, he seems so in control, certain of himself and the world, and Nate finds it easy to just let go and follow wherever Ras might lead him.

"Everything is going to be okay," he says, and Nate believes him. "I promise."

Nate takes a deep breath and lets it go in a soft half laugh. "Yeah?"

"Yes."

Ras slips his fingers under the hem of Nate's long-sleeve shirt and lifts it, and Nate raises his arms obediently and lets Ras pull it over his head. He's getting used to this—the vulnerability he feels when Ras's eyes move over his bare, scarred skin, dark with lust. Ras has his own scars after all, lines on his arms and one shoulder from the time he fell through a glass door as a teenager, and a bullet wound on the left side of his chest, just over his heart.

"You totally ruined both our clothes," Nate says. "You ruined two sets of clothes, the table, this chair, my shoes, and the carpet."

Ras looks up at him with a playful smile. "Small price to pay to get you undressed."

He dips his finger in the pool of ink on the table and writes his name across Nate's skin in thick letters, stretching across his chest so the S is over his heart, curled around the crow tattooed there. The lines left by his finger look like brushstrokes, full and sweeping. It looks nothing like the angular letters of the graffiti tags marking his territory across the city or the notes he signs in his sharp, sloping handwriting.

"You're a narcissist," Nate says, laughing. "You think everything in this city belongs to you."

"Am I wrong?" Ras has a wicked gleam in his eye, his ink-stained fingers on the buckle of Nate's belt. "Do you belong to someone else, then?"

"No," Nate says. "Just you."

And in this moment, Ras looking up at him with want and adoration, it comes out like a promise. The ink on his chest has a ritual feel to it, like marking, like laying a claim. Something with a degree of permanence, even though it's only ink that will eventually wash off skin, if not the carpet.

*

Ash sighs, shutting the front door behind him. It was a long day of classes, and then he spent most of the evening with a struggling student whose home life and personal tragedy are beginning to affect her academic standing. There's only so much he can do for students like her, and he always leaves feeling like it wasn't enough.

The lights are on in the living room, but he knows Ras isn't home. He's out with Scarlett tonight until late, doing whatever it is they do on the streets of the dark city that Ash tries hard not to think about. Instead, Nate is there, oddly enough, sitting stiffly on the sofa. The TV is on, but he doesn't seem to be watching it.

"Hey," Ash says. Nate startles and scrambles to his feet. "I didn't mean to scare you." He looks so miserable that Ash feels a little guilty.

"No." Nate clears his throat. "It's...it's fine. I just wanted to stick around until you got home so I could say sorry."

"For what?" Ash asks. A little pulse of pain has started above his left eyebrow, and he is not ready to play therapist to yet another wayward soul.

"For..." Nate gestures to the carpet beneath the kitchen table, stained a dull gray. "I spilled some ink. I'm really fuckin' sorry, man. I—"

"Is that it?" Ash rubs his forehead and gives Nate a half-apologetic smile. "Not a big deal, Nate, really. Go home. Don't worry about it."

Nate casts another pitiful glance at the stain, then nods and heads for the door like he can tell how unwanted his presence is. Ash feels terrible, watching him go. Another person he's not doing nearly enough to help.

"Wait," he says, and Nate pauses in the doorway. "You wanna stick around for a while? Have a drink? I've had a shitty day; I could sure use some company."

Nate hesitates, frowning, and Ash thinks it's completely unfair, that no one should have the right to look that attractive when being surly. No wonder Nate caught Ras's eye. Ash isn't ugly, but he may be the only one of Ras's lovers who couldn't moonlight as a model.

"Okay," Nate finally says and manages a small smile. "Sure. But I can't drink any booze."

"Me neither. But we've got some root beer. Okay?"

It's surprisingly comfortable, settling on the couch and talking with Nate, who is actually interesting and kind of funny when Ash manages to coax him out of his shell. He hasn't really been romantically interested in anyone but Ras for years, but he could see how, in a different world, he and Nate might have gotten along all right. They have so much in common, after all.

"It's how people look at you." Nate gestures with the hand that holds his root beer bottle. His right sleeve is rolled up to his elbow so he could show Ash his track marks. Ash understands the impulse—to share with a fellow addict because only they can really relate. "I can't even wear short sleeves."

"I understand." Ash unbuttons his cuff and rolls up the long sleeve of his dress shirt to reveal the thick lines of scar tissue that run down the inside of his forearm. "People see these and they already assume a thousand things about me."

"Yeah. I get that. I wanted to die for a while too. Probably would have if Jude didn't save me."

Ash glances at him, startled. "How do you know that name?"

"I knew him back then." Nate toys with the peeling label on the bottle, pulling it up with blunt fingernails. "When his name was Jude."

Ash's heart sinks. He's resigned himself to sharing Ras, and for the most part manages to be okay with it. But he thought Jude belonged entirely to him. "Did the two of you...?"

Nate shakes his head. "I think he had somebody."

"Oh," Ash says, softly relieved.

"He can't remember me. When we met he didn't even know who I was. And he looks so different I didn't know him at first."

Ash is quiet for a moment, wondering how much to reveal. Ras would prefer he keep it all secret, but Nate deserves to know at least a little.

"He used to be two different people," Ash says. "And then...something happened. I don't fully understand how, but he became neither of them but, instead, the man he is now."

"You mean like a split personality?" Nate asks.

Ash nods. "I think Jude...kept secrets from his other half. Things he wanted to protect. And some of those secrets just got lost. Like his memories of you."

Nate is quiet for a moment, thoughtful. "Could Jude come back?" he asks finally.

"I don't know. But I don't think so."

Something about Nate's countenance hardens, the set of his jaw, a subtle narrowing of his eyes, and Ash can tell Nate doesn't believe him, or rather, refuses to.

"Even if I could turn back time and make him into the man he was back then, I wouldn't," Ash says, meeting Nate's eyes with his own defiant gaze. "Jude was deeply unhappy. He wasn't a whole person. He was missing a part of himself."

"How do you live with it?" Nate sounds more baffled than righteous. "You're a good person. I can tell. How do you live with everything he does?"

Ash gives an easy shrug to hide his disquiet. "Ras and Scarlett do a lot of evil things. But there's good in them too. All of the money I use for charities around the city comes from them. And without them to unite and manage the city's criminal elements, there would be more violence, and more chaos, and more danger on the streets."

Nate doesn't look convinced, frowning intently out at the city sparkling beneath them in the night.

"You get used to it," Ash says, more gently. "They don't usually talk about it with me. It's not like he comes home at night covered in blood."

Nate gets up and goes to the window. He looks down at the scattered lights like he's trying to catch a glimpse of Ras, who is probably out there right now, hunting some unfortunate soul. Ash knows this in a cerebral, conceptual way, but in his heart, Ras is the man who holds him at night, who looks at him with such great tenderness, who puts roses on his desk and kisses him breathless. He'd sacrifice any amount of truth to keep that man by his side. Nate, on the other hand, doesn't seem like a man who makes compromises.

NADYA DE HAVEN, PORTRAIT. 2006

Acrylic on canvas

Ras and Nate stand before the large, ornately carved wooden door that leads to Ras's childhood home. It's framed by two-story columns above which sharply steep roofs rise. The wrap around porch cages them in, and the tall narrow windows are shuttered and eerie.

When they get inside, Nate glances warily around the dark Victorian mansion. It looks like a house out of a ghost story, with long hallways dimly lit, thick curtains drawn, dust motes heavy in the hair. Most of the rooms are unused, with sheets thrown over the furniture. He wonders what it was like for Ras, growing up in this dismal place. Ras gives brief, perfunctory summaries of each room's history, but it's not nearly enough to satisfy Nate's curiosity about where Ras comes from.

"What's in there?" Nate asks as they walk past a peculiar carved door with an ornate old-fashioned key sticking out of the lock.

Ras stops, regarding the lock like he's never seen it before. "I didn't know she had a key," he murmurs.

He turns the key, then the knob, and the door swings open to reveal a study that smells like dust and cigarette smoke. A somber wooden desk sits at the back of the room, while two plush chairs wait in front of the fireplace. A shotgun hangs on one of the walls, a large framed map of the city across from it.

"She cleaned it," Ras says, looking around in amazement. "She fucking cleaned it."

It's true. The desk shines like it's been freshly waxed, and the shelves displaying hardback copies of classic books have gathered no dust.

"Is it your mom's office?" Nate asks.

Ras glances at him, unreadable. "No. It's my father's."

"Oh." Ras has never once mentioned his father. Nate assumed the man was as absent as his own. "Am I gonna meet him too?"

Ras's mouth twists in bitter amusement. "If you like. He doesn't talk much to anyone besides me though. Here." He brushes by Nate, out into the hallway. "Come with me."

They walk out into the gardens and down a pale cobblestone path surrounded by rosebushes, the brilliant blooms and tangled briars like in a fairytale. The farther away from the house they get, the wilder the roses grow, until the path narrows and Nate's long sleeves catch on the thorns. Ras pauses to break a few white roses free from their bushes and bring them along.

They come to a little clearing and stop in front of an old, timeworn statue of an avenging angel, sword raised to the heavens.

At the foot of the statue is a cleared space of dirt the exact size and shape of a grave.

"Dad." Ras tosses the roses onto the dirt. "There's someone I want you to meet." He tilts his head the way he does when Nate has said something he finds particularly curious, but Nate hasn't said anything at all. Then he laughs, and for a moment he sounds like a child.

"Uh..." Nate tries to think of something to say because it feels like Ras is holding a conversation with someone else. "What was your dad's name?"

"Vance. Vance de Haven. He was the syndicate boss, before Scarlett."

Of course he was. Who else would have raised their child to become such a monster? How else could Ras step so seamlessly into this role, as though he were born for it?

It was his dad. It isn't him, not really. It's just what he's been taught.

Ras presses his palm to the angel's wing and it leaves a bloody stain behind, torn on the thorns of the roses he grabbed on the way in. He doesn't seem to notice, or if he does, he doesn't care.

"Um...maybe we should go back." Nate has seen Ras have dramatic mood swings, and he's always somewhat eccentric. But he's never acted like this. Like he's detaching from reality. Like his dead father is alive and standing right in front of them.

Nate takes Ras's hand and tugs, ignoring the tacky feel of blood between their palms. Ras turns reluctantly toward him, and together they make their way back through the brambles to the house.

In the kitchen, a woman sits in the sunlight falling in through the only open windows Nate has seen. She rises to greet them. Her long black hair flows past her shoulders, and her features are angular and severe, almost gaunt. Her eyes are a familiar shade of green, and Nate immediately knows who she is.

"Jude," she says, wrapping her arms around Ras. "It's good to see you." She speaks with an accent that must be Russian.

"Mom." Ras sounds like an offended teenager. "Ras is my name now, and I wish you'd call me by it."

"I like Jude," Nate says. A gentle name for a man who might have grown up gentle if not for the lessons of his father.

Maybe it's not too late.

"Don't you start." Ras gives him a dirty look.

"You are right, Jude." Ras's mother studies Nate with a sly smile on her face. "He is handsome."

Nate blushes and casts about for something to say.

"He is." Ras's smirk mirrors his mother's. "Nate, this is my mother, Nadya."

"Good to meet you," Nate says with a polite nod. Much to his surprise, she responds by pulling him into a tight hug. He's so stunned it takes him a moment to wrap his arms around her and hug her back. This must be where Ras gets his affectionate nature, his easy way of bridging the gap between them with a touch and a smile.

"How is your little girl?" Nadya asks. "Ras tells me she is wonderful child."

"She's okay," Nate says, the compliment warming something inside him. He loves to see Sierra and Ras together; the way Sierra has come to trust Ras and the way Ras has come to care for her.

"I'm glad to hear it." A wistful smile crosses Nadya's face. "I'm getting old and would like grandchildren soon."

Ras ignores that remark as he rummages in the many cupboards that wrap around the kitchen. Nadya sits at the little table by the window and gestures for Nate to sit beside her.

"Jude tells me you are artist. That's wonderful."

Nate smiles shyly. He doesn't feel worthy of the descriptor—artist—but he likes hearing it all the same. He likes that Ras describes him that way.

"Yeah. I guess so. I paint, mostly."

"You paint." Nadya claps her hands together in a show of delight. "I love it. May I see your paintings sometime?"

Nate pulls out his phone and shows her a few of the ones he's finished. She praises each one in a way that feels distinctly motherly, despite Nate's lack of experience with that kind of interaction.

"You did good finding this one, Jude." She glances into the kitchen. Ras is kneading some kind of dough on the counter, the front of his black shirt coated with flour.

"I know," he says.

"How did you meet?" Nadya asks, and Nate freezes, unsure if he should come up with a lie or tell the ugly truth.

"We just ran into each other," Ras says. "Literally. He was carrying a pile of sketches and I bumped into him on the street and sent them all flying. I helped him pick them up, and I liked what I saw. I'm putting together a few art shows, so I asked him to submit some work. From there...he just charmed me."

Nate nods, grateful but also a little unnerved by how smoothly Ras was able to lie to his mother. Does Ras lie to him just as easily?

*

"Mom." Ras is walking a quarter along the back of his knuckles, a restless habit he has when he's in a place where he can't play with his switchblade. A mostly empty plate of piroshky sits between them—it was delicious. "My knives are gone. The ones that were in my room."

"I got rid of them," Nadya says. "I am getting rid of all weapons in this house."

"You got rid of my knives? You didn't even think to ask me if I wanted them?"

"You do not have enough?" There's an edge to Nadya's voice that makes Nate think she might not be so blind to Ras's nature after all.

"Those were sentimental," Ras says. "Vance gave them to me."

Nadya's frown deepens. "I want no memories of that monster."

"Then why are you still here, in this fucking house?" Ras growls. "He is in every corner of this house. If you want him gone, you should leave and let me burn it to the ground."

Nadya doesn't flinch in the face of his anger. "You would never."

And just like that, the anger fades, and Ras looks down at his hands. "No. I suppose not."

"Go through the rest of the guns and knives. Take what you want. I get rid of the rest. I want this house to be a place where children can visit."

Nadya doesn't glance at Nate, but he feels like that comment was meant for him to hear, a quiet invitation to join a family.

"Fine," Ras says petulantly, oblivious to any deeper meaning. "I'll come by tomorrow and sort them out."

*

When Nate lets himself into the house, shutting the door quickly to keep out the blustery spring weather, Traci is on her phone, swearing loudly.

"The fuck you mean he's just gone? Where?" She listens for a moment, scowling. "Well I ain't gonna pay his debts, so you can just go fuck yourself." She hangs up the phone and turns to Nate.

"What was that about?" he asks.

"Troy's boss. Troy skipped town a few days ago, and now his people are calling me asking where the hell's the money. Like I got any."

"Troy left?" A suspicion stirs within him, a question he refuses to even put into words. It makes sense Troy would disappear if he owed money he couldn't pay back—it wouldn't be the first time. There's no reason to worry, or look too closely into it. Ras promised to leave Troy alone, and Nate forces himself to believe it.

"Yeah." Traci throws herself onto the couch. "Fucking asshole. And Sierra's in a fucking mood too. She won't even talk to me."

"I'll check on her." Nate is glad to be distracted from the question of Troy's disappearance.

Upstairs, Sierra is drawing at her little desk. Nate knocks softly on the door frame, and she looks up, startled. "Hi, Nate."

"Hey," Nate says, stepping into the room. "What are you drawing?"

"We gotta do a family tree at school." She shows him the worksheet with spaces for moms and dads, grandparents, aunts and uncles. "But I dunno who to put."

"Okay. I can help you with it."

"But who is my real dad?" Sierra blurts out the question like she can't contain it for another moment. She might pretend Nate belongs to her and her to him, calling him "Dad" when no one else is around, but she has no illusions about the reality of it. "All the other kids in my class have dads."

"Come here." Nate sits on the bed and pats the spot beside him. He isn't sure how to have this conversation or how to answer the question himself. He's probably grappled with it just as much as she has.

"At school the teacher said you were my dad." She grabs her stuffed shark and sits beside him, the toy in her lap. "But Mom always says my real dad is rich and lives in the Rise and is gonna come get us someday."

Nate is never sure what to say when Traci talks about Sierra's "real dad." He knows it's a fantasy Traci made up so Sierra wouldn't feel so desperately alone, but he doesn't think it's his place to dispel the myth. At the same time, it grates at him because he knows someday Sierra will find out the truth, and it will inevitably hurt her.

"There are two kinds of dads," Nate says carefully. "There are the dads that help moms make babies. And then there are the dads that take care of you and love you. Sometimes, that's the same person, but not always."

"Oh," she says softly, and begins twisting the fin of the stuffed shark, her fingers clutching its soft fuzz. "Why do you pick me up from school if you're not really my dad?"

Because I'm the only person who will. But that's not a satisfying answer, nor is it the whole truth.

"Because I love you. And because I have a car," he adds matter-of-factly. "What would be the point of my car if I didn't pick people up?"

"But I want to have a *real* dad. It's not fair."

"I know," Nate says, rubbing her back. He understands better than she can know. He's always wondered about his own absent father, though he has some suspicions—the hellfire-and-brimstone pastor who was at their dinner table more often than not.

Sierra cries a little, and Nate holds her, and when she goes to bed, he's left alone with his thoughts, filling the space around him like mist, threatening to drag him back, and back, to places he never wants to visit again.

ETHAN DRINKS COFFEE. 2006

Ink on paper

Nate has never had a friendship quite like what is developing between himself and Ethan. To be fair, he's never really had much in the way of friends—he has a few, but he's not particularly close to them. Ras isn't a friend, he's something different entirely, something darker and more passionate than such a wholesome word can describe.

"You look a million miles away," Ethan says with a smile. They're in their usual coffee shop at a little table with a handmade mosaic on it, brilliant red-and-blue tiles, uneven grout.

"Sorry," Nate mumbles, staring into his latte. "I stayed at Sierra's last night so I could help her get ready for school. I can't sleep too good in a bedroom I'm not used to." He's paranoid enough when the lights go off and his memories start to haunt him, and in a strange place, they seem closer than usual.

"It's going to make a difference for her. I'm glad she has you."

Nate looks down, a warm, pleased feeling flushing over him. "I dunno. I'm not really a good role model."

"I disagree. Every single day at work I see parents who don't deserve their children. I see children who have been made to think all of it is their fault. If each of those children had someone like you in their lives, it would make all the difference."

Nate wonders what his life would have been like if someone had stepped forward and adopted him as their responsibility, when he was ten years old and they took him away from his mom. But he was too filled with anger and fear for anyone to get close, too damaged for anyone to love.

"Sierra thinks it's her fault." Nate absentmindedly rubs the scar on his hand. "She don't say it, but she thinks she's a bad girl, deep down. I wish I could fix it."

"No child could ever deserve to be abused." Ethan's eyes are gentle and sorrowful. "Healing isn't easy, but I know a really good therapist. It would probably help Sierra a lot."

Nate hesitates, though he doesn't fully understand why the idea fills him with trepidation. He remembers when he was a kid, and the therapists they made him see, and how little good it did. "Probably can't afford it."

"Get your boyfriend to cover it," Ethan says with the wry twist to his mouth he always has when talking about Ras. "If you can't...the therapist will charge you on a sliding scale."

Nate nods thoughtfully. Maybe there is something to the idea. He was beyond help, but he desperately hopes Sierra isn't. "Thanks for the advice. I'll think about it."

Ethan changes the subject then, and they talk pleasantly about small things until Nate hears a familiar voice from the other side of the room.

"Nate," Sierra hurries to his table. She's alone, her bright, anxious face turned up to him. "Hi. Don't be mad."

Nate looks around the coffee shop, but neither Traci or Troy seem to be present. "Are you alone?"

She nods. "Mom dropped me off outside."

Nate suppresses the brief, hot fury that passes through him. He knows any kind of anger frightens Sierra, no matter who it's directed at. He'll be having a long talk with Traci tonight about leaving Sierra unsupervised in the city. What if he'd already left the coffee shop?

Sierra's gaze drops to the floor like she can tell he's upset. "I'm sorry," she mumbles, scuffing her shoe against the wooden floor.

"Hey." Nate puts his hand on her shoulder and squeezes gently. "It's okay. You're okay. I was just worried because I don't like it when your mom leaves you by yourself."

Sierra looks a little reassured. Her gaze darts to Ethan, then shyly away.

Ethan gets up, and for a moment, Nate thinks he's going to leave, annoyed by the entrance of a needy child into their usual time together. But instead, he retrieves a chair from the next table over so Sierra can join them. It's a simple gesture, but it warms something in Nate's heart regardless.

"Sierra, this is my friend Ethan," Nate says.

Ethan smiles at her. "Are you the artist Nate was telling me about?"

Sierra ducks her head bashfully, but this time, she looks pleased rather than intimidated. "I like art."

"Me too," Ethan says. "Do you ever go to the art museum?"

"Sometimes Nate takes me. He makes me look at boring paintings of people. But then we go to the sculpture garden. I like that best."

Nate sits back and watches as she and Ethan have a genuine conversation. Ethan talks to her as respectfully and thoughtfully as he does Nate, coaxing her slowly, gently out of her shell until she's giggling into her hot chocolate, drawing silly pictures for him on her napkin.

Watching them, Nate feels an odd sense of contentment. In this warm little bubble of a moment, there is nothing he needs that isn't right here in front of him.

*

Ethan smiles encouragingly at Nate as they sit outside the therapist's office where Sierra is being evaluated. He offered to come along when Nate confided his anxiety over the appointment, and Nate had desperately not wanted to be alone. Ras has a strange aversion to any kind of mental health intervention, and Nate didn't want to bring that up by asking him to come. Even though Ras is paying for this, he wouldn't want to actually be in the stifling little office with its pleasant Monet print hanging on the far wall and soft music playing in the background. Whatever happened to Ras—whatever broke his mind— he'll only ever allude to, and rarely, but Nate doubts it involved a setting like this. No one helped Ras, and it shows, but Nate is determined to see that Sierra doesn't suffer the same fate.

"Hey," Ethan says, hushed even though they're the only people in the little waiting room. "She'll be okay."

"She doesn't like being alone with strangers."

"Karla sees a lot of scared kids. Her whole job is helping families like yours. Sierra's going to be fine."

"You know her?"

"Yeah. She testifies for me sometimes in court." Ethan gives him a gentle smile. "She helps me put the bad guys behind bars and protect the people they hurt."

Nate smiles back. He likes the thought that somewhere in the city, the bad guys don't always win. He imagines Ethan in the courtroom, a white knight in a three-piece suit sending abusive parents and spouses to jail.

"Thank you, for this," he says, his voice rough. "For bringing us here."

"It's what I do."

After what feels like an eternity, the door opens, and Sierra steps out, stone-faced and surly. Standing behind her is a short woman with fluffy black hair and horn-rimmed glasses who looks a little like a librarian. Nate stands up quickly and holds out his arms, but Sierra walks past him and flops down on one of the waiting chairs.

"Are you okay?" he asks her.

"Fuck off, Nate." It's her new favorite saying, which Nate is sure she learned from Troy. "It sucked."

He can see little shimmering trails on her cheeks, and his heart aches at the sight. He wonders if that's good or bad and understands her anger entirely. They made him see a therapist when they took him away from his mom, and he felt just the same way after the first session. They never made him go more than once or twice when the therapist and the social worker found out what a resistant child he was. There was no saving him, but it's going to be different for Sierra. They're going to come back here, and back again, until she's healthy.

"Don't say fuck," he reminds her mildly, then turns to the woman Ethan introduced as Dr. Karla.

"I'd like to speak with you for a moment, Nate," Karla says. "Sierra, will you be okay out here with Ethan?"

Sierra shrugs, mumbling a quiet "Whatever."

Nate follows Karla into the next room. She turns on a little noise machine situated by the door, then gestures for him to take a seat. She sits facing him, clipboard in her lap.

"Everything Sierra tells me is in confidence," she begins, "unless someone is hurting her. In that case, I would inform you and the authorities immediately."

Nate nods, dread prickling the back of his neck. "Is someone abusing her?"

Karla shakes her head. "But I don't think it will come as a shock if I tell you it sounds like she's had a very difficult childhood."

"I'm gonna do better," Nate says, sitting up straight. "I swear to god I'm gonna do better for her."

"I'm not assigning blame. I'm very glad you reached out to me. I think Sierra and I have a lot of work to do together, and I think I can help her."

Nate nods, quietly gathering his courage. "Someday, I probably gotta get custody of her." It's the first time he's spoken the words out loud, even though they've been on his mind for a while. "If her mom keeps slippin' like this, then someone's gotta step up."

"I can testify, if I think it's in Sierra's best interest," Karla says carefully. "But I need to know both of you a little better before I do."

"I love her." It comes out like a plea. "Ain't nobody I ever loved more than her."

"I know." Karla smiles. "And that's going to do a lot to help her heal."

They set up a time for another appointment, and Karla gives him some instructions about how to take care of Sierra after—to not force affection on her, to give her space to process but be available if she wants comfort.

Outside in the waiting room, Sierra is holding up a pocket-sized notebook to show Ethan something she's drawn. It must be Ethan's notebook, but he looks happy enough to have her doodle in it, and the sight of the two of them together makes Nate's heart swell.

"Hey there," Nate says, and Sierra looks sheepishly up at him.

"I'm sorry I said a bad word," she mumbles.

"It's okay. We all get mad sometimes."

"I drew us at the coffee place." She holds the notebook out to him like an offering. Nate studies the two stick figures holding hands next to a smaller stick figure with short black hair. Beside them is a lopsided table with mugs sitting atop it, curvy lines of steam rising from them.

"It's beautiful," he says, swallowing an odd lump in his throat. Together, the three of them look like a family.

*

The dark city's district attorney is a weary woman in her late thirties with a nose like a hawk's beak and a withering stare that has made more than one defendant melt helplessly on the witness stand. Her name is Victoria, and she's almost always accompanied by the deputy DA, Hugh, a tall, hulking lawyer who has—if the rumor mill is to be believed—used his fists more than once to make a witness agree to testify. Their department is not well funded, and while their offices are large and marble floored, their furniture is shabby and worn, their computers ancient and ponderous.

Ethan studies the photograph of Ras on one wood-paneled wall. There are tiny holes in the wall around it, but very few darts have actually punctured the photo. The office staff don't usually play that game until after Victoria breaks out the bottle of whiskey in the bottom drawer of her desk, and by then, their vision is blurry and their aim completely off. Ethan doesn't usually play, as he doesn't work out of this office, but rather a smaller, newer building a few blocks away. Ras is too big a fish for a lawyer like him anyway. Most would consider his cases to be small time and relatively unimportant. Except, of course, for the people who are living them.

Around Ras's portrait, yellow sticky notes are tacked to the wall with tidbits of information. There's so much rumor and gossip surrounding him, but these notes contain the very few bare bones of what they know for sure.

"Not his real name," one reads. Another: "Ties to the Bancroft family." "Martial artist." "Russian."

"It's Ethan, right?" Victoria asks, standing in the doorway. "Come to look at our shrine?"

"Just curious," he says. "Do you think you'll ever catch him?"

Victoria shuts the door behind her and joins him at the wall. "Yes." Her eyes are fierce and furious as they scan over her notes. "Someday."

"I know where he is," Ethan says hesitantly. Nate might never forgive him, but this way he'll know Nate is safe from that monster.

Victoria barks a startled laugh. "Well, you've got a pair. Don't you know he goes around killing anyone who snitches?" She shakes her head, relenting. "We *all* know where he is. I've got plainclothes cops who keep an eye on him. But he gives them the slip before he commits a crime, or kills them after. Or he bribes them so they keep his secrets." The dark anger in her eyes makes it clear the last fate is the worst.

Ethan nods. This really doesn't come as a great surprise. "Some information, then."

She crosses her arms. "I don't deal in rumors. Only facts."

"I know." Ethan scans the notes on the wall, then turns to her. "He's running some scam in an art gallery downtown. He got into an altercation there. And...he's in love with a man."

Victoria's eyebrows shoot up and the corner of her mouth curves. "You got this man's name?"

Ethan hesitates. After a moment, he shakes his head. "He's not a criminal. He's not part of it."

"I'd still like to question him."

"No," Ethan says. He doesn't need to pause or think about it.

Her eyes move over him with a calculated coldness. "I don't think you understand, Ethan. I want this man in my office by tomorrow morning. If you can't do that, then I'm not sure there's a place for you on my staff."

Ethan turns back to the picture on the wall. "That's how Ras runs his empire. I thought we did things differently here."

"We are at war," Victoria growls. "And I will take him down by any means necessary."

Ethan fixes her with a level gaze. He thinks of Nate, and his resolve doesn't so much as flicker. "I'll tell you anything you want to know about Ras. But not his lover."

Her eyes flash with anger. "You'll tell me everything. Or else you'll find out Ras isn't the only person in this city who can be persuasive."

Ethan hesitates. He thinks of Nate, of the last time they were together, wandering through the sculpture garden at the museum, Nate leaning into him to speak softly into his ear with the kind of hushed reverence he always has around beautiful works of art. There's no way Ethan could betray him, not ever. "Have Hugh knock out my teeth, then." He meets Victoria's eyes. "It's not going to change my mind."

She sweeps her hand toward the door. "Get the hell out of my office."

Ethan does.

He spends the next few days waiting for word to come down from the DA's office that he's no longer employed, or for Hugh to pull him into a dark corner of the parking lot after work. But neither of those things happen, and after a week, he comes in to work to find a small bottle of very good whiskey on his desk. There's a phone number on a sticky note attached to the bottle he's sure goes directly to her private cell. She didn't add an apology, but he can read the gesture well enough, and he breathes a sigh of relief before tucking it into the bottom drawer of his desk for days when his workload—the sum of all the human suffering laid in neat manila folders on his desk—overwhelms him.

MOTHER. 2006

Crayon and paper

Ras is beginning to learn Nate's rhythms, the needs and wants he refuses to let himself vocalize. He's made a careful study of Nate, the way a predator might watch his prey, learning all of his behaviors and habits and coping mechanisms. He knows that nights like tonight—nights when Nate texts him and tells him to stay away—are when he's most desperately needed. He's never been good at boundaries anyway, just at picking locks.

He pushes open the door to the apartment and says Nate's name softly. Nate doesn't respond, curled in around himself on the bed, knees drawn to his chest, facing the wall. This is the fourth time he's found Nate like this, huddled and silent, usually on the bed but once, one particularly bad night, under the kitchen table. Ras isn't sure what triggers these episodes, only that they are brief but overwhelming.

He climbs into bed with Nate and holds him close. All he knows to do is wait for it to be over, and it frustrates him to be so helpless.

"What happened?" Ras doesn't really expect an answer—he doesn't usually get one.

But Nate shifts in his arms and speaks, his voice croaky and weak. "Mom called me."

Ras is not prone to anger, but he has seen enough of Nate's scars that the mention of the woman who created them is enough to make it flare hot in his chest. "What did she say?" He keeps his voice even. His fury, though justified, is not what Nate needs in this moment.

"Same thing she always says."

"Does she call often?" Ras had assumed Nate would be estranged from such a violently abusive mother. But then he thinks of his own father's fists, and that same father's fond smile, and understands why it would be complicated.

Nate's shrug is a gentle push against Ras's embrace.

"And this happens when she calls," Ras says, realization dawning. "She's still hurting you."

Nate doesn't answer, just curls tighter in on himself, and Ras lies there with him, thinking, planning. It's his job to protect Nate, to see him happy and safe and loved. But he can't slit Nate's mother's throat in her sleep. Nate would never forgive him. He's going to have to resort to diplomacy instead.

*

Ras knocks hard on the door to the pleasant little cottage where Nate's mother lives. She opens it quickly, looking harried, and draws in a sharp breath when she sees him.

"You," she hisses. "What are you doing here?"

"I came to talk. That's all."

She sets her chin. "I have nothing to say to you."

"I have something to say to you," Ras says, pushing her gently backward and stepping inside the house. He shuts the door behind him and locks it. "So sit, and we'll talk."

She glares at him furiously but sits when he does on an old-fashioned floral sofa with hard cushions and intricate stitching. "You can't tell me anything. I'll call the police."

Ras rolls his eyes. A tiny tabby, barely more than a kitten, rubs against his leg, looking up at him expectantly. He reaches down to run his fingers through its soft fur, and for a half second, it takes him back to his thirteen-year-old self, when his father asked him to kill something he loved, and he obeyed. It was the first thing he ever killed, and now this cat is looking reproachfully up at him as though it knows exactly how black his soul is.

I did what I had to.

The kitten leans against his hand and presses its little head into his palm.

"Susannah." Nate's mother glares at the cat. "Get away from him."

"Cute." Ras tenses as the cat jumps into his lap and begins to make herself comfortable.

"I just want you to know." Nate's mother leans forward to meet Ras's eyes. "There is no stronger force on this earth than a mother's love." She gives him a venomous smile. "You might think Nathaniel is yours, but the truth is he'll come back to me someday. Men always come back to their mothers."

Ras narrows his eyes at her, flushed with hot anger. Nate is *his*. "I would never hurt him like you did. You're worse than I am."

"He didn't tell you the truth?" Nate's mother gives him a look of wide-eyed innocence. "He lied to all those doctors, and now he's lying to you too."

"I've seen the scars."

"I didn't put them there." She pauses for effect. "He did."

Ras hesitates, remembering the way Nate had reached for the glowing coil of the burner on the stove the last time he was here, the glazed look in his eyes as he came within less than an inch of burning away the skin of his hand.

"There's a great evil inside him," she says. "He was born with a demon in his heart. Sometimes it overcame him, and he would do evil, and then he would atone."

Ras considers this, baffled. He has never met anyone whose inherent goodness shines brighter than Nate's. If he harms himself, it's because he's a martyr, not because he's a demon.

"He jumped out the window," Nate's mother continues, sniffing in an ill-considered attempt to earn Ras's pity. "He jumped out of the upstairs window and fell into the backyard. When the doctors saw all his scars they...well, they thought the worst. And they took him away."

"Of course he did," Ras says, and for a moment, it feels like he can't breathe. Of course Nate would save himself the only way he could, and have the courage to take that leap, even if it could mean his death. But finding out he almost died is like a deluge of icy water. Ras needs to see where it happened, to witness it as best he's able before he can put it to rest.

He carefully scoops up the cat and moves her off of his lap. "Show me the window."

She leads him upstairs to an austere room with a low, slanted ceiling and a child-sized bed. A kid's drawing of an angel is tacked up over a tiny desk, and a single wide window looks out over an unremarkable backyard, bare dirt beneath a dead tree. Ras draws in a sharp breath, looking out at the distance Nate fell in his desperate bid for escape. *My fighter. My martyr. My phoenix.*

He turns back to Nate's mother. She has her phone pressed to her ear, a smug half smile on her face.

"Hello, Nathaniel," she says. "I made a batch of your favorite cookies, and I hope you'll come soon and eat some." She pauses for a moment, listening. "I worry about you, honey. I just worry, that's all." Another pause. "I worry because I know that man doesn't love you. How could he? How could anyone love you except me?"

Her eyes meet Ras's, and he can't tell if she's crazy, or if she knows exactly what she's doing. "He's going to leave you in the end. But you'll still have Mommy. Mommy will always love you." She smiles sweetly. "Okay. I'll call you later. I love you."

She ends the call, and Ras takes a deep breath, trying to still the thrumming fury inside him. How dare she play so shamelessly with the man he loves? Nate almost died because of her cruelty, and even now, she won't let him go.

"You see?" she says. "It's never going to last. It will take me time, but I will take Nathaniel from you, and I will save his soul. He knows what kind of wickedness you have in your heart, and he'll never—"

Her words break off in a startled whimper when Ras slams her hard against the bedroom wall.

"Nate is mine," he growls. "Don't you fucking dare try to take him from me."

"You..." she gasps, eyes wide, breathless with fear. "You can't stop me. The Lord is on my side, and I am not afraid."

"You should be." Ras releases her, stepping back as a deadly calm settles over him like a sheet of ice, separating the layers of self yet again. "There's no demon in Nate, but there is one in me, and it wants to see you bleed."

She draws in a short, sharp breath, then begins to pray. "Yea, though I walk through the valley of the shadow of death, I will fear no evil."

Ras laughs, and it's truly delighted, like a child's mirth. He's twirling his switchblade in his hand. The long, elegant fingers bear thin, pale scars from when he was a teenager, practicing to get that trick just right. He puts the sharp side of the blade just under her chin, and lifts it, so she's forced to look up at him.

She meets his eyes and a shudder of fear goes through her, her prayer faltering.

He smiles.

The blood begins to flow.

*

Ras looks down at the limp body with something like horror. He leans down and presses his fingers to her neck, feeling for an absent pulse. Her profile is proud and defiant in the same way as Nate's, even in death.

Ras closes his eyes. "What did you do?" His other half, which is usually a part of him as naturally integrated as an arm or a leg, still dissociates sometimes, to pursue his own agenda.

His mind is darkly silent, more or less whole again— or as close as he comes to having a single consciousness.

He sighs, running a hand through his hair. "Nate is never going to forgive us for this."

But then, Nate doesn't have to know. No one has to know. Ras and Scarlett have perfected a system for disposing of inconvenient bodies.

Ras wipes off his knife on her dress and then calls the team he has on hand to clean up after messes like this. He's about to step out the door when he hears a soft meow, and something furry brushes against his leg.

He gets to his knees and looks down at the cat, who stares back up at him with wide eyes. "Trust me," he says, his voice rough. "I'm the last person you want to attach yourself to."

She answers with a plaintive cry, still looking expectantly up at him.

"I hate cats." He runs his hand gently over her head and down her back. "Everybody knows that."

She presses her head into his palm, mewing pitifully. He closes his eyes against the memory of another cat, black fur thick against his hands, cuddled in his lap, trusting him to do no harm.

"My father told me to do it. He knew the only way I could become the man I am now is to kill something I loved."

Ras scratches the kitten gently behind one ear, and she begins to purr. "But you're right." He feels stronger with every moment she doesn't flinch away. "He's dead. I don't have to play his games anymore."

He rummages in the hallway closet until he finds a hatbox. Tossing the wide-brimmed sun hat on the floor, he grabs the curious kitten, sticks her in the box, and quickly leaves the scene of the crime.

ZOO SKETCHES, VARIOUS. 2006

Graphite and colored pencil on paper

Children and their parents mill around the path leading in a wide arc around the north side of the zoo, peering into the cages and pointing excitedly at all the different animals. Nate holds Sierra's hand. She's bubbly and excited as she leads him to her favorite exhibit. Ethan is by Nate's side, a quiet, stalwart companion.

Sierra is transfixed by the scaly creatures, though Nate feels a little queasy after walking through the reptile house with its cool, damp air and cages of slithering creatures. She chatters eagerly about which she would like for a pet, and Nate plays along, debating the merits of an iguana or a snake. Ethan doesn't chime in, but listens with a soft smile on his face.

Nate had wanted Ras to come to the zoo with them, but Ras muttered something about how you shouldn't keep predators in a cage, and then told him Ash was having a reading for his newly published book of poetry. It was a little odd that Ras had to cancel at the last minute—usually he keeps better track of when he's able to spend time with Nate. It isn't like him, but Nate knows he's a busy person and is willing to forgive it, especially because Ethan had offered to come instead. And why not? Ethan has become a friend, a really good friend. The kind you can count on to always have your back, whose moods aren't as fickle as spring weather. And he's a good role model for Sierra.

They get ice cream at a little stand and sit at the nearby tables to eat it. Sierra devours hers in huge, ambitious bites, making adorable scrunched up faces when she gets brain freeze. When she's done, she runs off to the nearby fountain to play in the water with the other kids. Nate and Ethan hang back in the shade of the tall, colorful umbrella above their table and watch her.

"This really takes me back," Ethan says. "My parents used to bring me here all the time when I was a kid."

"Yeah. Me too. One time, my foster brothers tried to push me into the grizzly bear enclosure." Nate laughs, although the memory isn't really funny. "They wanted to get rid of me. My foster dad was pissed. He got his belt and none of us sat down for like a week."

"What a bastard," Ethan says, but there's more concern in his eyes than anger.

Nate shrugs. "Happens to everybody."

"It doesn't."

Nate gives him a skeptical glance. "So your parents never hit you? Not even once?"

"Would you hit Sierra?"

Nate feels something inside himself violently recoil at the thought. "No. Never."

"That's how my parents felt too. It's how every parent should feel."

"I'm not her parent. "That's probably why."

Ethan is quiet for a moment, studying Sierra as she darts among the spurts of water in the fountain. "It would be hard for you to get custody unless her mother decided to give her up. But you could fight for it. I would help you fight for as long as it takes."

"Why?" A strange and gentle warmth spreads in Nate's chest. "Why would you do that for us?"

"I think you know why." Ethan brushes his fingertips very gently over Nate's knuckles. "So don't make me say it, okay?"

He gives Nate his wide, charming smile and gets up to chase Sierra through the fountain until they're both soaked. Nate watches them, wondering if this is what it would be like to be a family. No sharp edges or sinister undertones, just love, simple and straightforward. Being with Ras feels like being high—shocking in its sweetness, its breathless embrace. But this is like standing with both feet on the ground.

"You know," he murmurs to Ethan as they stand in a crowd in front of the lions' enclosure. "Ras and I have an open relationship."

"I know," Ethan says but looks away. "If that makes you happy, then I'm glad, but it's not what I want. I'm sorry."

He turns back to the lions. In the ensuing silence, Nate feels like he's the one who should be apologizing. They move through the rest of the exhibits. If Sierra notices they're quieter than usual, she doesn't say anything, but talks eagerly about snake facts until Ethan drops them off at home.

"Did you have fun at the zoo?" Nate asks as they walk up to the front door. Sierra clutches the toy snake he bought her at the gift shop.

"Yeah." She bursts into the house with Nate following behind. "I really want a pet. I would take care of it and feed it and give it water and love it and—"

"That's lucky." Ras is on the couch in the living room like he owns the place—which, Nate supposes, he does. In his lap, a kitten dozes, an orange tabby with a torn ear and a distinctive dark spot over one eye like an eyepatch. "I was hoping this cat could find a home."

"A cat?" Sierra hurries forward and perches on the couch beside him, delicately running one finger over the kitten's head. "She's so cute!"

"I thought so too." Ras scoops up the furry bundle and settles her on Sierra's legs. The cat has a blue collar with a silver heart tag that jingles softly when Ras moves her. "What do you think? Will you keep her?"

Sierra looks up at Nate with dark, pleading eyes, and he realizes this is already too far gone for him to say no.

"I'll think about it," he says.

Ras Bakes Bread. 2006

Acrylic on canvas

Becky looks curiously around the house where Nate spends most of his time, peering at the clean, homey furniture and decor. She gives him a glance that is unreadable, but not hostile. "This is nice, Nate," she says primly.

"Hi Becky," Sierra says from the doorway leading to the kitchen, half hidden by the doorframe. She's never felt comfortable around Becky, and Nate senses the feeling is mutual.

"Hello, Sierra," Becky says. "I brought you a present."

Sierra carefully crosses the room to take the jewelry box Becky is holding out to her. "Thanks, bye," she blurts out, quickly darting toward her bedroom.

Nate doesn't have the heart to scold her. He understands how she feels. Becky's gifts never come without some sort of price or promise of guilt. This little black box probably contains another cross, which Nate will later find stuffed in the bottom of her sock drawer along with the others, never to be worn.

Becky frowns at Sierra's disappearing figure but doesn't comment on her behavior.

Ras steps out of the kitchen with a loaf of bread on a wooden cutting board, a little dish of butter beside it. "You must be the sister." He grins at her. But there's something cold in his smile, a glint of malice in his eyes. "I've heard so much about you."

"This is...Jude," Nate says. It's possible Becky wouldn't recognize the name Ras, being so far removed from the criminal elements of the dark city, but Nate doesn't want to take the chance. "He's my friend."

"It's a pleasure to meet you, Becky." Ras sets the bread down on the table. "I'm madly in love with your brother, so I suppose I'd better be civil to his family, don't you think?"

Becky chooses not to answer, instead turning to Nate. "I have some news. We need to talk. Just the two of us." She casts a meaningful glance at Ras, who makes no move to leave.

"I'm an excellent eavesdropper," he says with no trace of shame. "You may as well just let me stay."

It makes Nate uneasy, but he doesn't push Ras to leave. It might be nice, for once, to have someone act as a buffer between himself and Becky. Someone to keep him tethered to the present.

Becky sighs, smoothing her skirt as she sits on a cushioned leather chair. Nate sits across from her on the sofa, tense with worry. Ras settles lazily beside him.

"What's up?" Nate asks.

"Mom left the city," Becky says, her voice wavering. "She wrote me a note, but all it said was that she was going away and not to contact her again."

"Oh." Nate feels a relief like cool water flow over him, like he'd been holding his breath ever since he was a kid, and now, for the first time, he can breathe freely.

"I don't understand," Becky says, dabbing at her eyes. Absentmindedly, Nate slides a box of tissues toward her. "She never said anything about going away, did she?"

Nate shrugs. "We didn't really talk."

She called him, but most of the time he didn't answer. He used to listen to the voice mails she left, curled up on his bed in the late night, clenching his teeth against the flood of memory and the agony of craving. But lately, he hasn't gotten any. He thinks maybe Ras has been deleting them before he can torture himself with them. Even though it's an invasion of his privacy that he really should be angry about, he's mostly just desperately grateful.

Beside him, Ras picks up the bread knife and twirls it absentmindedly in his fingers, the silver blade flashing in the light. Nate's used to his quirks by now, and Becky seems to be pointedly ignoring him.

She draws in a shuddering breath, crumpling the tissue in her hand. "You don't even care, do you? She's your mom, and you don't even care that she's gone."

"She's our mom," ten-year-old Becky says, her hands on Nate's shoulders as he trembles with silent sobs. "She loves you. She does it because she loves you."

Nate feels a hot flash of anger that leaves him breathless. "No. I don't give a fuck. I hope she's dead."

As soon as the words are out of his mouth, he wishes he could bite them back, and not just because of the look of horror that spreads over Becky's face.

"Nate," she whispers. "How could you say that?"

"I'm sorry." Nate hangs his head, heavy with guilt and shame. "I don't mean it. You know I don't." But a cold, vengeful corner of his heart really does.

Ras starts to cut the bread, the shining blade easily sliding into the loaf. He keeps his knives extra sharp, takes great care in honing them to a perfect, flawless edge. Becky sobs softly into her tissue, and Ras offers Nate a still-warm slice of bread with butter melting into it, holding out the plate like an offering. His eyes—vivid, verdant green—catch Nate's, and he smiles. "I love you. You don't need anybody else."

"I know," Nate says, because what else can he say to such a simple, fervent display of devotion? Ras doesn't even seem to care that Becky is right there and can see them and hear them.

"Would you like a piece, Becky?" Ras asks, the knife gleaming in his hand. "This is Russian black bread, my mother's recipe."

"No," Becky says, wiping her eyes. She barely glances at Ras, lost in her own sorrow and fears. "I should go."

RAS AND CITY AT NIGHT. 2006

Ink and graphite on canvas

Ras is at that perfectly drunk place where all the sharp edges of the world have blurred into pleasant fuzziness, but he's still alert and aware enough to appreciate it. More importantly, he's drunk enough to almost—almost—forget what anniversary this day—this night—marks.

"You came," he says as Nate—who could easily be the most handsome man in the world—walks into the syndicate office, looking around suspiciously like Ras might have booby-trapped some of the corners.

Nate takes in the bottle of vodka and the bottle of wine on the table and gives Ras that disapproving frown of his. Nate is such a fucking saint, in this and all other things, and Ras still doesn't understand why that turns him on so much.

"You're drunk," Nate says. "You know I can't be around that."

But the commandments of the twelve-step program are no match for Ras's wily charms, and, anyway, he knows Nate's not an alcoholic. Nothing short of heroin is going to drag him back down. So Ras gives him a sincere, pleading look and asks him to stay.

Nate doesn't say yes, but sits on the sofa all the same. He picks up the bottle of vodka and pulling it out of reach. "You've had enough for right now," he says.

Ras flops dramatically onto the black sofa. "You are so mean."

He finishes off what little is left in the bottle of wine. Then he flings the bottle as hard as he can against the far wall. It shatters satisfyingly, leaving a red stain like blood on the white paint. Scarlett will be pissed when she comes in tomorrow, and that thought, too, is very satisfying. She should be here tonight; she should be mourning too. She should show some fucking respect for all they have lost.

"What was that for?" Nate asks.

"Redecorating." Ras eyes the bottle of vodka Nate snatched away from him. He gets up and moves over to Nate's sofa, swaying a little but light on his feet like a cat that's been drinking but has a high alcohol tolerance.

"Nate." Ras straddles him on the little couch. "Have I ever told you how handsome you are?"

In Ras's drunken haze, it feels like Nate's glowing with goodness—a martyr. A blinding point of light in the dark city. Idly, Ras wonders if Nate will let Ras fuck him tonight, or if Ras has pissed him off too much already.

"You're drunk," Nate says warily, but his hands move to Ras's hips, and he leans his head back when Ras runs his thumb over the bit of collarbone exposed by Nate's ratty old T-shirt.

"You're just as handsome when I'm sober," Ras says, which is true, even if Nate remains adorably oblivious. "If only you could see what I see..."

Ras presses his lips to Nate's neck, and Nate runs his hand through Ras's hair, making soft sweet noises. Nate always loses himself in their lovemaking, unable to remain guarded once Ras has his hands on Nate's body. It took them a long time to get here, but with Nate's skin hot beneath his lips, all Ras can think is that it was worth every moment of waiting. He wants to kiss the elegant curve of Nate's neck forever. But even with his intoxicating scent in Ras's nose and his fingers gently tugging on Ras's hair, it's impossible to ignore the ghost whose presence fills the room every time the sun goes down, and is especially potent tonight. So Ras takes advantage of Nate's distraction to grab the bottle of vodka and slip away, back to the other sofa.

When Nate opens his eyes and sees what Ras has taken, he sighs. "That was kind of shitty." He sounds so vulnerable it almost breaks Ras's black heart.

"I'm sorry." Ras really does mean it. "I shouldn't have called you. Tonight is...an anniversary, of sorts. It's difficult, and I'm not at my best. You should probably go home."

"You want me to leave so you can sit here and get alcohol poisoning?" Nate says, scowling. "I don't think so. We're both goin' home."

Does he always have to be such a righteous asshole? Just once, just once Ras would like to see him really fuck something up. Just to see what he'd do.

"I'm not leaving," Ras says coldly. "You can stay, or you can go. But I will stay here. And I will be drunk because if I have to do this sober, I'm going to jump out of one of these fucking windows."

Nate's eyes dart to the great glass windows and the night city outside.

"I'm being melodramatic," Ras waves his hand dismissively. "They don't open."

Nate studies him thoughtfully. "What kinda anniversary is this?"

Ras gives him a smile bright as broken glass. Why hide it? This should be a day of triumph, of celebration. "It's the day Scarlett and I took over the syndicate." *It's the day we won, and don't you fucking forget it*, he whispers to the ghost in his head.

"But...ain't there a parade or something?" Nate frowns in confusion. "I mean, isn't that what you always wanted?"

"Of course." Ras's voice is sharper than usual. It cuts through the still air between them. "This doesn't look like a fucking celebration to you?"

He gets up and walks to the window, looking out over the city that belonged to his father, the city that he took, the city he's bound to by blood and ambition and love. "Here's to you. You blackhearted son of a bitch. You're never going to let me rest, are you?"

Ras can picture his father easily, just as he was on the day he died, in a white shirt with the sleeves rolled up to the elbows, his hair graying at the temples. He can imagine his father's fondness and disapproval, the gentle resignation on his face when he bled out in Ras's arms. He can still hear his father's last words. *I love you, son. I'm proud of you.*

Ras turns away from him, back to Nate, to his hero. If anyone can save a villain as irredeemable as Ras from the ghost of his past sins, it's Nate.

"I still hear his voice sometimes," Ras says.

"Who?"

"My father." Ras washes the words down with vodka so they won't feel so much like shattered glass. "He was the syndicate boss before Scarlett. He trained me. He made me what I am, and then I killed him and took his place."

"Oh," Nate says, softly, a thoughtful expression on his gorgeous face. "Maybe that's why."

Ras raises an eyebrow. "Why what?"

"Why you're a monster. It's not you at all. It's just what you've been taught. You have a good heart, Ras."

He reaches out and puts his palm on Ras's chest, over his heart. The same place where Ras's father's bullet once landed, the same place where Ras's knife buried itself in his father's heart. Nate doesn't know that history—he can't know it. He could never understand it.

"You could be a good man," Nate urges him. "You just have to...you just have to try."

It's an absurd, impossible idea, but Nate looks angry when Ras starts to laugh.

"It's not funny," he growls.

"I'm sorry, love." Ras forces his features into a mask of seriousness and contrition. "But I'd much rather be the villain. You're the hero of this story." He links his fingers through Nate's belt loops and pulls him closer. "You're my knight in shining armor. My Prince Charming. My guiding light. My phoenix, rising from the ashes."

Nate gives a soft half laugh, his face turned away. Even drunk as he is, Ras can tell this is one of the times when he needs to be careful, when too many sweet words will make Nate defensive and tense. Instead of speaking, he buries his face in the curve of Nate's neck and breathes his musky scent, trying to forget the specter that haunts him, a reminder of his remorse.

Nate's phone rings, and he pulls away with a murmured apology. When he answers, the gentleness in his tone makes it clear he's talking to Sierra.

"No one is in your closet," he says, his tone low and soothing. "I promise. It's just your imagination. You're in a safe place now. Do you remember how long Ras spent setting up the security system?"

He's quiet for a moment, listening. Ras puts a hand on his shoulder.

"Where's your mom?" Nate asks. "Oh. Okay. No, you're right. Don't knock on their door if Joel is in a bad mood. Just wait for a little while, and I'll come over." He makes a few more sweet, gentling promises and hangs up.

"Monsters in her closet?" Ras guesses. It's an intense fear Sierra has had often.

Nate shrugs helplessly. "I better go check on her. Sorry."

"Who is Joel?"

"He's Traci's new boyfriend. He's trouble, but there's nothin' I can do about it."

Ras nearly offers to kill him but remembers just in time Nate's general aversion to his method of dealing with problems. "I'll come with you and keep an eye on him." It will be a nice distraction from the restless memories that haunt this office.

"You're drunk," Nate says with a gentle push on Ras's chest. "I don't want you to be around Sierra like that."

Ras wants to protest, but the room spins around him a few times, and he's forced to concede Nate's point. "If you need me, call me."

Nate gives him a small smile and says a distracted goodbye, his mind already on Sierra.

He almost asks Nate to stay, to keep him company as he rides out this darkest of nights. But he knows who Nate would choose, if the choice were forced upon him. So he stays there, in his tower above the city, alone with his ghosts.

*

"I'll look," Nate says, flicking on the light and peering into the closet, checking every corner. He turns to Sierra and gives her a sad smile. "No monsters. I promise."

She's huddled on her bed, her stuffed shark clutched to her chest. "Thank you for coming." Her voice is very tiny. She knows what a burden she is to Nate—her mother frequently reminds her. She doesn't want to call him in the middle of the night because she's afraid of the dark, but sometimes the fear overwhelms her, and she can do nothing else.

"I'll come anytime you need me," Nate says, sitting beside her and draping an arm over her shoulders.

She leans into his soothing warmth. He is the only person she has never been afraid of.

"Try to get some sleep." He squeezes her tight. "I'll be right outside if you need me."

He tucks her into bed and flicks off the light, bidding her a gentle goodnight.

She closes her eyes and tries to sleep. Nate is just down the hall in his bedroom, and he would never let anything bad happen to her. But even knowing this is not enough to calm her as she lies there in the suffocating darkness trying not to cry. Eventually, she gets out of bed and creeps toward his room, freezing when she hears the soft sound of his voice.

"She was afraid there were monsters in her closet," he's saying, and when she peers into the living room, she sees him on the couch with his phone pressed to his ear. "I wish I knew how to make them go away for good. You know what I mean?"

When the person on the other end of the line speaks, Nate smiles gently. Sierra has rarely seen him look so content, so peaceful.

"Thanks, Ethan. I mean it. You always know what to say." Nate looks up and spots Sierra in the doorway before she can shrink back. "Look, I gotta go. I'll call you later, okay?"

Nate murmurs his goodbye. He hangs up the phone and gestures for Sierra to join him.

"You can't sleep either?" he asks with a wry glance.

She shakes her head and crosses the room to join him on the couch. Nate is her safe place, her sanctuary. The one man she knows would never hurt her, could never hurt her.

"Want to watch cartoons with me?" he asks.

She nods meekly, glad he isn't mad at her for still being up. They sit together in companionable silence until loud, angry voices start to drift from upstairs where her mother's bedroom is. Sierra draws her knees to her chest and wraps her arms around them, tucking her head downward like a frightened turtle. Joel hits her mom sometimes, and yells a lot, and Sierra hates him with a burning fury matched only by her fear.

Nate puts a gentle hand on her shoulder. "I'll be right back."

She watches him walk up the stairs with her breath held, afraid that Joel is going to hit him too.

Nate's even voice comes from the stairwell, too low and level for her to overhear. Joel's response is a lot louder, and he calls Nate that word that she hates, the word that makes her cringe to hear.

"If you weren't fucking Ras himself, I'd beat the shit out of you right now," Joel shouts.

"You need to be quiet," Nate says loudly enough that Sierra can clearly hear him, though his voice remains mostly even. "If you gotta fight, you need to do it somewhere else."

"She ain't your little girl," Joel says. "Honestly, it's kinda creepy the way you hang around her. If I were her dad, I'd run you off with a fucking shotgun."

The wet tears on Sierra's cheeks splash onto her knees, still drawn tightly to her chest. Nate is not like that—he could never be like the men who pursue her mother, who leer at Sierra and say dirty things to her, promises for when she gets older.

"I don't give a fuck what you think." Nate sounds strong and unafraid. "I love her, and I'm gonna take care of her, and I'm more sure of that than I've ever been about anything. If you really wanna start shit, you can fight with me tonight, and then with Ras tomorrow. Or you can shut up so Sierra can get some sleep."

There's a long silence, and then Joel mutters some things too soft for Sierra to hear. The sound of the door slamming shut reverberates through the house.

Nate comes back to Sierra, frowning intently when he sees the tears on her face. "I'm sorry." He sits on the couch and puts an arm around her. He holds her close, and she breathes in the familiar scent of him. "I wish I could make things better for you. I wish I could fix all of it."

"It's okay," she promises him. "I'm okay." Maybe if she says it sincerely enough, it will come true.

SIERRA PLAYS WITH HER CAT. 2006

Watercolor and graphite on paper

It surprises Nate when Becky wants to visit again so soon after her last trip to see him. Maybe with their mother gone, Becky is trying to cling to the only family she has left.

As uneasy as Sierra is with Becky, she gets along pretty well with Becky's daughters. They're playing together in Sierra's room, their laughter drifting from down the hall. It feels good to hear Sierra laugh—it doesn't happen often enough these days. They're all walking on tiptoes around Joel. He hasn't done anything yet, but Nate knows it's only a matter of time.

He hasn't told Ethan anything about Joel because he doesn't want Ethan to bring the attention of the law to their home. He'd probably send the police out to investigate Joel's drug dealing, but Traci would get picked up as well. There's a strange tug in Nate's chest when he thinks of Sierra's mother behind bars. A kid should be with their mom.

Becky gives him a hesitant smile across the coffee table, and he wonders what she would think if she knew that drug deals go on in this house when she isn't around or that Nate's lover is a monster feared across the dark city.

"Have you heard anything from Mom?" Becky asks, setting down her teacup. She peers at him, eyes bright and anxious, obviously hoping for news.

Nate shakes his head. "She hates me. You know that. She's probably just tired of me." It makes him feel simultaneously rejected and relieved.

"She doesn't hate you." Becky takes his hands. "How could you say that?"

Nate shrugs and pulls his hands away. "You always take her side."

"I don't take anyone's side."

"Mom, look at this." The older of Nate's nieces bursts into the room with Bast in her arms. "Look, they found Grandma's cat." The kitten scrambles to get out of the girl's embrace, and the girl holds her tighter. "Shh, Susannah," she murmurs.

"Her name is Bast." Sierra tugs on the girl's arm. "And she doesn't like to be held like that. Give her back."

Bast hisses, and the girl drops her with an indignant squawk. "She scratched me!"

Sierra scoops up the angry cat and hurries off down the hall. The slam of her door barely cuts through the haze of shock.

"How did you get Mom's cat?" Becky narrows her eyes, glaring furiously at him. "I thought you hadn't seen her for years."

Nate doesn't have an answer for that—or rather, he does, but it's hard to hold it in his mind. It's unthinkable, but at the same time so obvious he feels like an idiot for not realizing it sooner.

"Susannah scratched me." Nate's niece pouts, holding her arm as though gravely wounded.

"You lied to me, Nate." Becky pulls her children to her. "How could you? You know how bad I wanted to see Mom, or at least hear that she's okay."

"You lied to me my whole life," Nate replies. He's furious, at her, at Ras, at the whole fucking world. "You told me I deserved everything that happened to me. You told me I was broken. You told me she was right. Everything you said was a fuckin' lie."

"Mom always said you were a liar. I should have believed her." Becky presses her lips together in a thin line, grabs her purse, and stalks out the door, her children obediently following.

Nate sinks onto the couch, heavy knowledge pressing down on him. There's only one explanation, only one reason his mother would disappear and Ras would show up holding her cat in his arms. His mother is dead, and what he feels—rage, horror, grief—overwhelms him. This is his fault; he brought Ras into his life, to his family, and he can't tell if what he feels is the guilt he deserves, or just a hollow sense of relief that she'll never be able to reach him again.

He puts his head in his hands and sits helplessly on the couch in the living room. He waits, motionless, as the sun slowly sinks behind the big oak trees lining the street in front of the house.

That's how Ras finds him, there in the dark. "What are you doing?" Ras asks with that tenderness that is not a lie, but is not enough of a foundation to build anything real on.

"How could you?" Nate is exhausted and helpless, and his voice comes out in a weary croak. "How could you?"

"Nate..."

"She was my mom. You fuckin' monster."

"She hurt you." Ras brushes his fingertips so gently over Nate's cheek, like there's some amount of love and affection that could make everything better. "I couldn't just let her hurt you."

"I don't want to see you." Nate jerks away despite the yearning he feels at Ras's touch, even now. "I never wanna see you again."

"You don't mean that." Ras sounds devastated, like he's the one who's been wronged, like it's his heart that has been broken. "Nate, everything I do is because I love you."

"Get out," Nate growls. "Get the fuck out of my house."

For once, Ras does as he's told.

*

Nate stands in the doorway, watching Sierra sleep. She's curled around her stuffed shark, which is starting to show some wear and tear at the edges of its fins. The soft sound of her breath, the rise and fall of her skinny shoulders, is soothing. Nate feels a love so deep and powerful he might drown in it, and a responsibility so weighty it could crush him. He wonders if he can rise to the challenge before him—if he can be the father she needs.

His phone vibrates in his pocket for the sixth time that night, and he relents, turning away from Sierra and walking down the hall to answer it.

"Stop calling me."

"I just want to talk," Ras insists.

"Talkin' to you is how I got into this fuckin' mess in the first place. Stop calling me."

"Do you wish your mother was still alive, then?"

Nate hesitates. He does and he doesn't. Her death brought him a deep sense of relief but also a harrowing guilt at how unburdened it made him feel.

"I did it to protect you. I did it because I love you."

"Bullshit."

"Fine," Ras snaps. "I did it because she made me angry. Because she was so certain you belonged to her. Is that what you wanted to hear?"

Nate doesn't answer. This isn't exactly surprising, but it's not as noble a motive as he would have wished for. With Ras, it never is.

"You are so fucking judgmental," Ras continues. "Do you think that was easy for me? Everything I did was just a little bit wrong, even though I jumped through every single hoop you wanted me to."

Nate takes a deep breath, clutching the phone tighter than necessary. "You never wanted to be a dad. We never woulda had a future anyway, because Sierra and me are always gonna be a package deal, and you don't want that."

Ras is quiet for a long moment. "Of course I want to be a part of your family," he says softly. "I just didn't think you would ever let me."

"What's that supposed to mean?"

"I don't want to talk about this over the phone. I want to see you." Nate doesn't answer, and Ras sighs wearily. "At least come pick up your things from my apartment. You left some sketchbooks and drawings here."

"Okay," Nate says finally. "I'll be there tomorrow morning. But just to pick up my stuff. After that, you're not gonna see me again."

*

Nate stands in before the large window lining the hallway just outside Ras's penthouse, taking in the view for what he's sure will be the last time. He'll miss drawing the city skyline from Ras's windows, the hard, bright quality of the light in the mornings. And so much more.

It's never going to be the same, not for him. Ras's love was like a river, the current easily sweeping Nate under, and he'll never regret drowning in it. That sweet water brought forth something he can't explain, a few white blossoms on a dead tree and a black bird that has seen to so many deaths, but brought one dead thing back to life.

He knocks, even though he has a key. It feels wrong to use it now.

Ras lets him in without a word. Nate had expected an apology from him for fucking everything up, but none seems to be forthcoming.

Ras gestures to the table where Nate's sketchbooks are neatly piled in a box beside his art supplies. There are a few pieces of paper on the glass table, and Ras taps one of them brusquely.

"The deed to the house," he says.

Nate examines it. Traci's name is the first thing he notices, and then the absence of his own. "You're angry." He glances at Ras.

Ras crosses his arms over his chest, leaning against the window. He somehow manages to look like a dangerous criminal and a sulky teenager all at the same time.

"I'm the one who's gonna have to figure out how to tell my sister our mom is dead," Nate scowls at him.

"It's already taken care of." Ras waves his hand dismissively. "I have one of my best people talking to her right now about how your mother died in a car accident. She was killed immediately in the collision, no suffering."

Nate feels a little weird about the cold efficiency of it but can't deny it's a huge relief. He doesn't like lying to his sister, but this truth would break her.

"Did Mom suffer?" he asks, his voice soft and tentative.

"Not as much as I would have liked," Ras says, and a chill runs down Nate's spine. Ras grins, showing his teeth. "Is that what you wanted to hear? Did you want me to remind you I'm a vicious monster? Now you can leave with a clean conscience and tell yourself you did the right thing."

"Why are you so angry?"

"Because you're breaking my heart. Because all I have done is love you, and now you're walking away. I gave you my best, and even that wasn't good enough for you."

"It's not like that," Nate protests, overwhelmed and flushed with an emotion he can't identify. "It's just—Would you give it up?" It's his last, desperate hope. "Would you give up the syndicate for me? Would you stop hurting people and killing and destroying everything in your path? That would...that would be good enough for me."

"No."

Ras doesn't even pretend to think about it. He actually has the audacity to look a little shocked, a little betrayed that Nate would even ask.

"Yeah," Nate says softly. "I know."

He takes a sketchbook off the pile in the box—it's worn from years of use, with a black cat on the cover. Inside are sketches of Jude and, later, of Ras, and notes he's written to them over the years, all the things he could never bring himself to say. He sets the book on the table and picks up the box.

Ras holds the door open for him but says nothing as he leaves. As he walks down the hall, there's a soft click behind him as the door swings shut.

TRIAL. 2006

Graphite on paper

"You quit?" Leo is perched on the edge of a chair in the office at the gallery, giving Nate a dismayed frown.

"Yeah," Nate says. "Sorry." No matter how much he loves this gallery, it's Ras's place, and Nate will never break free as long as he's tethered to it. Ras keeps making excuses to see him, and every time. Nate has to push him away all over again. So far, it hasn't gotten any easier.

"Something happen?"

"I just gotta put some space between me and Ras." Nate glances down at his feet, unable to meet Leo's eyes.

"Well, fuck." Leo scratches his head. "Good for you, Nate. I'm glad you got away. But I'm not gonna lie, we're gonna miss you around here."

Nate nods, looking around. "I'm gonna miss it too."

He keeps his hands in his pockets, hiding the skinned knuckles on his right hand. He'd punched a wall to dispel the building fury when he realized he had no choice but to leave the gallery for good. Not hard enough to injure himself, just enough to leave him with scraped skin like he's been in a fistfight, an embarrassing reminder of how emotionally unstable he's felt.

The air is frigid around him as he walks from the train station, and he's shivering by the time he gets to the house he's started to think of as home, even though Ras put the deed in Traci's name. Since they broke up, he's been by turns the tender, loving person Nate remembers, and a petulant child unused to being told no. But at least Traci has promised to let Nate stay in the house as long as he wants. She understands Sierra needs more than she can give and has started to accept Nate's help. Joel, however, has been doing his best to undermine Nate's influence wherever he can, determined to eventually drive Nate away, maybe because of some unwarranted sense of jealousy or possessiveness over Traci and her family.

Nate steps through the door to the house and stops, frozen in the doorway.

The coffee table is broken down the middle, the wood in splinters. Just past it, Traci is on the floor, groaning. She looks up at him with blood on her face, one eye swollen shut. A chair lies on its side, and the glass in the side window has been shattered.

"What happened?" Nate asks, though he already knows the answer.

Traci whimpers and brushes her hand gingerly beneath her eyes.

"She fuckin' asked for it, that's what happened," Joel steps out of the kitchen, drying his hands on a dishtowel before throwing it back into the room behind him.

"You can't do this." Nate stands straight and steady, unafraid. He once stared down Ras, his vicious smile and a knife gleaming in his hand. He has nothing to fear from scum like Joel. "You need to leave. And don't fuckin' come back."

"You think you can tell me what to do, you fuckin' asshole?"

Nate ignores him. He bends to help Traci. "It's gonna be okay," he tells her, and she sits still and dazed as he uses the long sleeve of his shirt to wipe some of the blood from her face. When he next glances back, Joel is gone. Good fucking riddance.

"This is the last straw," Nate tells Traci. "I don't fuckin' want to see Joel around here again. If I do, I'm gonna call the cops."

"Fuck you," Traci growls. "This is my fuckin' life. You don't get to tell me what to do."

"It ain't just your life. It's Sierra's life, too, and I'm gonna do whatever it takes to protect her. Even if it means sending you and Joel both to jail."

Traci gives him a look that is pure hatred.

The sound of nearby sirens resonates through the air and then flashing blue-and-red lights spill into the living room. The neighbors must have called the cops, perturbed by the explicit presence of violence in their quiet neighborhood. Nate hunches his shoulders, the familiar anxiety trapped in his chest, even though he has nothing to fear from law enforcement now that he's an honest citizen.

"Don't let them in," Traci says. "Don't you fucking open that door."

Nate answers the hard knock on the door and lets the police officer into the house without a word.

The officer is tall, with close cropped blond hair and the straight-backed posture of a soldier, and she introduces herself as Officer Wilson. With her is a shorter, rounder man who doesn't give his name. He's carrying a little first aid box, and he hurries to Traci's side and opens it.

"I'm fine," she mutters but doesn't pull away.

"Can you tell me what happened here, sir?" the officer asks, her steely gaze on Nate while her partner tends to Traci.

"It was—" Nate begins, but Traci sits up with a groan and interrupts him.

"It was him," she says and points directly at Nate. "He did this to me."

Nate steps back, stunned. "I didn't. I wouldn't. I—" He looks around wildly, but he knows Joel has likely already made a hasty exit through the back door and out the gate into the alley.

"Ma'am." The officer speaks gently, if somewhat impersonally. "Are you sure it was this man?"

Despite her anger, Traci can't meet Nate's eyes. She nods in his direction, tears spilling down her cheeks.

"No," Nate says, but the officers give him a long look that makes him think they're not going to believe a word he says. "I would never do that. I would never. Her boyfriend did this. I can tell you his name and—"

Officer Wilson is at Nate's side so quickly and gracefully the movement reminds him of Ras. "We're just going to go down to the station, you and me. You can speak in your own defense once we get down there. But I think you've done enough here."

Nate closes his eyes against hot, angry tears as she moves behind him, pulling his hands together and cuffing them with expert ease. It takes him back to that dark, misty night when he was seventeen, picked up in a park for soliciting. They had glared at him with disdain and disgust then, and now they do so again as Officer Wilson escorts him to the car with flashing lights and locks him into the back.

Troy had bailed him out then and, with a few bribes, got him a lenient judge and a quick trial. But now, he has no one to look out for him. He could call Ras, but he knows doing so would bring Ras right back into his life as though he'd never left.

Nate has spent enough of his life bending to the wind like a blade of grass. It's time for him to stand straight and strong for something that matters. It's time to do the right thing. So even as the police car speeds away from the one person left to him in the world, he refuses to compromise his integrity.

He sees Sierra's face in the window for just a second before the house is out of sight, and in his heart, he promises her he'll be back. They can't possibly believe Traci's lies for long.

*

Ethan sits at a broad wooden desk across from the precinct's police chief and forces a smile as the chief makes small talk. They've worked together on a few cases before and have a good rapport. Police generally like Ethan because they know if they bag their evidence right and present well on the witness stand, he can usually get a conviction.

"So you're here for Redfield," the chief finally says, setting a closed file on his desk. "I haven't gotten word from on high yet that it's your case, but—"

"It's not," Ethan says. "It's a personal connection. I need to know what's going on."

The police chief hesitates. "You're a good guy, or I would never do something like this." He gets to his feet and taps the file on his desk. "This is the case. I know if I go make us a cup of coffee, it will be right here on my desk when I get back."

Ethan smiles, relieved. "Thanks. I'll owe you one."

As soon as the chief leaves, Ethan grabs the file and quickly leafs through it. It seems so wrong—Nate's prints smudged black against the page, his name in black and white on the header. A prior conviction for soliciting at seventeen; Ethan wonders briefly about it before turning the page. He reads the account of Traci's testimony, the damning circumstances. The blood on Nate's sleeve and the skinned knuckles. Traci's claim that Nate flew into a rage because she kicked him out of the house and told him to stay away from Sierra. Ethan knows how furious that would have made him, how desperate. Nate is accusing someone named Joel, someone he claims is Traci's boyfriend. But he's never mentioned any such person to Ethan before, and no one else was present when the police officers searched the house.

It's impossible, Ethan tells himself. But still, he wonders.

He sets the file aside and seeks out the detective assigned to the case, who tells him she's pretty sure Nate is guilty. But like the chief, she owes him a few favors, so she unlocks the door to the interrogation room and lets him in.

Nate's head is bowed, the fluorescent light glinting madly off his chestnut hair. He barely looks up at Ethan before his hollow eyes return to the slate surface of the table between them. "I didn't do it. You believe me, right?"

Ethan is quiet for a moment. He believes one thing with his heart, but his head is telling him something else. He can't believe it, he can't—but he's spent his whole life living by the truth as revealed by evidence, and the evidence here is all pointing one way.

"Traci is getting a restraining order against you, but she's not pressing further charges," Ethan says. "The police will take you tomorrow to collect your things, and then you'll be free to go."

Nate glares at him, betrayal written across his face. "You don't believe me. You think I did it."

"I don't know what to think."

"You think I'm a fuckin' criminal." Nate jerks upright, the chains holding him to the table jangling as he does. "You think I'm a monster."

"Nate, I—"

"I don't fuckin' need a lawyer. And I sure as hell don't need you."

Ethan feels the weight of Nate's words as though they are stones hurled at his heart. "That's not what I meant."

"Then say you believe me," Nate growls. "Say you trust me."

"The officer I spoke to—"

"Just get out." Nate puts his face in his hands, deflating like a weary balloon at the end of a long day. "I don't wanna see your fuckin' face again."

Ethan gently presses a hand to Nate's shoulder. "I'll look in on Sierra for you."

The door swings open and creaks shut behind him. Ethan leans against the solid barrier—Nate trapped on the other side—and wonders why it feels like he was the one to betray Nate, when it's Nate who has betrayed everything Ethan thought he might be.

PHOENIX #5, RISING. 2006

Spray paint on stone building

After the hearing, where they stretch the ten-day restraining order into a thing of months and years, Nate takes the train to Ghost Town. He doesn't think about what he's going to do, but the awareness fills him all the same. There is no reason not to, nothing left to live for.

He gets off the train and the automatic doors slip shut behind him with a familiar hiss. He knows where to go—he's been down this road before. He knows a left turn from the train stop will take him down a brightly lit boulevard, and from there, it's a sharp right into a more dimly lit side street. An alleyway veers off to one side, three-story stone buildings on either side with walls like slate, windowless. It's even darker in this alley, and if he follows it farther, he'll come to an underpass. Waiting there will be a familiar face, a familiar toothy grin, a familiar knowing glint in the drug dealer's eyes. He'll get Nate high and ask no questions.

But as he turns a corner in the maze of alleyways, he sees hooded figures shifting guiltily, each carrying a box. They're bickering amongst themselves, their voices the high of teenage boys who have yet to settle into maturity. When they hear Nate approaching, they turn quickly.

"Shit," the tallest one whispers. He can't be more than thirteen. "He looks like a fuckin' narc."

"We gotta get out of here," says another. The three of them drop the boxes they're carrying with a disorganized clink of metallic cans and scurry out the mouth of the alley.

Nate shrugs, a little bewildered, then looks down at himself, at the suit he wore to the trial. He does seem out of place in this seedy neighborhood. He looks like a respectable citizen, and what a joke that is. Well, whatever. The illusion won't hold for long. He's about to take that first hit of dope—his hands shake in anticipation—and from there every fine and beautiful thing left in his life will turn back into a fucking pumpkin and a pair of unlucky mice.

The glint of the streetlamp on something in the boxes stops him, for just a moment. He reaches in and pulls out a smooth canister of spray paint, heavy against his palm. He sprays a brief, tentative color test on the wall. A shining, defiant silver.

The other two boxes contain more than a dozen cans of paint. Whatever these kids were planning, it must have been big.

Without thinking, he picks up a can of black and starts at the bottom of the wall, close to the ground. He paints a pile of ashes tossed askew, in the vague shape of an outstretched wing. Stark black lines like the bars of the cell he was put in when they first took him away from Sierra, like the shape of the despair taking root in his mind.

From that ash, a fire emerges, licking, crackling, burning bright. The red lines of his anger dance across the wall until they are waist high, vividly, vitally *alive* in their breathless fury. They rise and rise, and he's not even thinking as he tosses down an empty can of red and reaches for the next one, fingers stained but steady.

And then the bird begins to emerge. First, the stark, naked outline of the wings, rising and rising. He has to stand on a nearby dumpster to reach the top of the bird's head, turned triumphantly up to the sky. And then the silver, the white and the barest hint of gold, light as feathers and bold as day, until the painted phoenix covers the entire wall, deathless and defiant.

He lets the final can of spray paint fall from his fingers and clatter to the ground. He steps back and tilts his head up to see his masterpiece. His hands, streaked with red paint and smudged silver, clench and unclench as he stares at it for a long moment, as it looks back at him without flinching.

And then he laughs, and it's as clear and triumphant as the morning around him. As the very first red rays of the sun shine into the alleyway, the phoenix gleams in the light, and Nate leans his back against the building opposite it and brushes absentmindedly at his wet cheeks, leaving streaks of silver behind.

MUSEUM OF CONTEMPORARY ART.

2006

Mixed media on canvas

Leo looks around Nate's tiny apartment with dismay. His easel is crammed up next to the kitchen sink—the only slice of open space large enough to accommodate it in the narrow studio. There's no window, and the lighting is shit, but what he's got on the easel is still pretty damn good. It's a darker piece than he usually paints, a self-portrait in rich, vivid hues that bring to life the shadows beneath Nate's eyes, the weary turn of his mouth. It's one of the most honest and heart-wrenching self-portraits Leo has ever seen a contemporary artist do, and he feels guilty for not coming to see his friend sooner. Whatever Nate's been through in the last few months, it hasn't been easy. But he's survived it, and if this painting is any indication, found some meaning in it.

A key clicks in the lock, and the door opens. Leo doesn't take his eyes away from the canvas. "I'm not gonna lie. This is really fuckin' good."

"You picked the lock on my door," Nate says wryly.

"You weren't home," Leo says with a guileless shrug. "You didn't answer my calls. I had to make sure Ras hadn't killed you and buried you somewhere."

He turns to see Nate standing just inside the apartment, wearing the ridiculous uniform of the fast-food place down the street, and feels both anger and pity.

An artist of Nate's caliber should absolutely not be slaving away behind a griddle.

"Ras wouldn't hurt me."

Leo's not so sure. Ras is a monster, and Leo doesn't believe anyone can keep it as starkly compartmentalized as he claims to.

"Either way, I'm glad you're okay." Leo glances at the painting. "Well. I'm glad you're alive. But...is everything okay?"

Nate gives an expressive shrug. "Sure."

The shadows under Nate's eyes match the ones in his portrait, and there are new lines around his mouth, but even so, Leo keeps his skepticism to himself.

"Glad to hear it," he says. "Ras is a fucking wreck— not that I care." All Leo cares about is that Scarlett has to put up with the moody fucker.

Nate's mouth twitches in a movement that might be the slightest of smiles. "I don't care either."

"Ras and I had a...difference of opinion." Leo puts it much more delicately than it had played out in real life. "He wanted someone dead; I disagreed. So..." He waves his hand dismissively to avoid discussing the particulars of the situation, of the man he let escape. Ras probably would have killed anyone else for insubordination of that magnitude, but Scarlett held him back and saved Leo's life.

"So you're not running the gallery anymore?" Nate asks.

Leo sinks into one of the chairs by Nate's scratched wooden table. "Nah. They passed it on to someone else."

"Sorry to hear it."

"No big deal." Leo is used to letting things go. "I got a new project. I wanna open a museum."

Nate looks surprised. "A museum? What kind?"

"Do you love this city?" Leo leans back in the chair and puts his feet up on the nearby kitchen counter.

"Yeah." Nate frowns thoughtfully. "I guess so. I never lived anywhere else."

"That's why I need you. I'm starting a museum of local art. Collecting the best from artists all around the city and putting it in a place that's freely open to the public. So whaddya say?" Leo pulls his feet off the counter and sits up. "You in?"

Nate laughs softly. "I don't know shit about museums."

"But you know art. And you know this city."

"What would I do?"

"We're gonna be a small operation, at least at first, so you'd do a little bit of everything. You'd help me acquire art, go to shows, talk to dealers, that kind of thing. You'd also have to work with donors, maybe teach a class or two, and play tour guide. And help with the bookkeeping and shit until we get a little bigger. But I'd pay you pretty good. So what do you think?"

Nate hesitates, and Leo's pretty sure he's going to say no. But Nate just glances at the self-portrait on the easel for a pensive moment and then gives Leo a tentative smile. "Yeah. Guess so."

"Great," Leo says and holds out his hand for Nate to shake. "We start on Monday."

*

Sierra feels like she's cried enough tears to make an entire river of glistening salt water. She doesn't have any tears left, so she usually just lies on her bed after school, buried in a book until it's time to sleep. Joel and her mother come and go, and she barely notices them. She's lost the only person who really cared about her, so why should she care about anything?

Today is a dark, drizzly day, and the house is cold. She's sitting by the radiator with her knees to her chest when a knock sounds on the door. She opens it cautiously.

Ethan stands outside in the rain, his jacket soaked and his hair dripping. "Hey Sierra. Can I come in?"

She steps aside to let him in without a word. He seems worried as he looks around the dark, mostly empty room. "What happened to the furniture?"

She scuffs her foot on the carpet with a despondent shrug. Her mom and Joel have been selling it off bit by bit now that Nate's not here to stop them. "Nate's gone again. He went away."

"Yeah," Ethan says softly. "I know."

She sniffles and scrubs her hands over her face. "What do you want?"

"I wanted to see how you were doing. I was a little worried about you."

"I'm fine," she mutters, drawing her arms in tight to her body.

"Where's your mom?"

She answers him with a shrug. She doesn't know, and she doesn't care. She has never borne a grudge against Traci for the childhood lost to long nights alone in seedy apartments, for the nightmares she has in the dark, or the fear that consumes her during the day. But her mom lied, and they took Nate away, and Sierra will never forgive her.

Ethan sighs and runs his hand through his hair. He looks tired, like he hasn't been sleeping well, and really sad.

"Did they put Nate in jail?" Sierra asks. "Joel said he's going to jail."

"No." Ethan sinks onto the couch. "But your mom got a restraining order against him. That means he's not allowed to come close to her or you."

Sierra is glad he's not in jail, but this is almost as bad. She misses Nate every day, and without him, things are starting to go back to the way they used to be.

"I hate her," she mutters. She flops onto the couch beside Ethan and draws her knees to her chest. "If she didn't lie, they would have took Joel instead of Nate, and everything would be okay."

"She lied?" Ethan sets his words out carefully, cautiously. "What do you mean?"

"She told them Nate hit her," Sierra explains. "They were stupid and believed her."

Ethan is quiet for a moment. "Sierra, there's a lot of evidence that—"

"No!" Sierra shouts her protest into the darkened room. She thought Ethan was a good person, trustworthy. He can't possibly think Nate is bad like everybody else does. "It was Joel. I saw him, and then I went and hid like Nate told me to do whenever Joel got mad. And when I came back out, Nate was gone."

"Is Joel your mother's boyfriend?" Ethan speaks slowly, thoughtfully, and Sierra realizes her mistake. She hunches over and presses her hands to her mouth.

"I'm not supposed to say about Joel. Nate told me not to."

"Why not?"

Sierra draws her knees to her chest, her brow furrowed miserably. "'Cause somebody like you might try to take me away if they knew about him."

Ethan stares at her, eyes wide and shocked. "Is that what Nate thought?"

"Yeah," she says, hanging her head.

"God." It comes out choked, like a sob. "I should have known. I should have known. Sierra...I'm so sorry."

Sierra shrugs. She doesn't have any tears left. "Doesn't matter. Nate is gone forever."

"Not forever." Ethan turns to her. His forlorn slouch and sad eyes are gone, replaced by a straight spine and fierce expression. "I'm going to help him fight for you. I'm going to help him get back to you."

"It's not going to work." Sierra doesn't even care anymore. Her whole body is heavy, her heart weighing her down until she feels like she's going to sink right through the floor. "Nothing ever works."

"It might take a little while, but I'm going to do everything I can," Ethan promises. "Nate will too. He'll fight for you with everything he's got."

Sierra looks away from the hope on his face. Instead, she stares into the dark corners of the living room. She is so tired she can't bring herself to answer, to correct his foolish, noble assumptions.

"Will you draw something for me to take to Nate?" Ethan asks. "I know he misses you."

"I don't have paper." She refuses to look at him, refuses to be caught up in the story he's telling where the noble hero saves the heartbroken princess from darkness. It won't happen, and it will only hurt more if she hopes for it.

Ethan takes his small notebook and a pen out of his pocket and offers it to her. "You can keep this. I'll come back tomorrow with more paper for you. And I'll talk to Nate. Okay?"

She nods because it's easier than protesting. After he leaves, she sits on the floor, the notebook open on the coffee table before her, and draws dark, empty rooms and looming shadows with long, heavy strokes of the pen.

*

It takes months of scrambling, months in which Nate balances his painting and the time he spends seeing to the seemingly endless number of tasks necessary to start a brand-new museum from scratch. He's had bitter black coffee in a struggling sculptor's tiny, unheated studio, and sipped a fine merlot with a wealthy art collector in his chateau outside the city—grateful that Ras taught him about expensive wines, and how to be not at all intimidated by wealth. He's helped Leo build something entirely new, and today, as he walks through the space that will become the city's new museum of contemporary art, he feels a strange wave of

accomplishment that almost makes him queasy.

The walls are a blank white, ready for canvases to be placed on them, pedestals sitting in corners awaiting sculptures. There is a small theater with a projector, and a space for performance art just around the corner. Nate stands in the center of it all, struggling to contain the emotions inside him—pride, wonder, and as always, the underlay of grief for the little girl gone from his life.

Footsteps sound from the corridor outside. He expects Leo, and isn't prepared for the shock of anger and longing when Ethan turns the corner and gives him a slight, sheepish smile.

"Hey, Nate. I, uh, I brought you something." He holds out the large, stiff piece of paper like it has some great significance, and Nate takes it from him without a word. It's a drawing of Sierra's, two people holding hands at a playground, the swing set and the smaller figure's hair rendered in lumpy black paint. Nate studies the drawing for a long moment, trying to hold back his rioting emotions.

"Why do you have this?" he asks finally.

"I've been keeping in touch with Sierra. She asked me to bring it to you."

"How is she?" Nate's voice comes out hoarse and desperate.

"She's okay. Things could be better. That's why I'm here, actually."

"To blame me?" Nate steps back. His anger, always so quick to surface, boils fiercely against his ribcage.

"No. No. Nate...I was wrong. I was so wrong, and I don't know if you can ever forgive me, but I hope you will accept my help." He doesn't look away or down at the floor, but holds Nate's gaze, even as the shame in his voice makes it clear this is hard for him to say.

"Your help?" Nate asks skeptically.

"You need to fight for her. I don't know if we can win, but we have to try. Legally, you're her father, and that gives us a small chance."

"I got a fuckin' restraining order against me." A tiny flicker of hope lit itself in Nate's heart at Ethan's words, but he knows better than to trust it. "I can't even go see her."

"But Traci never pressed charges, and she might be persuaded to recant her testimony against you. Sierra knows what really happened, and she can testify to it. I can't promise you anything, except that I will fight for you for as long as it takes."

Nate nods, trying to reconcile the sick sense of betrayal he still feels with the newly awakened need for closeness with Ethan. He wants to shove him into one of the pristine white museum walls and he wants to embrace him and hold him closely enough to feel the beating of his heart.

"I'm so sorry," Ethan says softly. "I should have trusted you. I should have believed you."

Nate is quiet for a long moment, and then he nods. "Okay. Help me fight for her."

Ethan smiles, but it's laced with melancholy. "Anything for you."

ETHAN, PORTRAIT. 2006

Oil on canvas

Ethan never thought he'd make such a fool of himself for a man. But something in him is tuned to thrum dizzyingly at the very awareness of Nate's presence. He watches from the edge of the room as Leo proposes a toast and Nate shyly smiles at the gathered crowd. Ethan knows this museum is as much Nate's doing as Leo's, that Nate loved the idea of creating exhibits that were open for everyone in the city to see, art that was accessible for all.

Ethan lingers on the sidelines as the celebration goes on, out of place in his rumpled suit jacket and loosened tie—he'd hurried here straight from court, hoping to catch Nate's eye and see him smile. Hoping to celebrate this triumph with him. But so many people approach Nate, beautiful women and handsome men, brilliant artists and wealthy patrons, that it's hard to find an opening, or to believe his presence really adds anything of value.

Over the past month, as Nate has worked long hours to see this project come to life and spent an interminable amount of time waiting for the documents they've submitted to make their way through the legal system, he and Ethan have repaired what was between them. Nate smiles easily now when he sees Ethan, and that smile lights something in Ethan's heart. But Ethan doesn't think he'll ever be forgiven enough to have the kind of intimacy he yearns for. Someday, maybe soon, Nate will find someone else to love. He dreads that day and knows the inevitability of its coming.

Ethan has resigned himself to his position on the periphery of Nate's life. Nate is a shining star. His talent and inherent goodness open doors and hearts for him wherever he goes. Ethan has spent many sleepless nights telling himself he's done chasing that starlight, but when morning comes, he finds himself as hopelessly devoted as ever. If friendship is what Nate wants, then he will be a stalwart friend, and nothing more. He counts himself lucky that Nate has forgiven him for his mistakes, and that he's allowed to be in Nate's life at all.

Ethan wanders away from the celebration, threading his way among the paintings until he comes to one he knows must be Nate's. It's a portrait of Ras, who stands in front of the city's skyline, larger than life. The image is blurred, as though by a rain-streaked window, and in it, Ras seems to be both smiling and snarling, a glint in his eye that could be menace or charm. Like all of Nate's work, it's breathtaking in its complexity and emotional intensity.

Just past it is the phoenix, another rendition of the same bird as it soars above the fire that brought it back to life, indomitable and beautiful. Ethan raises a hand to touch it, the contours of the thick paint, shining a glimmering silver, but stops himself in time. He has never wanted like this, never yearned for anyone's touch the way he does now. It hurts, and makes him acutely aware of his own loneliness, but he wouldn't trade it for anything. Nate and Sierra have become an integral part of his life. Even if every interaction with Nate is tinged bittersweet, it's better than never realizing he had the capacity for this kind of love.

"Hey," Nate says, and Ethan, who had been entirely lost in the phoenix, startles.

"Hey. Congratulations."

Nate smiles at him. "Thanks for coming. I never woulda thought I could be somewhere like this, doin' something like this."

"I would have believed it." From the first moment he saw Nate's steady hands bringing graphite shapes to life on the drawing paper, Ethan knew it would only be only a matter of time before Nate accomplished great things.

"You always say nice things to me." Nate's gaze briefly drops to the floor. "Thanks."

"I love this phoenix." Ethan glances at the painting. "It's just as beautiful as the last one. Maybe more so. I was disappointed to see it's already sold."

"It's not," Nate says. "I set it aside. I, uh...I wanted to give it to you. If you want it, I mean."

"I..." Ethan is speechless for a moment, and Nate's shoulders slump. He looks away, frowning.

"Of course I want it," Ethan says quickly. "It's the most beautiful painting I've ever seen."

Nate gives him a skeptical glance. "I drag you to every museum. You see a lot of paintings."

"Sure. But this is the only one I've ever seen of you."

Nate glances from him to the phoenix and back. "Me?"

"No matter how bad things get, you can't kill a phoenix. They get burned to ash and then they come back to life, stronger than ever. Nothing can stop them. Just like you."

Nate stares at him for a moment, and Ethan chides himself for letting out the sentiment he's tried so hard to keep from Nate for all this time. But then Nate kisses him, and he forgets everything. It's a quick kiss, just a brush of lips, shy and chaste. But his heart leaps in his chest, buoyant, weightless.

"Is that okay?" Nate asks softly, tentatively, and Ethan answers him with another kiss, this one deeper, longer.

"Nate," he says, "we should talk first." But he offers no resistance when Nate drags him into the backroom and locks the door. In the cool, dark space, among blank canvases and boxes of paint, he surrenders to Nate's caresses like a man possessed.

It isn't until after, when their lips are still so close they're breathing the same air, that Ethan starts to come to his senses.

"I love you." He pulls away just far enough to see Nate's face, dear and close in the dim light. "But I don't think I could share you."

Nate smiles, lacing their fingers together. "You love me. That's good enough for me. I don't need anybody else."

"Then let me take you to dinner tomorrow." Ethan kisses the back of Nate's hand. "Let me take care of you. Let me be everything you deserve."

Nate buries his face in Ethan's neck. "Okay," he murmurs against Ethan's skin. "But you could take me home now if you want."

"Yes." Ethan breathes in the alpine scent of Nate's hair. "Let's go. Before I wake up and find out this is just the best dream I've ever had."

Nate laughs, hot breath against his neck, and holds him tighter.

*

Nate wants to be cautious. His every instinct tells him to be cautious, but when he sees Ethan smile, all of that fear is scattered to the wind. Being with Ethan is not a heady rush, dizzying or disorienting in its euphoria. Being with Ethan is like sailing on a calm sea, tranquil as breathing, deep and true. He wakes up beside Ethan the next morning, and the morning after that, until his toothbrush and a box full of art supplies and most of his clothes have made their way to Ethan's house.

He loves the place where Ethan lives—a home Ethan complains is too large for a bachelor, but of course, he's not a bachelor anymore. The house has three bedrooms, a spacious kitchen, and, most importantly, a large backyard with a little swing set that the last people to live there left behind. Nate loves waking up there, and in unguarded moments, he imagines what it would be like to call it home, and what it would be like to have Sierra there as well.

When Ethan asks him to move in, he takes a day to think it over. He never thought he could trust a man enough for this, but his relationship with Ethan feels like walking an even path—easy to follow even through the turns and twists because the light that guides him remains a constant. When he comes back before the day is over and says yes, Ethan's smile is its own reward.

Together, they pack up what's left in Nate's apartment. It doesn't take long—he didn't have much, but the canvases and drawings need to be moved with care.

"You drew Ras a lot," Ethan says, frowning down at a charcoal sketch Nate made in the early days of their relationship, while he was still wary but drawn to Ras like a summer bird to true south.

Nate shrugs. He still likes to draw him sometimes. He doesn't want to forget the contours of Ras's face—not the low-quality images they publish in the gossip rags, but what it was like to see him in real life. The playful glint in his eyes and the joy in his smile that no camera could reproduce.

Ethan doesn't press the matter, carefully placing the drawing with all the others. "Sierra's report card came yesterday. Traci sent it on to me without even looking at it."

Nate's heart aches like it does every time he thinks of Sierra. "How's she doin'?"

"Not very well. But it could be to our advantage. My private investigator is getting statements from her teachers. We're establishing a pattern of neglect that will make us a stronger case for custody."

Nate scrubs his hand over his face, sighing. "I fuckin' hate it. She's barely eight years old—she ain't gonna be able to wait for this bullshit to be over. Every day that she gets hurt is gonna matter."

"I know." Ethan puts his hand on Nate's waist and tugs him into an embrace. "But it's the best chance we've got."

Nate leans into Ethan's warm body. His eyes linger on the portrait of Ras lying on the table. It's a good one—he'd captured the warmth of Ras's smile, the frequent gentleness to his eyes. He has no illusions—he knows he broke Ras's heart, and from the way Ras acted after, Nate wonders if he was the first person to ever deny Ras something he really wanted. For his part, Nate had done his best to burn that bridge forever because, with Ras, it was everything or nothing.

He wants to do the right thing; he has always wanted to do the right thing. And he knows what Ethan would say if he spoke what was in his heart. Ethan would tell him to be patient because, in the end, the good in the legal system would prevail, and they would fight together until Sierra was safe. But Nate is running out of time. Sierra is his child—he knows this in the same primal way all parents do, down in his bones. He's done waiting. He will do whatever it takes to see that she's safe.

But he doesn't tell Ethan what he's resolved to do. Instead, he leans into the embrace and hopes when the dust settles, he'll be forgiven.

Ras Among Roses. 2006

Acrylic on canvas

Nate stands outside the imposing entrance to the regal Victorian mansion where, Leo assured him, Ras now lives. The exterior looks like it's been lovingly restored but it retains the solemn appearance it had the last time he was here.

He rings the doorbell and resonant chimes sound inside the house. After a few long minutes in which he contemplates running away so he won't have to do this, Scarlett opens the door.

Nate blinks, a little stunned at the sight of her—her hair tied loosely back and her dress flowing over a very pregnant belly. He doesn't know why it would come as a surprise that she and Ras would be having a baby, but it does. It hits him like a punch to the gut, throwing him off balance for a few seconds.

"Hey, who is it?" Behind Scarlett, Ash appears. He puts an arm around her with the ease of great familiarity, and together, they eye Nate suspiciously.

"What do you need, Nate?" Scarlett asks.

Nate clears his throat. "I, uh, I need to talk to Ras. Just for a few minutes."

Ash and Scarlett share a glance that speaks volumes.

"I think he's in the gardens," Ash says. "I'll show you."

He kisses Scarlett on her temple—a kiss that seems more brotherly than amorous—and leads Nate through the darkened hallways to the door leading out onto the back of the wraparound porch. "Follow the cobblestone path to the left. He's probably out there in the rosebushes."

Nate nods. He half remembers the way and hopes he won't come across Ras at his father's grave, acting as oddly as he had before.

Instead, he finds him in a field of red roses, the air thick with the sweet scent, petals littered on the ground. Ras has a pair of shears in his hand, and he's cutting a rose with a long stem to add to the collection by his feet.

Ras scoops up the pile of roses, adding the freshest victim to the bunch. The heads are a brilliant red, like blood, like the sun setting over the city, filtering through smog, like the flames licking at the feet of the transcendent painted phoenix. Nate studies the color, wondering if he can mix something like it when he gets home, and what he would want to make with it.

"Hello, Nate." Ras turns to him with the smile Nate remembers, the one he longed for with a dull ache that faded over time but will probably never disappear completely. "How are you?"

"I'm okay. I, uh, I wanted to talk. If you got a minute."

"I always have time for you. Let me put these in some water, and we can chat."

"Congratulations, by the way." Nate feels clumsy and awkward as they walk together back to the house. "Looks like you're gonna be a dad."

"It's a strange thought, isn't it?" Ras pushes open the screen door and lets Nate into the house. "It makes me think about my own father, more often than I used to."

"You're not gonna be like him," Nate says before he can stop himself. "You're not gonna make your kid into a monster."

Ras glances at him with a cold glint in his eye that makes Nate doubt his own words. He sets the flowers on the large butcher-block counter in the center of the kitchen and pulls off his gardening gloves.

"That ain't why I came." Nate hesitates, acutely self-conscious. "I...I gotta ask you a favor. I don't have anybody else I can talk to. If you still care about me, even a little bit—"

"You don't have to beg, Nate," Ras says sharply. "Just tell me what you need."

"Sierra's mom..." Nate hunches his shoulders and looks away. "Her boyfriend beat her up, but Traci told the cops I did it. She didn't press charges, but she got a restraining order. Now, I can't even talk to Sierra without gettin' in trouble. The judge ruled against me, and I don't know what to do. I can't just leave her, Ras. Her mom's no good for her, and she don't have anybody else."

"Take a deep breath." It isn't until Ras's fingertip brushes along Nate's wet cheekbone that Nate realizes he's crying. "Everything will be okay. Scarlett and I will get this sorted out as soon as possible."

"Thank you," Nate says, hit with a wave of relief so intense his knees feel weak and shaky. "Thank you. I can't say what this means to me."

"Anything for you, my love. Stay for lunch, and we'll work out the details."

"I'm getting married." Nate takes a quick step back, despite the wanting that flared in his chest at the familiar endearment.

The corner of Ras's mouth quirks briefly upward. "Congratulations."

"Thanks," Nate mutters. Ras didn't sound all that sincere.

"You know I...I want that too." Ras frowns down at the scattered flowers on the counter. He reaches into his pocket and pulls out two jewelry cases, each black velvet. He slides them across the table to Nate, who opens them to reveal, in one, a slender silver ring with a large, extravagant ruby surrounded by diamonds and, in the other, a platinum band engraved with tiny roses.

"I don't know how to ask," Ras says. "Or if it's something they would want."

"You're gonna marry both of them?"

"Why not? I love them both. It might not be legal, but when have I ever worried about that?"

Nate slides the boxes back across the table and tries to ignore the strange, sour jealousy. "I bet they say yes."

Ras brushes his fingers possessively over each box with a pensive frown, then tucks them back into his pocket. "Maybe. You didn't."

"I ain't gonna change," Nate says, with a casual shrug that hides the regret he still sometimes feels. "You neither."

"I suppose so. Let me find Scarlett. You can tell her the details of your case, and we'll figure out a way to get Sierra back to you."

"Thanks. And hey, Ras. It don't mean I didn't love you. I always loved you."

Ras steals a kiss, deftly as a pickpocket, so Nate doesn't even register the press of his lips until it's already gone. "I love you too," he says and disappears down the hallway.

BECKY SITS AT TABLE. 2006

Graphite on paper

After that it's easy, almost too easy. It's only a few days before Nate gets a phone call from a flustered social worker, promising they will remove Sierra from her mother's care as soon as possible and bring her to Nate. He hadn't expected the wheels to turn so quickly, if at all, and he hurries to get the house ready for Sierra to move in.

"What are you doing?" Ethan sounds alarmed, standing in the doorway of the room Nate has been using as a studio, watching as Nate packs away his paints, his easel folded up in the corner.

Nate straightens and gives Ethan a wide smile. He likes to see Ethan just after work, when he comes home with his suit coat rumpled and his tie loosened, weary from a long day but still Nate's white knight, dressed in his shining armor. "Sierra's comin' home." He knows Ethan will be as glad as he is, trusts Ethan to welcome Sierra into their life.

Ethan frowns. "How is that possible, Nate? We haven't even been to court."

"I, uh…" Nate's smile fades. Ethan won't approve of what he's done, even though he had no choice. "I asked Ras for help."

"Oh," Ethan says softly. "Well. I guess that's one way to go about it."

"I wanted to do it right. I woulda done it your way, but it woulda taken too long. Sierra needs to be safe now, and I don't give a fuck what it takes to make that happen."

Ethan nods, but he still looks upset. "And now you're packing up your stuff."

It takes Nate a few moments to get what Ethan is saying. And then he gives a soft half laugh at the absurdity of it. "I'm not leavin'. No fuckin' way. I'm just gettin' this room ready for Sierra."

Ethan runs a hand through his hair, mussing it further, and sighs. "I just don't like that he's back in your life."

"He's not," Nate promises. "I asked him for one favor. That don't mean I'm gonna see him again."

"Are you sure? He's persistent, and I know you really loved him."

Nate stares at Ethan, surprised. Jealousy and insecurity are new colors on him, ones Nate has never seen before. Ethan always seems so confident, so quietly self-assured that Nate assumed he was above such emotions.

"Sure." Nate crosses the room, holding Ethan's gaze. "I loved him, yeah. But I'm here with you, now. I wanna start a family with you."

Ethan smiles, then, and pulls Nate close for a kiss. "Okay. Let's give Sierra my office. I can set up a desk in the living room. You need this space to work."

Nate laughs softly and buries his face in Ethan's neck, so he can breathe in the familiar scent of his aftershave. "This is my happily ever after. Thanks to you."

"As much as I'd like to take credit," Ethan says, running his hand into Nate's hair, "the truth is you built this for yourself. I'm just glad to be along for the ride."

*

Ethan is by his side, but Nate still feels queasy trepidation as he knocks on his sister's white door, the pleasant lawn and hedges verdant around him. They've talked on the phone a few times, brief, tense conversations, but he hasn't seen her since the day he found out what happened to their mother.

Becky opens the door in her blue floral-print apron, flour in her hair and a mixing spoon clutched in one hand. Despite the anxiety raging in his chest, Nate smiles. He loves how passionate Becky is when she's baking. She creates masterpieces—massive multilayered cakes and delicate spun-sugar webs. When he completed his first year of sobriety, she made a meringue mountain, complete with marzipan trees, rocks, and a climber to represent the metaphorical mountain Nate had conquered.

"Nate," she says coldly, and doesn't move to let him in. "What are you doing here?"

"Hey, Becky." Nate takes a slow, deep breath, feeling as though his chest is starting to cave in on him. "I wanted to talk to you."

"Hi." Ethan steps forward and offers his hand with a friendly smile in an attempt to break the icy tension. "My name is Ethan. It's good to meet you, Becky. I've heard so much about you."

She doesn't take his hand.

"Can we just talk?" Nate asks. "Just for a couple of minutes?"

She hesitates for a long moment, then steps aside and lets them in. "Go, sit." She gestures to the living room. "I have to get something out of the oven. I'll be right back."

Nate and Ethan sit on the beige couch in the cozy living room, and Ethan brushes his hand over Nate's. "It's going to be fine. No matter what happens, you've done nothing wrong, and you're going to be okay."

Nate nods, and the knot in his chest eases somewhat.

Becky bustles into the room with freshly baked cookies on a tray, the smell wafting through the air. She sets it on the table so firmly it rattles against the wooden surface. "You may as well have some cookies while you're here."

The smack of their mother's hand against Becky's face echoes throughout the kitchen, and Nate shrinks back against the cabinets, wishing he was small enough to climb inside and hide among the pots and pans.

"Nate will eat when I give permission," their mother hisses. "You are not to feed him again. Do you understand?"

Becky sobs softly, tears rolling down her cheeks. "I'm sorry."

Nine-year-old Nate can still taste the cookie she had offered him when their mother's back was turned, crumbly and sweet on his tongue.

The cookies look magazine-perfect, a glittering sugar crust over fluffy shortbread, all a uniform shape and size. Nate stares at them, feeling as though he might throw up.

Ethan squeezes his shoulder and leans in to murmur in his ear. "Stay with me, Nate. We can leave whenever you want."

Nate looks Becky in the eye, the threads of their past spun chaotically around them. For once, there's something in his present solid enough to cling to. "I'm here 'cause you're my sister. After all the shit we've been through, I feel like I owe you somethin'."

"You don't," she says quietly. "You don't owe me a thing."

Nate presses on. "I'm gonna be a dad. I'm gettin' custody of Sierra for good, and I'm gonna take care of her. She's part of our family now and...I guess I just wanted you to know."

Becky's brow creases. "Nate—are you sure? A child is a huge responsibility to have all by yourself."

"He won't be by himself." Ethan puts his hand over Nate's. "He'll have me."

Nate is both grateful for the gentle touch and very aware of the way Becky's eyes linger on their hands before traveling up to his face.

Becky folds her hands primly in her lap. "You always had to be different, didn't you?"

Ethan sits forward and releases Nate's hand. "I want you to listen to me. Nate might have an infinite amount of patience for your bullshit, but I do not. If you want him to be in your life—"

"Ethan." Nate gently cuts him off. It feels good to have someone take his side, for once, someone who believes he's not the bad one, the broken one. "It's okay. I'm used to it."

"You shouldn't have to be," Ethan protests.

"The girls would miss you too much," Becky says softly. Nate knows that tone, the gentle look of surrender in her eyes. It means she's going to push past the things she can't understand and won't forgive in the name of a relationship that would otherwise be impossible. He recognizes the look because it's the same one she always used to give their mother when she would pretend that no harm had been done in their childhood. "They're going to be so excited to hear that Sierra is officially their cousin. And...congratulations, Nate. I mean that. I really do."

Nate isn't sure what to do with the funny mix of affection and resentment in his heart, but he smiles back, and Ethan gently squeezes his hand.

*

"You don't have to see your sister again if you don't want to," Ethan says in their cozy, warmly decorated bedroom. The visit has been weighing on Nate's mind, but he hasn't said anything about it. Still, Ethan must have been able to tell. "She was right—you don't owe her anything."

"It's fine. I know better than to expect anything."

"It's not fine. She hurt you. She continues to hurt you. That's not okay."

Nate shrugs, pulling off his shirt and reaching for his pajamas. Ethan puts his hands on Nate's bare shoulders, over a scar that looks a little like a hawk, jagged wings stretched from collarbone to shoulder.

"It ain't that." Nate struggles to get the words out of his tight throat. "It's just—every time I see her it takes me back. To bein' a kid. To that fuckin' house where we grew up."

Ethan runs his fingers gently over the hawk, and then lower, to a scar on Nate's bicep, and the one on the back of his hand. "Is that where you got all these scars?"

"Did you see how Becky didn't have any?" Nate says, his voice soft and choked. "It's 'cause she was a good kid, and I was bad."

"No child deserves this." Ethan sounds deeply sorrowful. "No child could ever deserve this."

Nate twists his shoulders free of Ethan's grasp and pulls on a long-sleeve shirt. "You don't know. You can't know."

"Sierra thinks the same thing, you know," Ethan says, calm and unruffled as always. "She thinks the things that happened to her happened because she was bad. She thinks she deserved all of it."

Nate turns to Ethan. He'd known this about Sierra but never made the connection to his own life. His circumstances were different. He knows this in a deep down, irrational way. He deserved it. She never could.

"You need to be a role model for her," Ethan continues. "You need to show her how it's possible to overcome this. And you can't do that by refusing to talk to me. You need to see a therapist."

Nate takes a few agitated steps, running his hand through his hair. This topic has come up a few times before, and Nate has always been resistant.

"You think I'm broken." Nate glares at Ethan from across the room. "You think I'm fucked in the head. Why the hell are you still here if I'm such a fuckup?"

"I think someone hurt you. And when people get hurt, sometimes they need help to heal. There's nothing wrong with that."

Nate shakes his head, unable to articulate why this makes him so irrationally furious and terrified.

"I'll call," Ethan says. "I'll set up the appointment. But you have to go. You can't expect Sierra to do this work when you won't do it yourself."

Nate tries to think of a good response but can't. Ethan's right. Nate is going to make Sierra do this, so he better be brave enough to do it himself.

Sierra, Portrait. 2006

Pastel and canvas

Nate shows Sierra around the new house, to the room they made up for her. She sets her little backpack on the bed—all the things she owns in the world, except what Nate has bought her in the hopes it might make up for the absence.

"This is your forever home," he says, sitting on the bed beside her. "I promise."

She gives him a look more skeptical than an eight-year-old should be able to give anyone. "I don't think Ethan will like me here."

"Sierra," Nate says gently. "I have messed up so many times in my life. Way more times than you. And Ethan still loves me. He loves you too."

She draws her knees to her chest, curled in a tight little ball. Nate's heart aches because he instinctively understands what she's afraid of. It was the same thing that scared him every time they put him in a new foster home. The certainty that there would come a day when he'd be thrown out on the street, not worthy, not good enough to belong. He used to force that day, causing trouble until the prophecy came true, as it always did.

"I held you on the day you were born," Nate says. "I carried you in my arms, and I promised you I was always gonna love you and take care of you, no matter what."

"You did?" she asks in a tiny voice.

"Here. Look at this." Nate rolls up the sleeve of his T-shirt to show her the mountain range that adorns his right bicep. Written in stylized letters along the peaks is a single word—Sierra. She's never seen the tattoo before, because he's only recently taken to wearing anything besides long-sleeve shirts, even in the privacy of his own home.

She traces the letters with her fingertip. "That's my name." She looks at him with her eyebrows raised.

"That's right. It's gonna be on my arm forever. And that promise is forever too. No matter what happens, I'm gonna love you."

She smiles, then, finally. Nate pulls her into his arms and presses a kiss to the top of her head. He's still clumsy when it comes to demonstrating affection, to giving free voice to what's in his heart. But he's working on it, learning how, because Sierra needs a dad who's always going to show her that he loves her. Nate has fears of his own as he embarks on this journey with her, but he also has a core of hidden confidence. He's sure of the integrity and strength of his love. It will not fail him.

He lets Sierra stay up late because he knows she's anxious about this new and different situation, but eventually puts her to bed with a kiss on the forehead and a promise of chocolate chip pancakes in the morning. While Ethan sits at his desk, determined to see right prevail over wrong in his newest case, Nate steps into the room that has become his, and stands before his canvas.

The broken places he's been, the sadness and the suffering that fell into his life, are still present in every painting he makes, each brushstroke casting a shadow. But now there are more colors at his fingertips—enough different hues to fill his palette to bursting. There is the sandy blond of Ethan's hair, the verdant green of Ras's eyes. The brilliant purple of Sierra's favorite crayon and the midnight blue that stirs his own heart. The colors of his despair and the colors of his joy.

Tonight, he adds feathering to the silvery bird on the canvas, barely-there strokes of perfect white, giving texture and depth to the wings, until a little hand tugs timidly at his smock. Sierra's eyes are full of hope and fear, her face tilted up to him.

He puts a hand on her shoulder, and together, they turn toward the door. Behind him, on the wide, tall canvas, shimmering in the light like an echo of his own soul, the painted phoenix rises.

ACKNOWLEDGEMENTS

My husband, for providing the practical so I could dream of the wildly impractical.

My mother, for reading this book a hundred times and believing that with each revision it would get a little better.

My father, for telling me, when I was very little, that if I was going to do something, I should take my time and do it right.

My sister and her son, for sharing with me that wondrous, fragile, breathtaking moment when he came into the world.

My brother, for failing to ever be anything less than fully himself.

My mother-in-law, for taking me to a youth homeless shelter to volunteer.

My father-in-law, for asking me to sign my name in a book that he owns.

My maternal grandmother, for teaching me to make Art.

My paternal grandmother, for placing in my hands the next story I'll tell.

More beta readers than I can count, who offered their kind, thoughtful critiques.

My editor, publisher, proofreader, and all the amazing minds that worked on this book before it was sent into the world.

And finally, Syl, my feline queen, who made me put the cat in.

About the Author

Sarah Kay Moll is a wordsmith and grant writer. She's good with metaphors and bad with coffee stains, both of which result from a writing habit she hasn't been able to quit. In her day job, she helps raise money for a small nonprofit affordable housing developer. She's passionate about books and has about five hundred on her to-read pile.

Sarah lives in a beautiful corner of western Oregon where the trees are still changing color at the end of November and the mornings are misty and mysterious. She spends her free time playing video games and catering to her cat's every whim.

Email: skmoll@gmail.com

Facebook: www.facebook.com/SarahKayMoll

Twitter: @skmoll

Website: www.sarahkaymoll.com

Mailing list sign up: www.eepurl.com/dwdxWb

Other NineStar books by this author

Dark City

Also Available from NineStar Press

Connect with NineStar Press

www.ninestarpress.com

www.facebook.com/ninestarpress

www.facebook.com/groups/NineStarNiche

www.twitter.com/ninestarpress

www.ingramcontent.com/pod-product-compliance
Lightning Source LLC
Chambersburg PA
CBHW061550100726
47898CB00002B/307